More Praise for

"Magical and mysterious, *Mermaid*'s twist on a classic tale is as ingenious as it is delightful."
  —CAROLINE LEAVITT, author of *Pictures of You*

"There is a part of every reader that longs to return to the days of reading fairy tales and myths, when imagination had no limits and stories were spellbinding. Carolyn Turgeon's *Mermaid* evokes just that feeling. She is one of my new favorite writers."
  —JO-ANN MAPSON, author of *Solomon's Oak* and the
    Bad Girl Creek trilogy

"This *Mermaid* is resplendent with shimmering details, the dark and thrilling story behind that comforting childhood memory. At once fresh and familiar, heartbreaking and full of hope, this dark retelling of Hans Christian Andersen's *The Little Mermaid* is like a gorgeous dream remembered."
  —JEANINE CUMMINS, bestselling author of *A Rip in Heaven*
    and *The Outside Boy*

"As moody and atmospheric as a Gothic novel, *Mermaid* is a heartfelt portrait of young love and all its sweet complications. Sweeping and lush, an inspired and imaginative reimagining of my favorite fairy tale."
  —TIMOTHY SCHAFFERT, author of *The Coffins of Little Hope*

"Turgeon's ability to breathe new life into the old bones of a beloved story we all think we know is unparalleled."
  —ANTON STROUT, author of the Simon Canderous series

Mermaid

Mermaid

A Twist on the Classic Tale

Carolyn Turgeon

BROADWAY PAPERBACKS

NEW YORK

BROADWAY

Copyright © 2011 by Carolyn Turgeon

Grateful acknowledgment is made to Farrar, Straus and Giroux, LLC, for
permission to reprint an excerpt from "Fable of the Mermaid and the Drunks"
from *Extravagaria* by Pablo Neruda, translated by Alastair Reid.
Translation copyright © 1974 by Alastair Reid.

Library of Congress Cataloging-in-Publication Data

Turgeon, Carolyn.
Mermaid: a novel / by Carolyn Turgeon.—1st trade paperback ed.
p. cm.
1. Mermaids—Fiction. 2. Princesses—Fiction. I. Title.
PS3620.U75M47 2011
813'.6—dc22   2010017038

ISBN 978-0-307-58997-2
eISBN 978-0-307-58998-9

Printed in the United States of America

Book design by Lauren Dong
Cover photograph © Andrea Buso/Gallery Stock
Mermaid's tail © Gary Braasch/Corbis

10 9 8 7 6 5 4 3

For my parents and sister

Scarcely had she entered the river than she was cleansed,
gleaming once more like a white stone in the rain,
and without a backward look, she swam once more,
swam toward nothingness, swam to her dying.

—PABLO NERUDA

CHAPTER ONE

The Princess

IT WAS A GLOOMY, OVERCAST DAY, LIKE ALL DAYS WERE, WHEN the princess first saw them. The two of them, who would change her life. There was nothing to herald their appearance, no collection of birds or arrangement of tea leaves to mark their arrival. If anything, the convent was more quiet than usual. The nuns had just finished the midmorning service and scattered to their cells for private prayer. The abbess was shut in her chamber. Only the princess was out in the garden, wandering along the stone wall that overlooked the sea. Here, near the old well, the wall dipped down to her knees, and an ancient gate led to a stairway that curved to the rocky beach below. She was bundled in furs, wincing against the blast of wind that swept up from the sea and made the bare trees rattle around her.

She was not supposed to be out here. She should have been in her cell, too, but she did not follow the rules the way the others did, and the abbess had instructed them to give her wide berth. No one knew why, only that she'd arrived one night on horseback accompanied by three armed guards, who carried in a large chest, placed it in a private double cell in the novices' wing, and disappeared as quietly as they'd come.

No one but the abbess herself knew that she was the Northern king's daughter, that she was in hiding after secret reports that the

South would be renewing its attacks. The others knew her simply by the name Mira, which was short for her given name, Margrethe. Most assumed she suffered some kind of ailment or melancholy, and the less committed novices had spent hours over the last months trying to guess which one. A few days after Margrethe's arrival, another new tenant had appeared: a bright, flame-haired girl named Edele, who became fast friends with Margrethe, almost as if they'd known each other for years.

Margrethe had never wanted to come to this desolate outpost, was not used to the barren loneliness of this part of the world. She missed the castle, the long dinners lit by fire and dancing, the sleigh rides, her childhood room with its little fireplace in which pinecones burned, the mantel lined with books. She especially missed those—her books, and the long hours she had spent with her father's adviser and old tutor, Gregor, poring over them, learning of ancient battles and loves and philosophies. But the kingdom was under threat, and this was the safest place for her, her father had said, here at the edge of the world, in the convent that her late grandmother had helped found and that her mother had been schooled in as a girl.

She thought of her mother now, as she stared out at this desolate sea. It had been two years since the queen's death, but sometimes it felt as fresh as a new wound. Margrethe pulled her furs close and stood stark against the wind, breathing in the thick air, which coated her tongue in salt. She wondered how her mother had felt staring out at this same sea. Was it like this back then? The ocean dark, wild? It seemed, to Margrethe, the color of grief.

Before coming here she had never seen the sea like this, as a living thing. Some trees had been uprooted by a recent storm, and they reached toward the water like gnarled fingers. She strained against the wind, hoping to catch sight of a Viking ship, a square flag, a dragon prow, but she was at the end of the world now, at the most northern point in the kingdom, and no ships came here.

How was she to know that this would be the most singular moment of her life? How can any of us tell when that thing comes that will make everything different? It seemed, to Margrethe, a moment like any other: waiting to return to her father's castle, looking over the gloomy sea, waiting for private prayer to be over and the convent workday to start. Strangely, she found herself looking forward to the hours she'd spend weaving that afternoon, listening to the clacking of the looms, the hum of the spinning wheels nearby, the voice of one of the sisters reading scripture moving over them. At first she'd hated the dull hours of work, but lately she'd found a certain comfort in them. She could forget everything, watching the wool transform in front of her.

The sky gleamed and shifted. The sun was a dull ache behind a veil of gray and silver.

And then, there. On the water! She breathed in quickly, afraid it was a trick of the sea.

A fish's tail shooting out. Bright, shimmering silver.

Margrethe squinted against the cold wind, trying to keep her eyes steady and focused. They say you can see things here, at the end of the world. Faces in the clouds and waves and leaves. Branches becoming arms and then branches again.

But there it was again, a flash of white.

Margrethe blinked repeatedly, and the sea air seemed to cut through her. She wiped tears from her eyes and cheeks and leaned into the wind. The sea seemed to shift from foam to water, from dark to light, swirling. In the distance, rocks jutted. It would be easy to mistake one for the monstrous fin of a great fish, the prow of a ship sinking down.

And then: a curving, gleaming tail flaring out of the water. A moment later, another flash and a pale face emerging, disappearing as quickly as it had appeared. A woman's face. The tail of a fish stretching out behind her. Silvery, as if it were made of gems.

Margrethe shook her head. The cold was making her see things.

She turned to look at the convent behind her, the cross and church spires stretching black against the sky. The other women were inside, next to fires and wrapped in blankets and furs. Only she was crazy enough to stand here staring into this impossible sea.

She laughed at herself, turned back to the sea. But the woman was still there, closer now, gliding through the water as if she had wings. Her hair the color of the moon and scattered through with pearls. Her skin shimmering out of the water, catching the light and turning to diamonds. And that tail propelling her forward, unmistakably. It was not human, this creature.

Mermaid. The name came to Margrethe automatically, from the stories that had rooted themselves in her mind, the ancient tales she had read by firelight as the rest of the castle slept.

She no longer felt the wind or the cold as she stood transfixed, watching the mermaid move through the water. Margrethe had not known such things could really exist, but the moment she saw the mermaid, it was as if the world had always contained this kind of wonder. *This is how it works,* she thought. *When the world becomes something new, it seems always to have been that way.*

She'd never seen anything so beautiful in all her years at court, not in all the grand banquets and dances, the festivals that lasted weeks at a time, the creations of musicians and storytellers, the rich spices and fabrics and jewels shipped in from all over the world. Not in all her years surrounded by handmaidens who bathed her and brushed her hair and laced her corsets and pressed powder into her skin. Nothing could compare to this creature gliding through the water, propelled by the tail of a fish.

As the mermaid approached the shore, Margrethe saw that she was carrying something. A man. Holding him in her arms and keeping his head above water.

The mermaid slowed as she arrived at the shore, and reached out to the rocky beach. In a graceful rolling movement, the man cradled in one arm, she moved from sea to land. The sharp rocks would have ripped a human's skin, but the mermaid seemed un-harmed as she released the man and gently, tenderly, laid him out on the shore next to her, her light hair hanging in long, wet ropes.

Now Margrethe could see clearly: the man's muscled warrior's body, covered with wounds. Human. The mermaid stretched out next to him—her pale, naked torso shifting to glittering scales as waist flared to hip, the curve of her tail like a perfectly fitted, exquisitely colored dress. A most wonderful silver, tinged with green. The mermaid sat up and pulled her tail to her side. She still didn't appear to be affected by the cold, despite the wind whipping all around her. Her skin seemed hard, like stone. As Margrethe realized this was the mermaid's *actual body*, a feeling of revulsion mixed with her wonder and awe. *What would it be like to be half a fish?* she thought. *How cold and hard was she to touch?*

The man was sputtering and coughing. The mermaid leaned over him, her breasts grazing his chest as she did. She kissed his forehead, stroked his wet hair. Even from a distance Margrethe could see the look of pure, radiant love that lit the mermaid's face as she gazed down on him.

This is what rapture is, Margrethe thought. That thing she saw come over the nuns' faces as they knelt in prayer. She'd tried turn-ing to heaven, the way the women surrounding her did, but her heart, she knew, was too tied to the earth.

Behind her the bells rang, announcing the late morning devo-tions.

Suddenly the mermaid looked up and saw Margrethe. Mar-grethe gasped, caught. She could see the blue of the mermaid's eyes, as if the whole scene had become magnified, feel it inside her despite the distance between them. It was as if, for one moment, the mermaid was right there in the convent garden.

Save him, the trees, the wind seemed to whisper. A voice inside her. *You, come now.*

Margrethe stopped breathing, could barely feel her own body.

And then, with one last look at the man, a last kiss on the lips, the creature pushed off from the rocks and dove back into the sea.

Margrethe cried out and, without thinking, ran through the convent gate and down the stone steps—hundreds of them—that led to the beach. She hugged the furs to her body, almost slipping, reaching to the thin iron banister to steady herself, the air rushing and whirring around her, the stairs streaming under her endlessly. She arrived at the beach, stumbled over rocks, but there was no trace of the mermaid. Only him, the man the creature had pulled to shore. And there, by his hand, one gleaming oyster shell.

Margrethe stood at the shoreline, then waded into the sea, not caring as water soaked through her boots. She stared out, but there was only endless ocean, cut up by rocks and ice and the worried, suffocating sky. Suddenly the world seemed entirely bleak and without hope. "Come back," Margrethe whispered. "Please."

But the sea was quiet now. The rocks pushed up from the water, motionless, like uncaring gods. The waves moved back and forth along the shoreline, slapping it, lunging to the earth, and then disappearing again.

CHAPTER TWO

The Mermaid

THE PALACE'S GREAT HALL WAS UNUSUALLY QUIET THAT afternoon. The ocean floor, dense with sea plants and anemones and coral plates, was still, and the amber walls swayed only slightly, sprouting flowers that brushed the mermaid's skin as she swam past. The high-pointed amber windows had been flung open, and schools of glowing silver fish with pointed teeth poured through, illuminating the dark water. Above, thousands of mussel shells opened and closed with the currents. If she squinted, looked as hard as she could, she imagined she could make out the dim glare of the sun above.

Her name was Lenia. She was the youngest daughter of the sea queen, and lived with her mother, father, grandmother, and five sisters in a large coral palace on the ocean floor.

She made her way to the end of the great hall, where a piece of heavy, clouded glass hung over the grand fireplace. Both glass and fireplace had been recovered from sunken ships full of human bones and ephemera and treasures. Lenia found it strange to see her own image, and she usually avoided the glass and its tricks. But today she felt so different and changed, she had to see if it would be obvious to anyone else.

Her sisters had badgered her all morning, their singing drifting through the water and every room of the palace, trying to lure her out to the garden, where they had all been waiting to hear her story. She had the most beautiful voice, everyone had always said, and it was she who'd been most excited, of all the sisters, to swim to the upper world. She was the one who had the human statue in her garden, a garden as round and red as the sun. She was the one who'd asked their grandmother countless times to tell her about men and women, about souls. But Lenia had waited in her room until she was quite sure her sisters had left for the day, until the only resident left in the palace was their old grandmother, who knew better than anyone that Lenia would talk when she was ready, and only then.

Lenia came upon the clouded glass. It took her a minute to focus on her blue eyes, her white skin, the glittering moon hair that flew out on all sides of her in the water, her small, pink-tipped breasts, her long silver-gray tail, the oyster shells lining it, symbols of her high rank. Behind her, an octopus swayed this way and that, and a group of sea horses floated past.

She leaned in until she was inches from her own reflection.

She pressed her palms into her waist, her smooth, cold skin. She had thought she might look more . . . human, she realized. But she was the same as she'd always been. She didn't even look older.

Her face stared out at her from the glass, as if it were mocking her. There was nothing human about her. Her skin was opalescent, changing color ever so slightly as she shifted in the water. Her lips were stained pink with the sea flowers that had been ground for her. Water moved in and out of the tiny gills on her neck. And right below the curve of her belly, her skin took on a high sheen and then turned, slowly, to scale. Long, thin silver fish scales layered down her tail.

She had wanted to go to the upper world for as long as she could remember. One by one her sisters had been allowed to travel to the surface of the water on their eighteenth birthdays, for the entire day, while she, the youngest, had to wait in the palace for their return. After each sister's visit, they'd all gather in the gardens and hear tales of the curiosities and wonders that lay above. The fish would slip past their shoulders and faces as the lucky sister wove her tale, and Lenia would listen breathlessly as her sisters spoke of the glimmering cities and clattering carriages they'd watched from the shore, the star-sprinkled night skies, the flying swans like long white veils over the sea, the mortal children with legs rather than tails, and the icebergs that glistened like pearls. Her sisters had been impressed by these things, but happy enough to return to the sea when their birthdays were over. But to Lenia, the whole upper world seemed so vast, so strange, so full, that she'd been determined to venture farther than any of her sisters on her own eighteenth birthday, memorizing every moment of it.

Once, mermaids had been able to visit the upper world whenever they wanted. They'd appeared to sailors, bewitched travelers, stolen beautiful young men from seasides, brought them down to the world below. But things had changed in the last few hundred years, as humans took more and more to the sea. After a group of mermaid sisters had been hauled up by fishermen and brutally killed, Lenia's great-grandmother had issued a royal decree forbidding any further interaction between the two worlds. "They are dangerous," she had said. "They will kill us all if they have the chance." Still, to honor that long-ago link between merpeople and humans, every mermaid and merman was allowed this one day, on his or her eighteenth birthday, to travel alone to the upper world, as long as they kept carefully out of view of humans.

To most of Lenia's kind, humans were base, predatory. They lived short, violent lives before dying and leaving their bodies to rot, which most merpeople found quite inelegant—as they themselves lived for three hundred years before turning gracefully to foam. The bloated bodies of humans littered the ocean floor; human ships sank and became tombs full of garbage and bones. In recent years, some merpeople had even elected to stay in the sea on their eighteenth birthdays, refusing any contact with the upper world at all.

Her sisters, more than anyone, had mocked Lenia's love for humans. Nadine would bring Lenia the bones of sailors and, whenever she could get to them before the fish, decaying body parts. "Look how disgusting," she would say, holding up a disintegrating finger, pieces of skin flapping off it like small sails. "Look what happens to them."

But none of her family's prejudices had lessened Lenia's desire to see the upper world for herself. She had anticipated her visit for so long that she had insisted on going the night before, right after midnight, in the middle of a terrible storm, one so strong and fierce they had felt it at the bottom of the sea.

"You might want to wait a few hours more," her grandmother had warned, the coral walls quivering around them, but Lenia had waved off her concern. The eve of her birthday had finally come, and she'd gone through the whole ceremony—the elaborate feast, the clipping on of oyster shells and pearls, the singing in front of the entire court—and she was not going to wait a second past midnight to visit the world above.

"I want to see all of it," she'd said. "Even the worst of it."

They had wrung their hands and tried to distract her with gifts and baubles. Her mother had had the cooks find giant clams and stuff them with monkfish liver and crab and roe, prepare lupe de mare with sea mushrooms, wrap crabmeat around imported rascasse, lay out platters heaped with the rarest caviar, and present a selection of oysters and percebes and periwinkles and crabs and lobster and conch on huge plates lined with starfish. Her father had given her a shell that, when held up to the ear, played the songs of whales and selkies. And her sisters had joined together to make her a bracelet strung with sea glass plucked from the oldest, most tragic shipwrecks.

The golden banquet table had tilted and shifted from the shaking of the storm above. Sand from the ocean floor had whirled up and spun around them as they feasted. The musicians kept playing their instruments made from coral and bones and shells, even as the palace swayed and the mussel shells above them snapped open and shut. No one had experienced such effects from an upper-world storm in hundreds of years, some of the merpeople whispered. This was extraordinary, and surely a very bad sign.

"Sing, Lenia," her sisters had insisted, trying to distract her, and, to defy them all, she opened her mouth and sang the sweetest song she could about the beauty of the world above them. She remembered details from her grandmother's stories, from her sisters' visits, from her own dreams. Creatures that flew through the air. Lightning that flashed across the sky. Souls leaving bodies and drifting up to the stars.

That is what the other merpeople did not understand, and what Lenia did: that humans had souls, and that their souls lived forever. It was not the same as when merpeople died, dissolving into foam and becoming part of the great ocean. Souls were webs of light that contained the essence of a human's life. Memories and loves, children and families. Every moment of a life, pressing in.

"Stop!" her mother had cried, seeing the effect Lenia's voice had on the court. Even those who had never been to the upper world and never wanted to go, who accepted it as a place filled with danger, had felt a deep longing within them when Lenia sang. They had all come from the same place, after all, humans and merpeople. No one could be whole in a universe so divided. Lenia's voice—so sweet and clear—had snaked into each one of them, filling their hearts and illuminating the parts that were empty.

Lenia had stopped singing, and there was silence as each guest struggled to regain composure.

"Just go, Daughter," her mother had said, resignedly, and her father had nodded beside the queen the way he always did. No one was even sure how much he actually paid attention to anything anymore, he was so used to echoing his wife. "It is almost midnight. Go and you will see that nothing is as wonderful as our dreams can make it."

And Lenia had left the palace and swum straight up to the surface of the ocean. Up, up, so fast it was like she was being pushed on a wave, as the water swirled around her. The surface was miles away, farther than she'd realized even on days when it felt so far from her it might as well have been another universe. The closer she got, the more intense the current became, thrashing her about, throwing fish and shells against her, wrapping seaweed around her limbs.

When she finally reached the surface and pushed her face above water, the sheer wall of sound nearly sent her back under. The crash of thunder, the pounding of rain, the rush of air as it hit her mouth and lungs. A strange, raw feeling—as if she were being hollowed out, the air swooping through her, invading every cell of her body. She struggled for breath as the waves rose and fell all around her, howling. The sky was black and then ablaze with lightning. She cried out, and flinched when her voice distorted as it hit the air. Even among the crazy cacophony of the upper world, the sound of her own voice seemed to shatter against her.

As her eyes focused, she saw something in the distance, tossing on the waves. She'd only ever seen ships at the bottom of the sea. It confused her, the force of it battling the storm. The dragon prow twisting this way and that.

She ducked back into the water and made her way to the ship. She cut through the wild water with ease and swam right under the vessel, watched in wonder as it tipped to the right and left, shedding oars and chests and other treasures into the sea. Like a monster riding the sea. She darted out from under the ship, pushed her head above water.

And then, there, on the vessel. Right in front of her.

Human men.

She watched their faces raging with life, as they fought to hold the ship steady on the impossible sea. But the vessel began to split apart beneath them. Whole chunks ripped off, twisting in the wind, crashing in the water, where they would sink to the bottom of the ocean and become new ruins for her and her sisters to explore.

A man fell from the ship. Just fell into the water like a bit of debris. She slipped her head below the surface and watched him being pulled under. He thrashed and struggled to get above water, to the air, and she wanted to tell him that he was safe now, that the world under the water was beautiful, that she could take care of him there. But, as she watched, his face became horrible, lurid. He stopped struggling. She swam to him. She wanted to help him, to pull him down to the palace and tend to him, but then his body stopped moving and she knew he was dead. She grabbed him and shook him. Her face was next to his, her hands under his shoulders.

It struck her, what she knew already: men could not survive under the surface of the water.

She'd seen many dead humans, of course, but she'd never seen a human die before. It was horrible. Merpeople had a different kind of death. Everyone knew when they would die, and it seemed long enough to them, their three hundred years. They passed gently, turning slowly to foam, fading into the water and then disappearing altogether, to become part of the sea. She'd seen many merpeople die, and those left behind always celebrated the passing with song and feast. But she believed it was even more beautiful when humans died because they had immortal souls. She remembered again, now, how her grandmother had described to her the way a soul would slip from a human body, shimmering and beautiful, and rise to something called heaven, where it would have eternal life.

But that was not what Lenia saw as she watched more men die

around her. These were awful, painful deaths. Limbs thrashing and going slack. Men struggling, with all their strength, for air, the horror on their faces as they began to drown.

It was the most terrible thing she'd ever seen.

She let go of the man's body in horror, watched him drop farther and farther, until he faded into the black of the sea.

She looked up. Men were falling all around her now, spilling through the water, clawing for land, for air. Dying. She pushed her way back to the surface. The ship was nearly gone, just slabs of wood falling into the sea. Men were swimming, trying to grab onto pieces of the ship. Their strange legs flailing, their screams ripping through the stormy air. She watched as a piece of ballast fell and smashed in a man's skull. Dead men floated past her. And the sky still crackled with lightning, like an angry god.

It was chaotic, terrifying. She did not know which way to turn.

Until she saw him. The one man clinging to a slab of wood. His eyes moved up and caught hers. Had she seen him before? He was so familiar to her. The water was pulling him. There were barely any men left above the surface.

Her body began moving before the thought crystallized: she would save him, this one man.

She swam to him, pushing past bodies and debris, and he was frozen, staring at her, stunned, the rain pounding down. He was so strong, clinging to life so ferociously, his powerful legs kicking to keep him above water. She found it moving, his passion for life. This will to live.

"Come," she said, holding out her hand.

He didn't move.

"Come to me. I will save you."

Her voice seemed to have some magical effect on him. He looked at her, his eyes wide with fear and wonder, a smile beginning to form on his face, despite everything. She smiled back at him. Her grandmother had told her this, how easily men were enchanted by mermaid sounds. How easily a mermaid could cast a spell on a man and lead him to his death. This made sense to her now. Her soft, beautiful tones in this harsh, loud world.

She put one arm behind his shoulders, the other winding about his waist.

"Let go," she said. "Hold on to me."

His face was right next to hers. She could feel his heart beating.

"My men," he said, his voice rumbling into her. "My ship."

"Shh," she said. "I will take you to shore."

He was wearing cloth over his chest, and the material felt strange under her palm. She loved the smell of him. Even over the sea and rain, she could smell his hair, his skin, feel the warmth of his beating heart. As she began swimming, she leaned her cheek into his wet hair, surprised at the feel of it. He was so soft, full of life. She had to stop herself from pulling him down to her garden and wrapping herself around him. *He will die there,* she repeated to herself. *Take him where he will live.*

She swam harder, pushing against the current, leaving the wreckage and the bodies far behind. She realized that she knew where to go, that her body could sense it.

It was wonderful, swimming for the first time between the two worlds, half in the air and half in the water, as the rain beat down against her. She liked the challenge of the crashing waves, the way the lightning cracked the sky open, the beauty of the night and the rain and the moon, faintly visible. She liked the feeling of him in her arms. For a human it'd be hard work, carrying a man of his size, but he felt easy in her arms. He had slipped from consciousness, but she was aware at every moment of his breathing, the air moving in and out of his lungs, how crucial it was to keep him above water and not let his breath stop.

She swam as her body told her to, slipping into a kind of trance between his breathing and the churning of the storm-ridden sea.

After a while, the rain stopped, the sea calmed, and there was no sound but the lapping of water and his faint breath. Above her, the black sky cleared, until she could see the thousands of stars strewn across it. Even in her most vivid imaginings, she had not understood the vastness of this world, how far it extended. She looked down at the man in her arms, his soft, perfect face, and a ferocious love moved through her.

I will save you.

She pushed her powerful tail behind her. She swam harder than she ever had, holding the man as if he could break, her arms under his shoulders. And then, finally, in the distance: the glimmer of windows. Humans. The way her sisters had described it. There was a wall of rock, and above it, a large stone structure. The sun was coming up behind the structure, on the top of the cliff, splitting the sky into pink and cream and blue.

"Look," she whispered, and his eyes fluttered open. "Look at the sky."

He turned his head, looked right at her, and, in the breaking sunlight, she could see the strange tawny color of his eyes. There was so little life in them now.

She shoved her tail against the waves and swam as hard as she could, to the shore, to where he would be safe.

Her eyes scanned the cliff, the building, and then rested on a lone human girl, standing on the cliff, near a long staircase that wound down to the rocky beach. Lenia focused in on her.

Save him, she thought.

She reached the shore and pulled him out of the water, onto the rocks.

She had only seconds.

She lay beside him and stroked his face and his hair. His eyes fluttered open and shut as she leaned down and kissed his lips, his eyelids, his forehead. The feel of him under her lips, combined with the sunlight, the air that swept along her bare skin, her wet hair—all of it filled her with a kind of euphoria she'd never before felt. The material of his wet shirt tickling her breasts as she leaned against him. His open mouth and warm tongue.

He was so beautiful. She had never seen anything so beautiful.

But she could feel the life leaving him, and knew that she had done all she could do, that it was time to let other humans take care of him so that he could live. She looked up at the girl on the cliff, standing there watching them, transfixed. Her black hair blowing around her, her pale skin and brown eyes, her furs.

You, she thought again. *Come now.*

CHAPTER THREE

The Princess

THE MAN WAS SOAKED THROUGH AND SHIVERING WITH
cold. His arms and legs were wrapped in seaweed. There
was a strange shimmer, Margrethe saw, where the mermaid had touched him, on his face and arms. He had a warrior's
body, though his clothes were those of a civilian. Even sprawled
as he was on the beach, half dead, he looked like a soldier about to
go into battle.

She knelt beside him, her knees pushing into the rocky beach,
and touched his face the way the mermaid had done moments before, running her fingers along the trail of shimmer the mermaid
had left on his cheeks and lips. There was no feel to it, no particles
that rubbed off onto her fingers. His skin was smooth, like stone,
and his light hair had already formed into ice. Just as she poised
her hand to touch his eyelids, to trace their curve, he blinked and
stared up at her.

His eyes hit her like an open palm. In them, she could see the
same glint that was on his skin. She jumped back.

"You," he said, in a strange accent, his voice like a growl. He
grabbed onto her furs, and she saw how weak he was. The rocks
around him were stained with blood. She did not know what to
do. She thought of her childhood nurse, who had been able to heal

with a clove or a piece of bark or a dried herb she'd plucked from the castle garden. But she had never been trained in the healing arts. She was the daughter of a king, she was not made for such things, she had never learned anything useful at all. She was alone, and no one would be able to hear her over this wind. She wanted to cry. Why did she know so little of the world? But she knew enough to see that the man was blue, his teeth clacking, that he would die, and her heart burst open, with grief, with love, and she jumped to her feet.

She winced as she slipped off her furs and placed them over the man, carefully tucking them under his arms and legs. Immediately the wind beat against her. She was wearing only a light wool tunic, as all the young nuns did, with a white robe over it. The thin wimple did little to protect her head from the cold. The man stared up at Margrethe as the cold slipped into her skin, into her blood and bones. "I will be back, with help," she said, and she spun and raced up the stairs as fast as she could, her body turning to ice, her hair to icicles that clanked together, and finally, after what seemed like days, she reached the garden, the gate, and then she was inside the abbey, gasping for air.

She pushed past the few nuns outside the abbess's chamber. "Quick! I need help!"

Margrethe pounded on the abbess's door as the others gathered around her.

The abbess opened the door, startled—then panicked to see the young princess before her, wet and shivering, in a dangerous state of cold.

"Mira!" she cried. "What has happened to you?"

"There is a man, at the beach, by the water. He needs help!"

"Come in here," the abbess said, pulling Margrethe inside, making her sit by the fire. She called out to the others, "Get blankets and furs! Get the nurse!"

"Please," Margrethe said. "We have to go to the beach, to help him. I told him I would go back!" She knew she could not let the man die. The mermaid had brought him to her, to save him.

One of the nuns ran in, breathless. "Mother, there *is* a man on the shore."

"Go to him." the abbess said. "Get him inside before he dies. A group of you, go!"

As the cloisters erupted into chaos behind her, the abbess leaned down and looked into Margrethe's face. "You cannot risk yourself like this, no matter what. You are not like the rest of us. Don't forget that. I promised your father you'd be safe here. Think of what would happen to us, if any harm were to come to you."

Margrethe nodded, woozy. The abbess was an imposing woman, with snow-white hair and pale eyes, and there was a stricken quality about her face, as if she'd just witnessed something awful. "He is down there dying," Margrethe tried to say, but her words came out in tiny gasps. "I saw . . ."

"Shhh. Drink."

Liquid burned down her throat. Vaguely, she sensed others coming in, wrapping her in blankets, leading her back to her cell. The abbess helping her as she lay on the pallet. Outside, the wind howled and howled. Suddenly, she was exhausted. Maybe there was something in the drink, to calm her and make her sleep.

∽

WHEN SHE WOKE, the room was bathed in darkness. Outside all she could hear was wind, the crashing of rain. Bells were ringing for prayer. It took her a moment to orient herself, remember where she was. Was it Vespers? Had she missed the whole workday? She rose, pulled on a clean tunic. Her fingers shook as she secured the scapular, then attached her wimple and veil.

She'd been dreaming of her mother, she realized. She was a child again, curled up in her mother's arms, taking in her lavender scent, the warmth of her voice, the softness of her palm as she smoothed down Margrethe's hair. A terrible sense of loss moved through her. And there was something else . . .

A mermaid, yes. And a man.

Margrethe shuffled down the corridor, still groggy from her long sleep. Her body felt like it had been wrought from flames. Slowly, she made her way to the chapel—stopping, for a moment, to peek outside, into the convent garden. She pressed open the door, and the wind rushed around her. It felt good, the cold. Rain lashed at her face, and she could hear the crashing of the sea.

It was dark. The stars were visible past the veil of white that covered them. The sea shone black in the distance, all its secrets hidden away.

She shook her head. What dreams she had had! The mermaid on the rocks, bent over the dying man. Her mother, singing her to sleep. She must have fallen into a fever, the way the abbess had only the week before, taken ill from the cold. Margrethe laughed, but not without a tinge of longing. She had been raised in a court where troubadours seduced them with magical tales, where she spent afternoons with her tutor, Gregor, reading long, ancient stories of heroes and conquerors, the dead come back to life. Now here she was, living against the most desolate sea, with women who spent hours each day speaking to heaven while she herself made up fantastical creatures.

She closed the door and hurried to the chapel, already late, taking her seat in the choir stall next to Edele, her old friend and most favored lady-in-waiting, who caught her eye and gave her a look of barely contained panic.

"Are you well?" Edele whispered, ignoring the sharp looks from the others.

Margrethe nodded and put her hand on Edele's to reassure her. She felt more than ever that she was at the end of the earth, where dream and reality mixed.

She mouthed the words along with the others. She closed her eyes, felt the sweat collecting at her brow. She had dreamed the wonders she'd seen earlier, she thought, but things were still lovely in this part of the world—these women, this place, the feeling that every moment contained something of the miraculous. And Edele, sitting beside her, one lock of her wild hair peeking out from the wimple that covered it.

After the service, Edele pulled Margrethe aside. "You shouldn't have risked yourself like that," she whispered, "running about in the cold. Remember who you are."

Margrethe's head shot up in surprise. Her heart began to beat frantically. "He is real?"

"The man on the shore? Of course. He is safe, because of you. But you should have called to the others, not gone yourself."

"I thought I had dreamt him."

Edele looked closely at Margrethe, her round eyes full of concern. She shook her head. "Are you sure you are well?"

A few of the others were gathering round. "He is a foreigner," one of the nuns said.

"There are no signs of his ship," another said. "It's a miracle that he washed up on our shore and that you found him there."

"A miracle," Margrethe repeated.

And then she felt his wet skin, under her palm, saw the mermaid's blue eyes, her white-blond hair, her silvery green tail glinting above the rocks.

"Maybe you should go back and rest," Edele said. "I will bring you tea and bread."

"I'm fine," Margrethe said, her eyes shining. "Where is he?"

"The man?"

"Yes, I want to see him."

Margrethe could see the women giving each other looks, but she didn't care. The man was her responsibility.

"The infirmary," a young nun said. "The last room."

"Excuse me," N
see you at supper

She crept dov
ways were dark
wind continue
ghosts on all

She arriv
paused, try
rain must
rooftop.

She st

The roo
a fire in the corner. The
body wrapped in bandages, furs su
faint light, she could see he still had the sheen o
him. His chest bare and glimmering.

She stared at him in wonder. The mermaid had come to him in the water, carried him to shore, placed him on the rocks. That shimmer—if anything, it seemed more pronounced, sparkling as the firelight hit it, on his cheeks, his eyelids, his chest. As she moved forward, to the edge of the bed, his face came out of shadow. Up close she saw his lips, the outline of them: the top lip perfectly shaped, coming down in a $\vee$, the shimmer extending across his bottom lip, which was more full.

He was as beautiful as the mermaid, she thought, studying him.

His chest rose and fell with his breath. She moved closer. Slowly she reached her arm forward and lightly, with just the tip of her index finger, traced the curve of his shoulder. *Who are you?* she wondered.

She looked back to his face and realized, with horror, that his eyes were open, that he was watching her now. Gasping, she yanked her hand back, moved away.

"Please," he said. "Don't leave."

24 Carolyn

Again she was startled. His fa
eyes, a green-brown-yellow, th
The lights from the fire c
strange. He looked at her
turned away, embarrass
"What is your na
She almost tol
"Mira."
"Mira," h
my savior
"It

ce was surprisingly soft and his
e color of a dying weed.

st his shadow on the wall, jagged and
as if he could see her thoughts, and she
ed. No one had ever looked at her this way.

me?" he asked.

him her given name, then remembered herself.

e repeated. He seemed to taste each syllable. "Mira,
. I am Christopher."

as a terrible storm," she said. "You are lucky to be alive."

hat was no storm," he said, raising his eyebrows.

"What do you mean?"

"Have you ever seen a dragon?" he asked.

"A dragon?"

"A monster who breathes fire," he said, lowering his voice. "As big as a glacier, maybe two. They live in the sea. We were sailing along, and everything was fine. Me, my men. There was music, dancing. We'd done hard battle, nothing to talk about to a lady. And then suddenly, there was a rocking. Water dropped from the sky. And the boat swayed and kicked, like a horse trying to throw us off. When I looked up, I saw it. The most terrifying monster in the world. Eyes of fire, skin like plague."

She stared at him, breathless, waiting. His eyes grew large as he remembered the terror of the beast.

"I slayed him, Sister, but not before he took every last one of my men. I never saw anything like it."

He finished his story, smiling. For a moment she just looked at him before smiling back. "You, my lord," she said, "are a spinner of tales."

"Oh, my lady," he said, putting his hand to his heart. "I am only telling you what I saw."

"And then a *mermaid* saved you, I suppose," she said playfully, watching for his reaction. Did he remember? "And left a trail of diamonds across your skin."

He laughed, delighted. The way he was looking at her—it was like she was a goddess, as if she had emerged from the sea like Aphrodite in the stories Gregor had told her. "Is that what you are? Is that why you wear that habit, to hide your true nature?"

"Perhaps," she said.

"I will never tell."

"Where do you come from?" she asked.

"Far from here," he said, waving his hand. "My men and I have gone to many distant lands. We have seen wonders you would not believe. Men with eyes in their foreheads, women with snakes for hair."

She shook her head with amusement. "Hmmm, I think I've heard of you," she said. "Did you enter an enemy city inside a horse as well?"

"Yes!" he said, nodding vigorously, "back when we fought a most terrible war. After, an enchantress put me under a spell and kept me on her island for seven years. I lived on nothing but the fruit I shook down from trees. Can you imagine, Sister? And once, in the middle of the ocean, we saw a woman stepping out of a clamshell, right there on the surface of the water."

"That must have been very awful for you."

"Yes, more than the most ferocious battle. Seeing a woman, in the middle of a long journey . . . It almost killed us all from shock."

She smiled, and then suddenly the whole room seemed to shift. "You . . . Wait." A terrible feeling rose in her, a suspicion, and her amusement faded away. She had been too blinded by that mermaid sheen, that beautiful glimmer marking his skin, to notice how sun-drenched he was underneath. His warrior's body. "Do you . . . come from the South?"

"I do. From a much warmer land than this."

"The Southern kingdom?"

"Yes." He was smiling at her, and then his face changed. "Are you well, Sister? What is it? I am not an enemy to you here, in a house of God."

Suddenly the door, the hallway, the other nuns—all of it seemed miles away.

"I have to go," she said.

"Sister? Forgive me. I do not mean to offend."

"I . . . have to return to my chores," she said, trying to keep her voice calm, prevent her hands from shaking, her legs from running, as she went to the door and pushed through.

"Sister!"

She rushed down the hall, to the main part of the convent and back to her cell, where she leaned against the wall, trying to catch her breath, stop the racing of her heart.

She had never met one of her kingdom's enemies before. The men from the South who had wended their way up to her own land when she was a child, leaving heaps of bodies in their wake.

CHAPTER FOUR

The Mermaid

LENIA'S EYES PEERED BACK AT HER, IN THE GLASS, HER hair swarming around her face and lifting into the water above. She could still feel him in her arms. That warmth, that beating heart. The sensation of wet hair, wet skin, under her palms. As soft as a mussel.

Then behind her, another face appeared. Vela, the next youngest sister to Lenia, her pale face pressing through the water, like a memory, or a ghost.

"You scared me," Lenia said, turning. "I thought you were in the garden."

Vela wrapped her long, silvery arms around Lenia's shoulders. "Did you have a good birthday, Sister?" she asked. "I was worried when you wouldn't come talk to us. I was afraid you'd been disappointed."

"By the upper world?"

"The storm. We could feel it down here long after you left."

Lenia smiled. Vela was the sweetest of her sisters. Anyone who didn't know them—though of course everyone knew them, they were daughters of the sea queen—would have thought that Vela, with her round cheeks and little bow mouth, her bright hair and peach-colored tail, was the youngest instead of Lenia. Vela loved the sea's creatures more than any of them and could spend whole days discovering hidden life in the ocean's crevices. Leaf-crowned sea dragons with long, glowing needles for teeth, tiny red octopi that spun like stars, glassy see-through creatures shaped like flowers. Even now she had a giant shell on her shoulder with a pulsing, gooey creature inside, suctioned to her skin.

"No," Lenia said, gently removing Vela's arms. "I wasn't disappointed. I liked the storm. I would have liked to stay longer."

"You would have?"

"I would have liked to stay forever."

Vela made a face. "Very funny. Come outside, come tell us all about it. We've found something, too, that you will like."

Lenia turned her head and kissed Vela on the cheek. "What?"

"Men, everywhere, from the storm. I found them this morning, by the cave. One body, then another and another, and the ship they were on, too." She smiled, raising her glittering brows. "And a chest of treasures."

"Oh!" Lenia said, wondering if she could find something of his, and then immediately felt horrible, remembering what she'd seen.

"What's wrong?" Vela asked. "You love human treasures."

"This is different," Lenia said. "I saw it happen. The shipwreck. It was terrible."

Vela's eyes widened. "You saw it?"

"Yes, the storm, the ship, I saw it break apart. I saw men die."

"Oh," Vela breathed. "Let's go to the others, you must tell us everything!"

She grabbed Lenia's hand, and the two swam together, through the long hallway where sea plants streamed around them, filled with small, phosphorescent creatures that lit up the dark. In front of the palace, in the main family garden, the rest of the sisters waited: Bolette, Nadine, Regitta, who was holding her son, and the oldest sister, Thilla, who was carrying a platter of baby soft-shell crabs left over from the birthday feast.

Lenia swam over and popped one in her mouth, liking the feel of the shell as it cracked between her teeth. She reached for another, suddenly starving.

"Didn't you find anything to eat up there?" Thilla asked, laughing.

"Look, Sister," Nadine said. She shifted, letting the electric eel in her arms cast light on a wooden chest, perched on a rock beside her. The chest was open. The insides of it splendid, as if it contained all the night stars spread across the sky.

"So when are you going to tell us about your adventure?" Bolette asked. Bolette and her twin sister, Regitta, were the next oldest, after Thilla. Bolette was the fastest swimmer of all of them, with the longest, thinnest body, which could slice through the water like a sharp blade. "Was it wonderful, like you thought it'd be?"

Nadine flicked her tail against Bolette's side. "I am attempting to give our sister a gift, if you don't mind," she said. She dipped into the chest and held out a gold necklace with a huge red stone hanging from the center. It was stunning.

The red stone flashed in the water, catching the faint light. A few small fish darted up to it, and Nadine caught them in her palm, stuffed them into her mouth.

"It's beautiful," Lenia said. She took the necklace, placed it around her neck. Nadine swam behind her and fastened it, kissing her on the shoulder.

"It looked like you," Nadine said. She swam back around to the other sisters, admiring her work. "That is how your voice sounds to us."

Lenia laughed, tracing the stone underneath her fingertips. She looked at her sisters' five expectant faces. They were all so lovely. Behind them, a thousand fluorescent fish swam upward in one motion.

"Well?" Vela asked, unable to contain herself any longer. "What was it like? Seeing them die?"

"Seeing what die?" Thilla asked. She looked from Vela to Lenia. "You saw . . . not humans?"

"Humans, yes," Lenia said. "A whole ship full of men. I saw it break apart in the storm. They were clinging, screaming. Their voices! My ears are still ringing from it. I swam right up to them. I looked into their faces. One of them was struggling in the water. I watched him die, and then his body went limp."

"How strange," Vela said, wonderingly. "To be alive one minute, and then—"

"Yes," Lenia said. "And they were fighting and trying so hard to live. It was beautiful. I mean it was horrifying, at the time, but then I saw that they just wanted so much to stay there, in the upper world."

"That sounds terrifying," Regitta said. Instinctively she rocked her tiny son, asleep in her arms, as if he could understand. "I think I would have turned around and come home rather than see that."

Bolette leaned into her twin and reached out to stroke the baby's shock of red hair. "I can't believe you saw humans up close at all, let alone dying ones. Weren't you nervous?"

"No," Lenia said. "Of course not. They were busy dying, they were not trying to hurt me. Plus, they are so soft. You would not believe how soft they are."

"Wait. You touched them?" Thilla said. She froze, a small crab dangling in her hand, next to her mouth.

"One of them," Lenia said. "Only one. I saved him."

She watched as her sisters reacted with horror. "I wish you all could understand," she said, "how lovely it was."

"But why would you do that?" Bolette asked, genuinely perplexed.

As Lenia was about to answer, a flurry of minuscule neon fish hailed down, attracted to her lilting voice. She swatted them away.

"I don't know," she said. "There was something about him. At one point I just focused on him, clinging for life, and I thought, *I can save him.* I pulled him from the wood he was holding and carried him all the way to land. I could tell he was strong, for a human, but, Sisters, he was so soft, and warm."

"Where did you take him?" Vela asked, mesmerized now.

"I took him to land. I held him for hours, against me, until we arrived. There was a human girl there, watching me, and I called for her to come down to him. She had to come, or else he would die. It was strange. I could feel her. Just like I could feel him. Every beat of his heart, every breath."

"I've heard of that," Thilla said. "That we might be able to read their thoughts. That we used to be able to do that."

"I would hate to read a human's thoughts," Bolette said.

Lenia thought back to the girl, the cliff. "It was less her thoughts, more just . . . as if I were inside her, a little. But I was more focused on him. I wanted her to save him. All I could do was bring him to land. He needed a human to help bring him back to life."

"You are too kindhearted, Sister," Bolette said. "If he could have, that human would have ripped you apart with his hands."

At that, Regitta gasped, holding her son to her chest.

"You two are awfully melodramatic," Lenia said. "I don't think he would have done that at all. In fact, he seemed rather enchanted by me."

"Well, at least you are home safe," Nadine said, digging back in the chest, bored.

Vela swept forward, the distress apparent on her face. "I can't stop thinking about dying, the way humans do it. Imagine! If at any moment, you could just stop existing. How different everything would be. Wouldn't it? If the world were that dangerous?"

"They don't stop existing," Lenia said. "Remember what Grandmother said? That they have souls that live forever. Even knowing that, they fought so hard to stay alive. I think it's so beautiful. Imagine: being that fragile, that permanent."

It *was* beautiful, she thought. She hadn't seen it, right then. The men's deaths had been so horrible. No souls rising to heaven, no eternal life. Just destruction and that heartbreaking will to stay alive. But when she'd moved through the water and the air with the man in her arms, feeling his fragile heart underneath her, she'd felt it. His soul moving into her.

Her grandmother had told her about souls: webs of light inside of every human, light that escaped the body and rose to something called heaven when a human body died. "And when two humans fall in love and marry," her grandmother had said, "a priest joins their souls together, and it is wonderful when that happens because that light becomes very strong." Lenia had always loved her grandmother's fantastical old stories, which she told the girls on long swims when the queen and king weren't around. "Priests can actually see souls, though souls are invisible to everybody else. And when a soul talks to God, that is a prayer." Lenia had often dreamed about these webs of light, wondered what it would feel like to have one inside her.

And carrying the man through the water, she had felt exactly like that: as if that light were entering her, too, the beginnings of an immortal life.

"That is what the sea witch says," Vela said. "That they live forever."

Thilla slammed the tray of crabs so hard on a rock that the water shuddered with it. "First humans, and now Sybil? What has gotten into you two? She's a *witch*. She was banished by our own great-grandmother, Vela."

"Some of the others have gone to her, for spells and potions. It's not a big deal."

"I can't believe you," Regitta said.

"She has tricks to make a merman fall in love with you," said Vela.

"You don't need tricks for *that*," Bolette said, laughing. "At least not from a witch."

"She was banished for a reason," Thilla said. She banged the rock beside her again in frustration. "Don't any of you care? She is dangerous, to all of us. And, Lenia, you're lucky to be alive. If you think dying like a human is so beautiful, go back to them. Let them kill you. They will, you know."

"I would, if I had a soul," Lenia said, crying out. The others stopped and looked at her, surprised by the intensity of her reaction. "I would go back right now."

"Lenia!" Bolette said. "What about us? The sea? You are a mermaid."

"Souls aren't even real," Thilla said, raising her arms in frustration. "It's just a pretty story Grandmother tells us, the way she tells us about sea fairies and talking flowers."

"Stop it, all of you!" Nadine said, lifting a heap of jewelry from the chest and tossing it out at them. Heavy gold and silver, gems of every color, streaking across the water. All manner of sea creature appeared suddenly, from under rocks and amid the coral, attracted by the flashing stones. "It's over. Lenia's back. We're arguing about nothing."

Bolette laughed as a bracelet knocked against her cheek, then fell onto a tentacle of a passing squid. And then they all began to laugh, twisting onto their sides, batting jewels and stones and coins, hundreds of coins from the bottom of the chest, back and forth.

Just like that, the argument was forgotten.

Only Lenia remained quiet, watching as an eel slunk by, catching a twinkling silver ring in its open, gaping mouth.

CHAPTER FIVE

The Princess

MARGRETHE BARELY SLEPT BEFORE LAUDS, THE EARLY morning office. She lay in bed wrapped in furs, her eyes wide open, starting at every sound. The branches crackling outside, the pounding sea, the occasional soft footstep. She slept with a knife blade flat against her belly—the knife her father had sent with her which she'd kept under her bed until now.

She'd heard about the barbarians in the South for as long as she could remember. They had sharp, pointed teeth, her old nurse had told her, and would drink blood straight from an infant's slit throat. She'd grown up having nightmares about being attacked in the forest, or the barbarians slipping past the city walls, across the moat and drawbridge, past the sleeping guards, into the castle and her private chambers. These people had killed her ancestors, her mother had told her, back when she'd told her stories at night, when she was alive—they'd slashed through villages, burning crops and houses, even churches, and danced among the flames. No one alive had seen these things specifically, but the stories had been passed on for generations now. Margrethe herself had spent countless nights lying awake, imagining these horrors, just like any peasant child.

She tossed in her bed. She rose, as she had done at least a dozen times, intending to go straight to the abbess, who could call her father's soldiers from the village below.

But the man had not seemed barbaric. There'd been something gentle about him. The way he'd looked at her—as if she were the one with glimmer on her skin, instead of him. As if she'd been the one to carry him through the water and to shore.

A fire burned in the corner of her cell, throwing everything into shadow.

She lay back down again. Did he know who she was? It would be a great coup, wouldn't it: to capture the daughter of the enemy king? They were not at war now, and yet there had been reports that the South was planning new attacks. That was why she was here. She thought of her father's men positioned in the village below. Disguised as civilians but ready to come to her aid at any moment. And the abbess—a powerful woman with old ties to her own family—had vowed to protect her at all costs. She could call all this aid to her in an instant, if she needed it. But instead she turned the events of the last day over and over in her head. Who was he? What he was doing here?

He was so close to her. Outside her locked door, past the cells of the novices, through the main cloisters, and past the abbess's chamber, he slept.

She reminded herself, again, of what she'd seen: the mermaid had saved him and brought him to the shore. To him, she was a "woman of the cloth," a girl who'd left her family to take vows and spend the rest of her life in this convent by the sea, and that was all.

She fell asleep, finally, imagining those moments in the water, the mermaid's arms wrapped around him. The cold sea, its ice and jagged rocks. The mermaid's silver tail, moving through the water. The blue of the mermaid's eyes as they met her own.

The bells seemed to ring only moments later, and Margrethe woke shivering and disoriented.

She quickly washed in the basin, then grabbed her breviary and headed to the chapel, where all the others were gathering.

They were watching her as she slid into place, crossing herself and kneeling to the floor. They nudged each other, gave her side-long glances.

Margrethe looked away quickly, tried to act as if none of it affected her. As if nothing could distract her from the sacred call. Her heart pounded. She opened her breviary to the correct page and stared at it intently.

Around her, she could feel their eyes boring into her. Many of them were girls from noble families that could not afford to marry more than one daughter off and so sent those more or less fortunate offspring, depending on one's view, into the church's care. Despite their crisp habits and plain, unpainted faces, most of them could have been her own ladies-in-waiting, playing cards or chess with her in her castle chamber. Others, like the elder nun standing in front of them now, had received a real calling, one that made them lie awake at night trembling with love, but even this nun was watching Margrethe now. Wondering about this mysterious young novice who'd rescued a man on the rocks.

The abbess signaled the beginning of service. After lighting a candle, the elder sister began reading through the day's office. Margrethe closed her eyes, listened to the nun's soft voice whispering against the stone walls. Even on a day like today, the presence of all these holy women around her was reassuring, comforting.

When the sister led them in prayer, Margrethe spoke with more fervor than usual, liking the feel of Latin as it filled her mouth, the cold hardness of the stone under the soft soles of her shoes. Here in this bare room, in these sacred garments, surrounded by these women, she felt safe. What had happened to her was God's will, all of it. The world was larger and stranger than she could ever imagine—the mermaid proved it. If death came to her here, it was because God had meant it to be so. A rush of bliss came over her—unbidden, a gift. Finally her body started to relax.

At the end of the office, as the women all began to move from the chapel to the refectory, where the morning meal awaited them, Edele slipped to Margrethe's side and grasped her hand. "How are you?" she whispered fiercely. "Would you please stop worrying me all the time?"

Margrethe looked into her friend's pale, freckled face, her round cheeks and huge green eyes. It always surprised her how unmistakable Edele was, even with the habit concealing her mass of red hair and large, curving body, whereas most of the others seemed to blend into one general person. "There is no need for you to worry so much," she chided. "It does not suit you, you know. I am in excellent health and spirits."

"Perhaps you could try to stay that way?"

A nearby nun shushed them, and Edele made a face. Margrethe stifled a laugh. Seeing her old friend try to adapt to this environment was a constant source of amusement for her.

They took their seats. The novices all sat at one end of the long wooden table and the older nuns at the other. Huge fires burned at either end of the room. One of the nuns sat reading scripture, her voice ringing out above the quiet clang of the dishes. Talking was officially forbidden at mealtimes, but this was one of many convent rules that was not strictly enforced.

As they ate, Margrethe heard snippets of news about the man and his fast recovery. The village doctor had been called for, to treat the man's wounds and apply cleansing leeches to his body.

"He is very strong," whispered one of the younger nuns, a woman who'd been sent to the convent by her family to rid her of the devil's touch. "He has the most wonderful eyes. Doesn't he, Mira?"

They all looked to her, waiting.

"How did you see his eyes?" Margrethe smiled.

The other novices giggled and received a sharp look from one of the older nuns seated nearby.

"I offered to bring him water and cloths," the young nun said, looking down at her plate.

"You are quite generous and kindhearted, Sister," Edele said.

"How *did* you find him?" one of the others whispered to Margrethe.

She looked at them, all of them watching her, fascinated. If only they knew how wonderful it'd been. For a moment she wished she could tell them everything, let them share with her the wonder of those moments, standing over the sea. She looked at Edele and suddenly missed the long hours they'd spent together at the castle, in complete freedom. There, she would have already told her friend every detail of the event several times over, reliving it again and again. She was not used to this silence and secrecy, pretending to be someone she wasn't.

"I was in the garden," she said finally, "and I saw a man lying on the shore. I don't know why I didn't call to anyone. I just ran down the steps, to him."

"You gave him your furs, I heard. You could have died in this cold."

"Imagine him, lying there, almost drowned!" someone else said. "It's a miracle he survived."

"I heard he's some kind of Viking."

They were all talking at once, and Margrethe leaned back, glad that, for a moment, they had almost forgotten her.

The abbess entered then, and a hush came over the room.

"I would like you to come with us today, Mira," she said, approaching the table, her black habit swishing about her legs. "To the village, to deliver help and blessings to the families . . ."

"Yes, Mother," Margrethe said, standing.

"A group of us are going. And then you and I will make a few visits alone."

Margrethe nodded. She knew what this meant: that they were to visit her father's men who waited in the village below, most likely to discuss what had happened. It was normal for the novices to accompany the older nuns on these visits, and no one seemed surprised. The abbess's appearance had instead sobered the group, and they quickly finished their bread and fish.

⌒

THAT AFTERNOON, a group of holy women walked from the convent into the village. The convent was at the top of a mountain, and the path was rocky and curved sharply down, bordered by bare, thick trees. The wind was brutally cold, and they were all bound in furs, the black and white of their habits flailing out beneath. Like the others, Margrethe carried a basket of goods to take to the villagers: furs and blankets they'd woven.

She stepped carefully along the path, behind the abbess. Her eyes watered from the wind, but she could just make out the village: its main street lined by shops, the pointed rooftops, the smoke funneling from the chimneys. The sky grew more and more dark as they walked, shifting from silver to gray, and she felt something nagging at her, that something was not right.

"It looks like another storm," someone said, but other than that, it was quiet except for the howling of the wind, the crunching of their shoes along the rocky pathway.

As they wound their way down the hill, the village unfolded in front of them. They passed a stone apothecary, and some small shacks. Villagers stopped and crossed themselves as the line of holy women walked by. Despite herself, Margrethe could not help but thrill at being out in the world. She'd not left the convent grounds since the night she'd been rushed through on horseback, three months before.

She remembered that night. She'd been covered in thick black cloaks, clinging to the back of one of her father's soldiers, flanked by them on either side. They'd left the castle in the dead of night. She'd had so little time to prepare, but she wasn't allowed to bring anything, anyway, that could give her away. It had been terrifying, being that exposed—she was so used to being pampered, adorned, protected—but her father had insisted that she go into hiding. "It is the only way to keep you safe," he'd said as she clung to him. "We must prepare to defend ourselves against the South's attacks." Later, as the world rushed past her and the horse under her strained against the wind, she'd felt the weight and fear that came with her position more than she ever had before.

"Mira?"

She started, looked up at the abbess, who was motioning for her to stop. The old woman's pale eyes reflecting the washed-out landscape. The others were walking ahead while the two of them stood in front of a shack, next to the blacksmith's. The sound of clanking metal filled the air.

"We will stop here," the abbess said, "before we visit your father's men. There's a boy here who's very ill."

Margrethe nodded. "Of course." She looked around. The village appeared peaceful in the daylight, and she felt inexplicably happy, being out in the world. Suddenly she realized what had been nagging at her. She hesitated, then spoke again. "I have been thinking," she said, "and I do not believe it is necessary to tell them about the wounded man. I fear they might react strongly for no reason."

"But your safety is of our utmost concern."

"I do not think he is a threat to me, Mother." She thought of the knife under her pillow and blinked the thought away. She had to have faith that he'd been brought to her for a reason. "I spoke with him—"

The abbess gave her a sharp look. "You need to stay away from him," she said.

"Yes, Mother," she said. "You are right."

The abbess stared at her, her face grave. "He is from the South, my child," she said. "Do you realize that?"

"Yes," Margrethe whispered. "I spoke with him."

The abbess was looking at Margrethe more carefully now as she responded. "As did I. He claims he was on a journey to explore the Northern islands. But it is clear he is, or once was, a soldier, an enemy to your father."

"But we are not at war," Margrethe said. "We are at peace."

"Child, you know as well as I that this can change at any moment. It's why you were sent here." The two women looked at each other, and then the abbess turned away, sighing. "I have already sent word to your father's men that we are housing a wounded man. But that is all." She looked back to Margrethe, as if she expected her to argue. "We have sworn to protect and care for the sick and the wounded. I do not want to break that vow, or make the cloisters a battleground for men who care for power more than they do for God."

Margrethe nodded. "Good," she said. "I would not like to feel responsible for an innocent man's death." She felt relief move through her, as well as astonishment, and admiration. Also a tinge of fear——what if the man *was* there to kill her? The abbess was more cunning and defiant than she'd thought.

"But for now," the abbess said, "let us get out of the cold." She turned to the door and knocked.

A tired-looking young woman opened it. Her face changed when she saw them, and she immediately crossed herself and bowed.

"Welcome, Reverend Mother," she said, moving aside to let them in.

"Good afternoon, my child," the abbess said. "We've brought some treatments for your sick one, and some food to nourish you."

Margrethe followed quietly, stooping to pass through the front door. She nodded at the woman and watched as the abbess blessed her and began handing her loaves of bread and small packages of herbs from her basket. In the back of the room, three children sat huddled on the dirt floor. A fourth was lying on his side on a thin mattress, moaning. The sick boy's eyes were closed, his hair damp, a sheen of sweat shining from his forehead.

It was Margrethe's first visit to a peasant home, and it was hard to hide the shock that she felt. She'd never seen conditions like it. There was one small room, with a low ceiling. A fire burned but did little to alleviate the cold. The boy's pain was palpable, and seemed to color the walls of the house.

She walked over to the children and knelt down next to them. Behind her, the abbess and the woman spoke in low tones.

Margrethe saw then that one of the children, a young boy, was drawing with a stick in the dirt floor. When she saw the picture he'd created, she nearly gasped out loud. "What are you drawing?" she said. "What is that?"

He put down the stick. "It is a fish lady, Sister," he whispered. And it was: crude as the lines in the dirt were, the woman's head and torso connected to the tail of a fish were unmistakable. *Mermaid*.

She caught her breath and spoke in a whisper, matching his. "Why have you drawn it?"

"The last time I went fishing with my father, we caught one in our net, Sister."

"You caught one in your net?"

"Yes," he said. "My father thought we'd caught a giant fish, and then we hauled it up, and there was a beautiful lady, like you. But she had a fish's tail."

Looking down, Margrethe saw a faint dust of shimmer on the boy's hand, even under the dirt that coated his skin and nails.

"Did you touch her? You did, didn't you?"

"Forgive him," the woman said, rushing over before the child could answer. "He is just a boy. The villagers tell these stories.

My husband . . . He was a good man, but he encouraged these fantasies in the children . . . He is, was a fisherman. He went to sea some weeks ago and has not come home, and now we have to fend for ourselves."

"He disappeared the day after we saw the fish lady," the boy said.

"Philip!"

The boy looked down, scared suddenly, and wiped out the drawing.

The abbess was stern. "You must instruct these children that it is a sin to indulge these fantasies. Clinging to the old goddesses, you keep the world in darkness. It is only one way the devil works through them."

"It is so hard to keep watch over th—"

"That is your duty," the abbess said, cutting her off.

The woman nodded her assent and knelt on the floor. "Forgive us, Reverend Mother."

Margrethe watched the boy. She smiled when he looked up at her, trying to comfort him. But the boy's shame was clear, and she wished there was something she could say to reassure him.

"Let us go," the abbess said, but Margrethe hesitated. Without thinking, she took a fur from her basket, knelt down, and wrapped it around the boy. "God be with you, child," she whispered and then set out all her furs and blankets in front of him.

"Thank you, Sister," the woman said, and Margrethe nodded. She would remember this family, she vowed, all of these families that suffered.

As they left, Margrethe could feel the abbess's disapproval.

"I will pay for them," Margrethe said. "For the furs and blankets. But they are so poor. I don't . . . I don't understand. How can they be that poor, when our kingdom is so rich?"

The abbess looked at Margrethe, her passion evident. She

hesitated, and then spoke clearly. "It's the war," she said. "I am sorry to be so plain, but I do not know how else to answer you. The king, your father, he's ruined the people, left them penniless."

Margrethe felt herself stiffen. "What do you mean?" she asked, an edge creeping into her voice. "We have been at peace for three years."

The abbess answered in the same clear tone, defiant. "There have been years of fighting, with many losses. Even during this peacetime, your father has been steadily building ships, and amassing an army, filling it with new blood. How do you think he's paid for this? He's raised taxes on the people so much that they can barely live."

"But, I thought . . ." Margrethe stopped. She had not thought anything, she realized. Suddenly she was angry about having been kept so far from the world—angry at the abbess, at her father. At everyone.

"I am sorry to speak ill against your father. But I only tell you the truth. Life is very hard right now, for many people," the abbess went on. "I know that you meant well, to give so much. But there are many in need here."

She had been naïve, Margrethe realized, assuming that everyone lived . . . if not as well as she did, then at least almost as well. With enough to eat. With a warm place to sleep.

She straightened her back and looked into the abbess's wise, weathered face. She would do well to learn from this woman, she thought. "I understand," she said, "and I appreciate your directness." She paused, then spoke again. "But I am here because the South is planning to attack us again. If anything, my father is rebuilding his army to protect us."

The abbess hesitated. "Yes. It is only a matter of time before the fighting begins again. But it is . . . Many people doubt these reports about the South, and believe it is your father who is hungry for war. Your father who has never really been committed to peace. Understand that it is illegal to speak against the war. I tell you this only so you will understand what happened here, and why the people suffer as they do."

Margrethe nodded, swallowing hard.

"Though, lest we forget, there *is* a Southern man lying in our abbey. We do not know if he was part of a planned attack that went wrong, even if he claims otherwise. On both sides, the resentment runs very deep."

"Yes," Margrethe said. She could not deny it.

They walked in silence to the next house, each lost in her own thoughts, past the main line of shops, near the fields and woods that opened behind the village, where many of the peasants lived. The abbess nodded to a house by the trees. It seemed just as dark and grim as the first. Ice dripped from the edges of the roof as they walked to the front door.

They knocked, and a man appeared and bowed to the abbess. Margrethe almost didn't recognize Lens, her father's favorite guardsman. He was dirty, disguised as a village fisherman. When Margrethe had last seen him, the night they fled the castle, he'd been a strapping man with bright blond hair and the neat blue and white costume of the castle guard.

"Your Highness!" he said, whispering and ushering her into the house. He smiled and bowed deeply. It was strange and wonderful to feel, for a moment, like herself again, back in the world as she'd known it before. They were joined by the other guardsman, Henri, who had been similarly transformed—his skin weathered, his clothes ragged and dirty.

"We are worried for you," Lens said, showing them to the kitchen table. "We want to know more about this man who washed up to shore. But you have assured us, Mother, that he is harmless, no matter who he is."

The abbess looked quickly to Margrethe and then back at Lens. "Yes," she said. "He claims he was on an expedition to the islands up north. He has no weapons."

"What islands?" Henri asked.

"There are rumors that land exists to the north, that no man has ever set foot on."

The two guardsmen nodded but looked unconvinced.

"How long will he stay?" Lens asked. "How close is he to re-covery?"

"He has made an extraordinary recovery," the abbess said, "and will soon leave. I have promised him the loan of a horse and provisions. He may leave as early as tonight."

"Tonight?" Margrethe repeated, unable to stop herself.

The word sank into her like a stone, and an anxiety rose from it, sweeping through her entire being. The thought was irrational. She should be relieved, calmed. He was her enemy. And yet all she could think was: what if she never saw him again? If he was planning to leave tonight, he could be gone even before she and the abbess returned. The thought filled her with an inexplicable grief.

But if he stayed any longer, these men—her friends, men whose only task was to protect her—could learn the truth and destroy him.

"Your safety is all we care about," Lens said. "We are sworn to the death to protect you."

"I know," she said.

That was what worried her.

~

THEY BEGAN THEIR walk back to the convent in late afternoon. Margrethe tried to hide her anxiousness, but the abbess turned to her. "Let him go, child," she said, softly. "No matter who he is, you must not dishonor your father."

"You do not need to tell me such things," Margrethe said, her voice more haughty than she'd intended. The abbess seemed to want to say more but stopped herself.

Margrethe kept her own words back, too. A *mermaid*. She wanted to tell the abbess that it was a mermaid who had brought the man to her. She wanted to turn and shake her, cry out, *I need to see him again!* Tell her that the mermaid had brought him to her, for a reason, and that she needed to understand what it was before he disappeared.

Instead they walked in silence, Margrethe struggling to remain calm beside the abbess when her body was nearly shaking with the desire to run.

The sky hung silver over the mountain, the convent just barely visible above them. The trail up to the locked gates seemed endless. Every sound was the sound of horses' hooves clomping on wet ground, the sound of him leaving.

Finally, they passed through the great gates and into the warmth of the convent.

The novice mistress was waiting for the abbess with urgent news, it seemed, and Margrethe took the opportunity to slip away. She raced down the hall to the infirmary, to find him. She came to the door and stood outside it, pressed her forehead against it. Her heart was pounding. After a few moments, she knocked. Once, twice, then pushed the door open.

He wasn't there.

It was Edele who came up to her as she was rushing back to the office of the abbess. "He is requesting you," she said, taking Margrethe's hand in hers. "He wants to see you. He is waiting for you in the garden."

"Is he leaving?"

"Yes," Edele said. "There is a horse ready for him." Edele paused then, as if she wanted to say something more. "You know he is—"

"I know," Margrethe said, stopping her. Impulsively, she leaned forward and kissed Edele on her freckled cheek, smiling at her friend's surprise.

Our enemy.

"Margrethe . . ."

She took a deep breath, ignoring Edele, not even noticing that Edele had used her real name, and then pushed open the stone door and entered the garden. The cold air slammed against her. It was snowing. When had it started snowing? Big, fat white pieces of snow, drifting down.

He was standing by the stone wall, looking over the water. His back was to her, and she stopped a minute, watching him. Massive in the snow-filled garden, wrapped in furs. She realized this was the only time she'd seen him standing.

She was terrified, she realized. She was not behaving at all like the daughter of the Northern king. Standing in the garden with her heart racing, like a schoolgirl, as she prepared to meet her fate. She stopped and straightened her back, lifted her chin, before going to him.

He turned as she approached, the sun catching his eyes, which seemed almost golden now, in the bright light. The shimmer on his skin was nearly blinding in the sunlight. Why had no one mentioned it? Didn't they see? His skin, like jewels.

"Hello, Sister," he said.

"I was afraid you had left," she said, immediately embarrassed by the panic in her voice. She paused, composing herself.

"No," he said, looking at her. "Not before thanking you. For saving me."

He walked toward her, and instinctively she backed away. He was so present. His smell, his hands.

He continued. "I felt you, you know. In the water. I saw you. You coming up under me and lifting me, carrying me to shore, and when I opened my eyes and saw you, I thought you were an angel.

I thought I might have dreamed all of it, but I remember now. You carried me. You told me to look at the sky."

She stared at him, stunned. He did not remember the mermaid, only her. She didn't know what to say. Part of her wanted to correct him, tell him the truth. But another part of her loved the words he was saying. The vision of herself, in the water.

He knelt down then and looked up at her. She watched the snow fall into his hair and furs, then disappear. His eyes like weeds, those strange lips. "I owe my life to you," he said. "I've seen many things in this world, Sister. But I never thought one day I'd be rescued from the sea by a creature like you, an angel." He smiled then. "I was starting to think there was no holiness left in this world. There has been so much hatred, and war. It had begun to feel like there was no beauty left, no bit of God left."

"Please stand," she said, her voice shaking. "If I did anything at all, it was only a stronger force working through me."

"I will always be indebted to you," he said.

"You've healed so quickly," she said. "I will be sorry to see you go." The words beat at her lips: *Why were you brought to me?*

He took her hand then, and it shocked her, the feeling of his skin on hers. Before she knew what was happening, he was turning her hand and pressing his lips into her palm and wrist. The wind lashed around them, and the snow fell harder, blocking the sun and turning the world to white.

And before she could react, he stood. At his full height, he was nearly a foot taller than she.

She stepped closer. She had these few moments, and then he would disappear. Suddenly she didn't care about his answer, why he was there. All she wanted in the world was to kiss him. Her first kiss, right here, and she a girl who'd never dreamed of such things the way other girls did. She was a princess after all. Her father's sole heir. At her birth, a prophet had announced that she would raise a great ruler, one who would bring glory to their kingdom. Yet without even thinking she lifted her face, and he bent his to meet hers. His eyes right next to hers, and she could not help but think that it was this, *this* was rapture, right now, and she felt like a mermaid lying on the beach, her body exposed to the sun and her tail gleaming.

There was yelling suddenly, from inside, and Margrethe pulled quickly away from him, feeling her cheeks flush with shame. A moment later one of the senior nuns appeared at the door to the garden. Margrethe could see the abbess coming up behind her.

"Your horse is ready," the nun called out. And then, looking at Margrethe: "Perhaps you should come in now, Sister."

He tightened his grip on her hand. "I must go," he said. "But I am eternally grateful for all you have done, all of you. I am forever in your debt. And I hope I may one day see you again, Mira, though I know your heart belongs only to Him."

"Mira!" the abbess called from the doorway, and Margrethe could hear the hint of panic in her voice.

He paused, waiting, it seemed, for some sign from Margrethe, and the moment pressed down on her. She wanted to stop time, keep him there until she knew how to respond, what to feel, how to behave with him for this moment, this one moment she had left, but then he let go of her hand.

"Good-bye," he whispered. "I will not forget you."

"Good-bye," she said.

He was already moving away, the snow dropping all around.

CHAPTER SIX

The Mermaid

THE SHIP JUTTED UP FROM THE OCEAN FLOOR LIKE A strange, otherworldly creature tilted on its side, its masts and sails stretching in every direction, like misshapen limbs. Small sea animals had already attached themselves to the rotting wood on the prow. Schools of fish glimmered from the wreckage, streaming in and out of it, attracted by decaying flesh. All kinds of human ephemera lay scattered around the ship, twisted in seaweed and hanging from the coral already growing up the sides of the vessel: weapons, utensils, oars, coins, boots, bodies, bread. The whole mess of human life.

Lenia hovered over the ship, peering down at it, brushing up against the tallest mast, and then swam to the main deck. Men were piled on top of each other, as if they'd been running to the side of the ship when it went down.

She tried to take in the death and devastation around her. The men who'd dropped through the water, who'd come to rest wrapped around the masts and ropes. She'd seen this kind of wreckage plenty of times before, but it felt different now. A young man's body was wedged sidelong in an open doorway. He'd been climbing up a ladder from below when he died. His hair was long and blond, swaying in the water around him, and his eyes were open, staring up toward the surface of the water. Had she seen him screaming during the storm, struggling for life? At what point had his soul left his body?

She moved in closer to him. *I'm sorry,* she whispered. His body was clothed in green and gold, a dark green jacket with a line of brass buttons down the front. He must have been important. She ran her fingers along the brass, felt the crude design stamped into it. Some kind of creature she did not recognize. Did the man she'd saved dress himself this way, too? She reached up and touched the dead soldier's hair. It was not just blond. It was brown and yellow and cream, all at once, and she could see he'd lived and worked outside, the sun beating down on him.

Did you know him? Who is he? What is he like?

She almost waited for him to respond, but the world stayed silent, and the only movement was from above, as a stream of translucent jellyfish wended their way down.

She moved her face right next to his, slipped her hand around to the back of his neck, the skin there.

This body. So full of secrets, of the world above, of men.

Who are you? she breathed. *What were you like?*

Was there any of him left, in this decaying flesh?

Beneath the bloated skin, she could see how beautiful this young man had been in life. She stared at his lips, traced them with her fingertips, and then again her mind went back to the other man, how his lips had felt against her own. That bliss that had moved through her. She shivered, remembering. And, without thinking, she pressed her lips against the dead young man's.

A mass of tiny fish fluttered by, brushing her face.

As she pulled away, she imagined what her mother and sisters would think, seeing her like this. Though they had once caught Vela, as a tiny mermaid, holding a human skeleton in her arms and pretending to dance with it. But Vela had been innocent then, a child, not a marriage-aged mermaid, as Lenia was now.

She swam to one of the other openings to the galleys below and pressed her body down through it. She'd been in plenty of similar spaces, of course, but this was where *he* had lived, and the hammocks, the chests of clothes, the wooden beams and tiny windows—as enchanting as she'd always found such human objects—all took on a special significance to her now.

A jug of amber liquid lay tipped over on the floor, and she went to it, uncorked it and lifted it to her mouth. Her first sip was straight seawater. She drank until the spirit hit her, burning down her throat, and she spat it out. Awful. She grabbed a fish swirling by and stuffed it into her mouth, bit down on its sweet flesh, its crunching bones, but the taste still lingered in her mouth. It took a few more fish, plus some sea flowers that were already growing through the galley floor, to get rid of the taste.

She shook her head and swam along the line of hammocks to the other end of the room. Some of the ship's structure had broken off completely here. A few bodies had been caught, and one had been lanced by a broken beam, a giant wound blossoming from where the beam pierced flesh, alive with sea creatures feeding from it.

She swam to one of the hammocks that was intact and moved into it, let her body rest against the thick rope. She stretched out. Closed her eyes and pretended that she was sleeping here. She thought of the black-haired girl she'd seen on the cliff, the only human girl she'd ever seen alive, and in her mind she became that girl. Resting her fragile body against the rope, that black hair spreading around her, her long legs reaching to the beam the hammock swung from on the far side.

She opened her eyes, looked out at the vision of her silver tail glittering in the dark room, against the old, rotting ropes.

Her sisters would think she was crazy. In love with ropes and bodies and rotten rum, horrible things that littered the immaculate ocean floor. But what they wouldn't understand was how this decay was attached to something so beautiful she could barely stand to think of it.

Eternal life.

She scanned the room from her hammock perch. The splintering walls, a chest of drawers spilling open, more bottles filled with amber liquid wedged under some fallen beams, an eel slithering along the floor and then disappearing through one of the cracks, a team of glowing fish falling down into the room like raindrops.

An unbearable feeling opened up in her, and all she wanted was to see him again. The idea that he was *there,* now, existing in the world above her, the world she was not supposed to return to, made it impossible for her to stay away any longer.

She sat up and, just like that, made a decision. She started swimming, pushing upward. Leaving the ship and the palace behind. Past mountains and cliffs and sea caves, giant squids and whole lines of transparent medusas unfolding through the water. She let her body relax. She could have been anything, any creature that was at one with the sea and its movements. She closed her eyes, let the dark water fall in streams on either side of her. Her powerful tail pushed behind her.

She tried not to think about what would happen if her mother found out. Merpeople had been banished, even put to death, for crossing to the upper world on any day other than their eighteenth birthdays, but that was long ago, back when the decree had first been issued and merpeople still wanted to visit humans. No one ever tried to go now, it seemed, and, besides, Lenia was the queen's daughter. *What could really happen?* she asked herself. And wasn't it worth it, for true love?

It took longer than she'd remembered, but eventually the water grew warmer, she could see the surface of it, and she swam faster, reaching up to it and the dull ache of the sun beyond it. And then her face hit the air, and the silence of the sea was broken.

She blinked her eyes, stared out all around her. Hardly believing she was actually here. It was so simple. Once, mermaids had passed in and out of the upper world as if doing so were nothing at all. Just like this. *This is how it was meant to be,* she thought. It felt silly, suddenly, that she had waited eighteen long years to go. It was all wrong, the separation that existed now, this fear that something terrible would happen if a merperson entered the upper world. And now here she was. Perfect, alive, free. The air caressing her skin, sweeping her into itself.

She was careful to let the air enter her body slowly, naturally. This world was more peaceful than it had been before, despite the glare of light, but a variety of new sounds blared into her ears even so. The crash of waves, the whoosh of wind, the caw of birds flying overhead.

And there was so much light! As her eyes adjusted, she realized that something was falling from the sky. Big white flakes falling to the water and melting into it. She watched for several long moments, transfixed. They rushed down to the water, vanishing against the surface.

Water extended out from her in every direction, as far as she could see. It was so silver and pure from this vantage point, lapping and rushing, full of life. The sound of it! The foam funneling down the waves. The sky was pure white, almost blinding. Lenia had never seen so much white. She stretched out her arms, opened her mouth, and let the flakes fall on her tongue. Sharp and cold, and then gone.

She laughed out loud—it was all so wonderful—and then began to sing. Softly at first, and then with more vigor. The water around her started to swirl, and she raised her voice until the water began moving in quick circles, little tornadoes reaching deep under the surface.

And as she sang, she thought how each thing entering her—the air, the flakes falling from the sky, all this sound and *feeling*—now felt like a soul. As if it was this euphoria that had filled those men at their birth and left them in the sea, and it was this that had filled the man she'd brought to shore and had started to fill her, too, as she carried him in her arms.

In the distance, now, she could just barely make out a shape of land. There! She stretched her tail and pushed through the water, heading toward land, toward him, and, as she approached, the land came more and more into relief. The same rocky beach, the sheet of rock, the wall, the building behind it, spread out, the torches, flickering to life. All of it coated in shimmering ice and snow.

Was he in there? Could he see the same light from the torches?

Come to me, she thought. *Come back.* Concentrating, so that he would hear her.

When she reached the shore, she closed her eyes and tried to imagine the feel of him under her, the warm, soft skin . . . She put everything she could into it, that feeling, that memory, to call to him. Never before then had she longed for legs, the strange appendages that allowed men to walk along the earth. Legs that would carry her to him.

How far does this world stretch? she wondered. Was it as wide and vast as the sea? What could possibly be inside that building on the cliff with the torches surrounding it, a giant cross extending from the roof and seeming to tap the sky? She had seen those crosses before, small ones, large ones, among the shipwrecks in the sea, and she knew, from her grandmother, that they had to do with souls.

The beach was deserted, rock-ridden, white with snow. She pulled herself onto the shore, dragging her body across the rocks, and stretched out her tail before her. For a moment, she was dazzled as the pale light hit her own body. How odd—the greens and blues that glittered from her tail, in the light. She held up her arms and laughed as they changed color. Maybe she would stay here forever, she thought, live on crabs she plucked from the rocks. He could stay here with her, and she could sing to him, and he could tell her of his travels in this bright, loud world.

She heard a sound and flinched. Was someone here? She looked up and down the shore, but it was empty. In the back of her mind, a shadow memory stirred, mermaid sisters being hacked apart by men. She closed her eyes, willed the image away.

And then suddenly, a figure appeared, on the cliff, at the top of the stairway. Lenia gasped, twisted her body around, toward the water.

"Please, stay!" she heard. The voice was strange, piercing. "Wait!"

The panic in the voice made Lenia stop. She turned back again and saw it was the girl from before, wrapped in furs, her dark hair blowing around her. Rushing down the stairs now, nearly tripping as she clutched the thin railing.

Lenia watched, fascinated, her body poised to return to the water in one leap, as the girl descended the stairs. A real human girl, right in front of her.

The girl reached the bottom of the stairway and began crossing the shore, to where Lenia sat. Walking tentatively over the rocks. She was beautiful, her movements graceful and light. Even with the furs swaddling her, and the long white garment underneath, stretching to her feet. Her black hair whipped around her face. Her skin was so delicate, like it could split open in an instant. Raw. Lenia could smell the girl, the smell of warmth and blood. The girl's fragility, so much like the man's. And yet the girl did not seem fragile, but confident and sure as she approached.

Lenia relaxed her body. Alone, this girl was no threat to her, she realized. Lenia could lift one of these rocks and smash her head in an instant. For a moment she imagined it: how the girl's soul would leave her body and slip into the air, beautiful and pure, a shining web of light. Surely here, in the daytime, Lenia would be able to see it, watch it rise to heaven.

She watched the girl's eyes widen, heard her pull of breath as she stopped halfway across the shore. For a moment they just stared at each other. The girl's dark eyes moved up and down Lenia's body, sweeping over her long tail, her torso and bare breasts, her long, ropy hair. When her eyes rested on Lenia's, the girl looked away quickly, embarrassed. And then back again.

Lenia tilted her head. She could feel the emotions of the girl. So strange, how they affected her . . . in ways the air and the cold could not. But the girl was shivering, like she had no skin at all. Was *this* a soul? This fragility, this absence? And that smell. Cold and wind, but, under it, other things. Spices, warmth, blood.

Lenia tried to calm her. *Talk to me,* she thought, concentrating. *Tell me who you are.*

After a few moments, the girl stepped forward, then knelt down on the rocks. "My name is Margrethe," she said.

Lenia smiled. "My name is Lenia," she said. "Len. Ee. A."

"Lenia," Margrethe repeated. "You are not cold?" She gestured awkwardly at Lenia's torso.

"No."

"I'm so cold my skin burns."

"You are softer than I am," Lenia said, smiling, touching her own skin self-consciously.

Margrethe smiled back then and seemed to relax. "Yes. I've never seen a . . ."

"A mermaid?"

"Mermaid." Margrethe repeated the word, whispering. "I wasn't sure if you . . . I wasn't sure if you, if your kind, even existed. I heard stories, when I was a child. But I thought they were only stories."

Lenia cocked her head. How strange. She'd always imagined that humans thought about her kind, too. They were always taking off to the sea in their giant ships, after all. "Well," she said, "we are not supposed to come to your world. We are allowed to visit when we turn eighteen, but we're supposed to remain hidden, not let you see us. . . . A long time ago, things were different."

"But you came . . . to save him?"

"Yes. I suppose I did."

"Why?"

Lenia stared up at the girl's open, curious face. *Why?* "I just . . . I saw the men, they were dying. It was my first time. In your world, I mean, above the ocean's surface. Men were dying all around me. And then I saw him, and he was dying also. I knew I should save him. I couldn't let him die."

And because I loved him, she thought.

"Why here?" Margrethe asked.

Lenia shrugged. "I just knew to bring him here."

"To me?" Margrethe asked, shyly.

Lenia hesitated. It seemed important to this human girl to think that the man had been a gift, from Lenia to her. She spoke slowly. "Well. I saw you standing there, and I called to you."

The girl leaned back, seemed to let the information sink into her. "I heard you, I think," she whispered. "A voice, in my mind. Did you do that?"

Lenia nodded. "Yes."

Margrethe's face changed, and she visibly relaxed. "I've been waiting for you. I thought you might come back. Maybe to see him."

Lenia looked down at the icy rocks, and then up again. "Is he still here?" she asked.

"No. He is . . . He was in danger here. From an enemy kingdom. And so he left."

"He is your enemy?" Lenia asked.

"Yes." Margrethe paused and then continued rapidly, explaining. "I'm in hiding here. My father is the king of the North. The Southern king is his enemy, and they have fought great wars against each other. They both feel this land is theirs." She paused then. "I don't know why I am saying this to you. I cannot talk to anyone else. I mean, I am not myself here."

Lenia took it in, what this girl was saying. *A princess,* she was. Lenia imagined that, in the human world, this was something even more fine than in her own. She thought of all the treasures glittering under the sea—the jewels and gold, the chandeliers and giant ships, the glass bottles of amber liquids. A thousand different wonders.

Margrethe leaned forward. "What did you mean when you said things were different a long time ago?"

"When we were all the same race," Lenia said. "Things were different then, between us."

"The same race?"

"Us," Lenia said, pointing at herself and then at Margrethe. "When humans were part of the sea. When the world was entirely sea. You have not heard this?"

"No."

"It is something we are all told about," Lenia said, "when we are young. How the world was all sea once, ruled over by a king and queen, until there was a terrible battle between them, and the king ripped up the ocean floor and left to found the upper world, changing his tail to legs so that he could walk upon it. They say that is why the ocean is filled with caverns and crevices."

The girl had never heard any of these things, Lenia realized. She had not even been sure that mermaids really existed, before now, outside of stories.

"Full of caverns?"

"Yes, everywhere." Lenia smiled, noticed that the girl was not shivering anymore despite her red, chapped skin.

Margrethe shook her head. "I feel like I'm dreaming. I have heard so many stories about mermaids, since I was a small girl. I always dreamt of what it would be like, to disappear in the ocean, learn its mysteries. I wish . . ."

The girl's longing was palpable, and it seemed to match Lenia's own. For a moment, Lenia saw the sea through this human girl's eyes. She imagined pulling the girl underwater, showing her the palace made of amber and mussel shells, the underwater volcanoes that shot fire into the sea, the ancient shipwrecks full of the bones of her ancestors, the impossible monsters that lived in the corners of the ocean, and then she thought of the blond soldier's body, bloated and peeling, which she'd kissed, and she remembered . . . This was as far as she herself could go into the upper world, only this beach, and the girl would die in the sea.

"What is it like?" Margrethe asked.

Lenia leaned forward, thought for a minute, but there was so much to describe, and she had almost nothing to compare it to. "I don't know . . . ," she said. "I wish I could show you. Just as I wish you could show me."

"I would like that. I wish I could show you my home, where I live usually. It is so beautiful there, and there is a big, bright sun, not like this."

Lenia could not imagine anything more bright, and she laughed. "How strange," she said. She pointed to the building on the cliff. "And what is that building, where you are hiding?"

"A convent. I'm staying there until it's safe to go home. That is why I'm dressed this way, like a novice." Margrethe opened her furs, gestured to her white dress. "Normally . . . well. I'm much more elaborately attired. Gowns in every color, with beads and lace and corsets. There are women who spend all day every day sewing gowns for me."

Lenia breathed in. "What is a convent?"

"A convent is a house for women devoted to God." When she saw Lenia's confused look, Margrethe continued. "It is a place for constant prayer and devotion. The women inside do not live lives like other people in the world. They are married to God, not men."

"Oh yes, how wonderful!" Lenia said, excitement rushing

through her. It was all true, what her grandmother had told her. "I know about God, and souls, and heaven. Are you also . . . married to God?" She thought of it: not just two webs of light joining together but all the light in the world strung together, shining at once. She blinked. She could not imagine it. It must be the exact opposite of the world at the bottom of the sea, where everything was dark and muted.

"No," the girl said. "I pray and worship, but I will marry and have a life in the world."

Lenia was overcome, by the beauty of the girl's words, the white sky that was shifting to silver above them, the ice-covered rocks surrounding her, the air hitting her skin and causing the girl's hair to blow about her face, the idea that there were human women who could spend their life in prayer, speaking to a being they could not see or touch. She was so beautiful, this human girl. The man must have loved her. Could he have? Even with the memory of her own voice in his ear?

"Did you love him?" Lenia asked suddenly. "Do you love him?"

"Do I love God?"

"No. The man I carried through the sea. Do you love him?"

The girl's face shifted entirely. She looked behind her, as if they weren't there alone, on the most desolate stretch of rock in the world, as if she had not just revealed many other secrets to her, this creature from the bottom of the sea. "I don't know if I love him, but there is . . . something."

"What? Tell me." Lenia realized she was holding her breath. "Tell me about him."

The girl looked at her nervously, and Lenia focused her mind. *Tell me. Please.* Again, the girl visibly relaxed. "He is . . . an adventurer. Like Odysseus. Do you know who that is?" When Lenia shook her head, she continued. "He tells stories, stories I have read in ancient texts. Most men do not have time for such things anymore, but he is learned, I can tell he has a curiosity for everything. The way he sees things makes everything seem different. There is something magical about him. And his eyes, the color of weeds, or stone. And he has . . . I mean, you touched him. His skin, where you touched him, it shimmers."

"What do you mean?"

"Where you touched him, where I saw you touch him, it's like there are jewels on his skin."

Lenia looked down at her own skin, and then at the girl's. They were so different. Hers thick and shining, almost hard, the girl's so soft and thin and flat. Delicate. Like petals.

"I don't know if anyone else can see," the girl said. "I don't understand it . . ."

Lenia lifted her hands in front of her. They both watched the light reflect off of them.

"Your skin is beautiful," the girl breathed.

Suddenly, the girl's eyes turned to water. It was the strangest thing Lenia had ever seen. Water, running from her eyes, down her cheeks.

Lenia reached out her hand, held it above the girl's hand. "He's the only human I've ever touched," she said. "May I?"

Trembling, the girl pushed up her sleeve, revealing the pale skin of her forearm. "Yes," she whispered. "Please."

Softly, Lenia placed her palm on the girl's skin. She saw her flinch as their skin touched, but the girl remained still as Lenia moved her palm up and then down, the heat of the girl's arm moving into her. Even in this cold, Lenia could feel the girl's blood pulsing underneath her skin.

"You're so cold," the girl said.

"I can feel your heart beating beneath your skin," Lenia said.

The moment seemed to stretch out. When she lifted her hand away then, it was unmistakable: the trail of diamonds on the girl's skin.

"There," Lenia said. "Is that what you saw on him?"

"Yes," the girl whispered.

A sound clanged through the air, and Lenia was quick to cover her ears. Still, the sound seared through them, through her body. "What is that?"

"Those are the bells," the girl said. "It is time to pray."

The girl did not notice Lenia's discomfort. She was mesmerized by her own skin, where Lenia had touched it. Lenia studied her again: the dark eyes, soft, pale skin, the shimmer on her arm. The furs wrapped around her, the white cloth that hung down to her slippers. Her hair, which blew in the wind, in front of that silver, darkening sky.

Margrethe looked up then, her eyes still full of water. "I have to go, or they will come searching for me in my cell. But I want to stay. I fear I will wonder if I dreamt all of this."

"I am real," Lenia said. "I promise you. All of us are. It was our ancestors, not us, that made our worlds separate and created the land you live on, that separated you from the sea."

"Thank you," the girl said. But she did not move, just sat and stared at Lenia, her eyes tracing Lenia's hair, her glimmering tail. "I . . ."

Lenia nodded. "I know." She could see that the girl would freeze to death if she stayed outside any longer, could sense that the air was getting even colder as the sky went from white to silver, to black.

Go, Lenia thought. *Go, and warm yourself.*

"Good-bye," Margrethe said. "I hope we will meet again."

"As do I."

And then Lenia watched the girl pick her way back over the rocks, to the staircase that wound up the cliff, to the world above, under the stars.

CHAPTER SEVEN

The Princess

D URING THE LONG AFTERNOONS, EVERY WOMAN IN THE convent was at work. Some swept and cleaned, some cooked in the massive kitchen. Some bundled themselves in furs and tended the garden or the sheep. The sisters from better backgrounds worked in the scriptorium, or sang in the choir, or spun or wove wool into blankets to distribute, along with furs, to the villagers below.

Margrethe sat at her loom, lost in thought. She performed her work rhythmically, steadily throwing the shuttle and moving her feet on the treadle, watching the shafts go up and down. The clacking of the looms, the hum of the spinning wheels, the dank odors—hours could pass this way, quite easily. Overflowing baskets of raw wool were gathered by the door, giving off an earthy, animal scent that penetrated the room. Margrethe was not used to the odor of wool, but she found it not unpleasant. Edele and a young novice were working at looms alongside her—Edele only barely masking her impatience with the work, occasionally muttering under her breath as the fabric knotted beneath her fingers— while another group of nuns spun raw wool into yarn on the far side of the room.

One of the sisters sat by the door, reading a passage from scripture, and the sound of her voice was lulling, soothing, but

Margrethe did not hear any of what she was saying. It had been more than two weeks since Christopher had left. A week since she'd met Lenia. Ever since she'd sat with the mermaid, she'd felt unwell, like something was off-kilter, and she'd stopped waiting by the stone wall, looking for her. She couldn't close her eyes without hearing the crash of waves. Over and over again she saw the mermaid swimming to shore, with the man in her arms, delivering him to her . . .

I called to you, she'd said.

Suddenly, there was a terrible commotion from outside. Voices shouting down the corridor.

The nun who'd been reading to them trailed off in midsentence, and the room went silent as the rest of them stopped their work to listen.

There was one moment, two moments of silence, and then they heard a voice calling: "The barbarians are here!"

At that, they all jumped, and one of the nuns cried out as a spinning needle pierced her finger. All but Margrethe and Edele rushed out of the room, crossing themselves, their work forgotten as they headed down to the main cloisters. Wool unspooling on the floor.

Margrethe sat petrified, her heart pounding. Automatically, she reached up, made sure the wimple was covering her dark hair.

Edele ran to Margrethe's side, her eyes wide with horror. "What should we do? What if he has returned?"

Margrethe took a breath, remembered herself. Surely, if there was any threat, her guards would be close by. No one could approach the convent without them knowing. "Let us follow the others," she said calmly, reverting to her royal demeanor.

Edele nodded, and they walked slowly down the corridor, their slippered feet padding on the cold stone. Listening.

Could he have come back? Realized who she was?

"If anything should happen to you here . . . ," Edele whispered. Margrethe squeezed her hand. Though Edele could annoy her like a sister, Margrethe knew that her old friend loved her ferociously, would die for her in an instant.

"Let us stay calm and find out what is happening," Margrethe said.

They slipped down a set of stone stairs into the main cloisters. The whole convent was in disarray. Nun and novice alike were racing about, gathering outside the abbess's office. The abbess, wrapped in furs, her face flushed and worried, was striding in from the courtyard, followed by the novice mistress. It was in such sharp contrast to the usual silence and calm inside the convent's walls.

"The king!" someone cried. "The king is here!"

Margrethe and Edele exchanged looks. "Which king?" Edele whispered.

Almost as soon as the words were spoken, a host of soldiers swept through the front doors. Margrethe recognized them immediately. Pieter, her father's main military adviser, and a handful of the royal guard, including Henri and Lens dressed in the telltale blue and white of the Northern king. They all seemed so huge and menacing in the hushed space of the convent.

And then, to Margrethe's astonishment, the king himself stormed into the room in a sweep of pomp and fury. His presence filled every crack and crevice, like an assault, like a hand around her throat.

King Erik was a tall, bearded man, with gray hair and weathered, battle-hardened skin. He seemed always on alert, aware of every movement around him. His eyes were deep set and the color of coal. Once, he had been renowned throughout the kingdom for his good looks. Her mother had told her stories about him from their courtship, when he was a dashing young prince who'd won her hand in a jousting match, but there was little left now of that long-ago charmer.

"Margrethe!" he called.

Edele breathed in next to her as Margrethe stepped forward

from the stairwell, terror coursing through her. Hiding had become second nature to her, and now here was her father and his men, revealing her to everyone in one fell swoop. The person she'd been all these weeks dismantled in an instant.

What was he doing here?

Trying to remain calm, she walked toward him. "I am here," she said, feeling the others' eyes burning into her.

The king saw her then, focusing in, clearly surprised by her appearance as she stood before him unadorned, in her novice's habit, her rich, dark hair out of view. His relief was palpable, but then he immediately turned his attention away from her and to the abbess.

"What have you done?" the king yelled, before the woman even had a chance to kneel at his feet. "I send my daughter to you for protection and you take in the *son of my enemy?*"

Margrethe looked from her father to Lens and Henri, confused, and saw them drop their eyes. She turned to her father. "I do not understand. I have been safe here—"

"The man that these women took in and housed in the infirmary was Prince Christopher, of the South. We're taking you from this place immediately. Our enemies know you're here. It's only through the grace of God that you're alive now."

"My liege . . . ," the abbess began, clearly as shocked as Margrethe was.

Margrethe just stared at her father, his fury like a wall in front of her. "How do you . . . ?" she began, stumbling over her words. For once she could not call on her royal training and was at a loss.

"We've received reports that he returned to his father's castle," the king said, "some days ago, on a horse given to him by this convent." He nearly spat the last words.

Margrethe's head spun. *Prince Christopher.* She'd heard stories about the Southern king's son, already legendary though he'd come of age only a few years before. At her father's court they'd spoken of his temper, his passion, his facility with words—though always as a warning. They said he was a sensualist who surrounded himself with women and food, and she'd heard all the stories about life in the South: the feverish dancing and lovemaking that lasted late into the night, the great feasts that went on for days, the tables overloaded with salmon and pheasants and capons and veal, candied figs and oranges and dates and lemons, cakes and tarts and spices coated in sugar, the endless vats of wine. She'd heard about the fountains scattered through the castle in which naked slave girls bathed, the flowers that were shipped in from the east and that burst from every room, the elaborate art that hung throughout the castle and lined all the roads leading to it, full of unholy scenes from myth and folklore. Her father's religious adviser preached such things as examples of all that they had been fighting against in the war.

Her mind filled with him, the image of him—this prince, this son of her father's enemy—spread out on the beach, under the mermaid, him lying in the infirmary, that shimmer on his skin, him standing in the snow in the garden, waiting. No wonder he had been in such a hurry to leave.

"Go search for any sign of him, anything he left behind," the king instructed his men, who obeyed immediately, scattering from the room.

The abbess stepped forward, clearly brimming with emotion. "My liege, please," she said, kneeling now. "We knew only that the man was dying and needed our help. This is a house of God."

"You housed the son of my enemy. Of all our enemies. There is no room for such a man in the kingdom of God."

The abbess looked up at him, and her expression was strong, despite her submissive posture. She spoke calmly. "It is our code, Your Royal Highness. We must take care of the ill, the wounded. He was not armed. He was almost dead when we found him."

The king stepped forward. "We do not care for the enemies of God. Do you dare to think you know better than I, your king? I sent my *daughter* to you for safekeeping."

Margrethe cringed. It was excruciating to watch. The others stood around, wide-eyed, shocked at the display before them. Margrethe prayed that no one would reveal how close she'd been to the Southern prince. She had no idea what her father would do if he knew that she'd been in his room alone with him, in the garden alone with him, that he'd kissed her hand by the ancient wall.

Margrethe looked to the others, who dropped their gazes when their eyes met hers. Of course. No one else would look at her. They would all feel betrayed by her, nervous about what they had said in her presence.

"Forgive me," the abbess said. "But, Your Highness, in the eyes of God we are all equal . . ."

Her words made the king angrier, and his guardsmen stood, waiting for his instructions. But Margrethe could see their discomfort: they did not know what the king would have them do here, in a house of women and God. Even she, his own daughter, no longer knew what he might be capable of.

He responded to the abbess slowly, doing nothing to hide his contempt. "You are fortunate, Reverend Mother," he said, "that my mother thought so highly of you."

"We have loved your daughter as one of our own. Broken bread with her, knelt with her in prayer."

"She is not one of you," he said, his voice booming against the stone walls. "The prophets said at her birth that it would be she who would bring forth the next heir to the kingdom."

Many of the nuns visibly started to hear such blatant heresy from the mouth of the king.

He looked around, indifferent to their shock. "Did any of you collaborate with the enemy, or have knowledge of him?"

Panic moved through the room, a sense that something horrible was about to happen. Margrethe did not know what to think. She'd never paid much attention to the stories about her father: what he'd done in battle, the ferocity for which he'd been praised and rewarded. The rumors about how he had come to the throne. She realized now that he was capable of anything.

"Father, please!" Margrethe said. It was unbearable, watching this. These were holy women. She was shocked to see the abbess spoken to this way. It was she who oversaw these women who spent their life in devotion and prayer, for the whole kingdom, for all of them.

He turned to her, his face red and eyes bulging, his cape whirling behind him, and she willed herself not to shrink from him. No matter that he was her father: he was the king, appointed by God to rule over His favored land.

But she was his heir. Her child would one day be a great ruler, greater than he.

"Father," she repeated, "I am the one who found him nearly drowned, on the shore. Do not blame these women!"

"What?" He stared at her in disbelief.

It was like the whole world was crumbling apart and it was up to her, her words, to stop it.

"He was not here to hurt me," she said. "He did not know who I was. I found him on the shore, and I ran to the abbess for help. I begged her to help him."

"You were alone, unguarded?" he asked. His rage like a physical presence in the room.

"I was outside, getting fresh air, and I saw him. Barely alive, all his men dead, brought here by . . ." She did not know how to tell them. Her father would think she had gone mad, living here by the sea, and the nuns would think she was a heretic, first a child of prophecy and then a girl who spoke to mermaids.

The men rushed back into the room, like a murder of crows hailing down.

"We did not find any sign of him," Pieter said. "The place is secure."

"Then we will leave," the king said. "And praise God that no harm came to my daughter in this place, even with the son of my enemy inches away from her."

Margrethe could feel her shoulders relax. Her father would not hurt these women after all.

The abbess stood then, smoothed her habit. "Thank you, my liege," she said, her voice shaking.

"Thank you, Reverend Mother," Margrethe said. "For all you've done for me."

The abbess nodded, her face softening as she looked at Margrethe. "I am sorry that events happened as they did. None of us were aware that an enemy so dangerous was in our midst. We would never intentionally expose you to danger, and I give thanks that you are in full health and safety here today. We have grown to love you very much, and will be sorry to lose you."

"We need provisions," the king said, almost cutting her off, "and fresh horses."

"Of course," she replied. "We will make preparations now. All that we have here is at your disposal."

Margrethe stepped forward. "Perhaps you will rest a night here, Father?" she asked, trying to keep the panic out of her voice.

Now that the immediate threat was gone, the reality of the situation was hitting her. They were leaving. Now. She was going back to the castle, and her old life.

Far from this sea at the edge of the world.

"There is no time, Daughter," he said. "We have urgent business at the castle. We will not let the prince's insolence go unpunished."

She listened in horror. The image of the sick boy and his family, the war-ravaged village shacks, flashed into her mind.

Something beautiful had happened here—she knew it, down

to her bones, the mermaid had brought *the enemy prince* to her, and she had loved him—and her father would use it as a reason to cause even more suffering and destruction than their kingdom had suffered already.

"Please, Father," she said. "Please let me just gather my things."

Pieter rushed in. "The horses are ready, Sire."

"We do not have time, Daughter. You do not need anything from this place."

"Please!" she said. "Please, Father! There is something I must do. I . . ." She racked her brain. "Let me just get Mother's necklace, which she left for me."

He paused, and she saw something flash over his face. It still pained him to think of her.

"Go with Margrethe." He nodded to Pieter, who followed as she rushed through the stone corridor back to her cell, thinking all the while, feeling that same sense of loss and confusion she'd felt when the warrior left, and she knew she had to see the mermaid once more.

"There is something I must do . . . ," she said over her shoulder to Pieter.

"I cannot leave your sight, my lady," he said firmly. "It is very dangerous for you here. He could be on his way back, even now."

He had not yet finished his sentence when she broke away and raced through an open doorway to the cloisters, then through the hall and into the garden, to the stairway that wound down to the sea. As she burst outside, the air assaulted her, as if it were full of knives, cutting through the thin sheath that covered her.

He was right behind her.

"Lenia," she screamed to the water, her voice dying in the wind. "Lenia!"

"Margrethe!" Pieter called.

She knew she was only making matters worse, but it could not be helped. This was her last chance. She knew that the prince being sent to her, being brought to her by the mermaid—all of it meant more than what her father, or any of them, could ever know.

She ran out to the sea. "Lenia!" she called. "Please come to me!"

The ocean sighed and breathed, churned silver water. Full of mysteries and secrets it would not reveal to her. She stumbled down the stairway that led to the rocky beach, ignoring the cold that sliced through her skin.

"Please!"

The wind whisked around her.

"Margrethe!" Pieter called. "What has come over you?"

Her eyes smarted against the wind so that she could barely see. There were faces all around her, in the trees and the water and the clouds, but when she blinked and looked again, racing all the while, they were gone.

She was crying now. She ached to be in the sea. Almost as if that ancient part of her longed to return home. She knew now that everything the mermaid had said was true. She had been part of the water once, a creature of the sea.

She reached the shore, stumbled over the rocks to the sea. Knelt down, put her fingers in the water.

"Lenia!"

If she went back—to the castle, to more war—would she ever again see magic? The magic of this place where mermaids washed up from the sea and told her stories, left shimmer on her skin. The peace of the nuns who whispered and prayed.

It was like the world before, the world from myth, where bliss was possible. The stories she had read out loud, in Greek and Latin, as her beloved teacher, Gregor, listened. She waited, inhaled the faint scent of the water, the cold, let the wind ravage her body.

"Lenia!"

But the mermaid did not appear.

And then he was holding her, his face buried in her hair, his arms around her waist, and it was all over.

"Lenia!" she screamed once more, and just as Pieter turned her from the sea to the cliff, she was sure that she saw a face looking out to her from the water, that beautiful moon hair and shimmering skin, the deep blue eyes, and then he was pulling her up, up the stairs, and she could not see anything else for the tears blinding her.

CHAPTER EIGHT

The Mermaid

THE SKY SHIFTED COLOR, FROM BLUE TO GRAY TO A BRIGHT silver, as massive clouds scattered across it, assembling into elaborate shapes and collapsing back again. The sun shot through from behind them, dull and steady. In the distance, the cliff seemed to rise straight from the water. In front of it lay a thin strip of beach, vanishing into waves.

A few miles out, Lenia waited. It was more familiar now, all of this, but she could not imagine ever being unmoved by the beauty of the upper world. Her tail stretched behind her, skimming the water. Her eyes kept moving from the clouds to the cliff in the distance, the convent sitting upon it, the bare-branched trees swaying over it, and the rocky shore beneath. But they were not there. No one had been there for days, and she could feel it, somehow she knew: he was not coming back. But where was the girl? What had happened to her?

She looked to the sky. She remembered stories about the ancient mermaids who could read their own fates in the clouds, back when it was acceptable to visit the upper world. All the legends of the first humans visiting the sea, the merpeople slipping into the upper world. It had taken a long time for the separation that existed now to come to pass.

Only Lenia seemed to feel an emptiness inside her, a sense that she'd lost something she could not get back. Why was she the only one who felt it? None of her sisters did. They were all content to find their mates, lay their eggs, and prepare for family life. They were happy with the riches of the sea, the delights of the palace, all the abundance they had been born into. Even her grandmother, who loved these old tales more than any of them, had never had any desire to visit the upper world after her eighteenth birthday.

Now that she, the youngest of the queen's daughters and the only one who had yet to find a mate, had reached her nineteenth year, they all expected it from her, too—that she would find her own mate and start her own family. Her behavior of late—singing songs full of longing as they dined on tentacles and seaweed and sea urchins—had only increased their expectations. It was natural that her mother and sisters would notice, and that they would all come to the same conclusion: Lenia had fallen in love. And she *had* fallen in love, and it made her voice bigger than it had ever been before, as huge as the empty spaces inside her.

They'd watched her when she was not looking, whispered about her when she was out of earshot, and they were all brimming with it: the excitement of watching a new love take shape, seeing their youngest sister find the same gift they had all found when their own times came.

And they'd all felt confident about the identity of the merman who was causing such a change in her: Falke, one of the men of the court, son of their mother's cousin. A beautifully formed creature, with a long golden tail and dark torso, glittery eyes flecked with gold. For some days they'd watched quietly as Lenia neglected her normal pastimes and smiled to herself when she swam by, unaware of what surrounded her, her face changed by a dreamy look that spoke of new love. And they'd watched Falke gaze at her whenever she was near and attempt to be beside her at every feast.

It was Thilla who'd approached Lenia yesterday and posed the question directly. Arching her brow, her dark hair swirling around her broad face, she'd asked, "Are you in love, Sister?"

They'd been floating outside the palace, watching over a gorgeous set of Thilla's bright blue eggs hidden in the rocks. A group of giant squids whirled about nearby, their long tentacles swishing back and forth like sea vines.

"Yes," Lenia had replied. The question had clearly caught her off guard, but she'd answered openly, her voice soft and small.

"I knew it! Oh, Sister," Thilla had said, reaching over and embracing her. "We were all so worried. You just seemed so . . . distracted, ever since your birthday and that horrible business with the shipwreck, and the human man."

Lenia had looked at her sister, radiant with pleasure and love. She'd been surprised that Thilla, with her gift of sight, did not already see the truth. "That was when I fell in love," she'd whispered.

Thilla had looked at her, confused, her expression hovering between excitement and worry. "What do you mean?" she'd asked.

"That night, in the upper world. The man I saved."

"But . . . aren't you in love with Falke? He is the best of the mermen."

"No," Lenia had said. "I do not love him. I love the man I held in my arms and carried to shore. Now all I can do is think of him."

As the impact of her sister's words hit her, Thilla's face had changed. "Lenia! That is impossible. It is forbidden."

"I know. That is why I am suffering so much now."

"We all thought you were happy, that you and Falke . . ."

"No, Sister," she'd said. "I am not happy."

"You only think this because the man was not conscious. Believe me, if you'd known him . . ." Thilla had shuddered. "He would have hurt you. That is what men do. You only saw a man who was weak, and so you thought you might love him."

"I do love him."

"No, Sister." Thilla had shaken her head, brushed away the starfish floating past. "And even if he was not dangerous," she'd said more gently, "it cannot be. You are a mermaid. He is a man. You are an adult now, too old for this fantasy."

"But, Thilla," Lenia had said, leaning in. "It is not a fantasy. It is something inside me. I've always had this feeling that there is something more. A longing for a soul, for eternal life. I don't want to become nothing, a handful of foam, the way Great-grandmother did, the way Grandfather did. After all those years and then . . . nothing. And when I carried him through the water, I felt it. His soul. Leaving his body and entering mine. I felt the way it could be, and it felt like everything I've ever wanted. And I saw snow, Thilla. Like Grandmother told us about. Snow! Snow and ice falling from the sky. And I felt their souls, in all of it."

"But it is not nothing, Lenia, to become part of the sea. In this way we, too, live forever."

"It is not the same," Lenia had said, wanting to cry with frustration. How could none of them comprehend the beauty of a human soul, shining in heaven for eternity? Where it would be whole again, as they all had been once, in times past? "We disappear. Nothing of what we were or did or felt remains."

"Oh, Lenia," Thilla had said, taking her sister into her arms. "Why do you long for such things? Why are you so unhappy with what you have here, when we have so much?"

"I don't know," Lenia had whispered, wrapping her arms around Thilla's slender waist.

THE WAVES LAPPED around her, breaking against the rock. Above her, the clouds were becoming less dense and dark. The storm seemed to be passing. Suddenly, she heard screaming. It ripped through the air and into her body, made her let go of the rock and fall underwater.

"Lenia!"

She pushed back up to the surface and looked out. It was Margrethe, frantically running along the cliff, under the trees, to the gate, dressed all in white, her head covered but her voice and her face unmistakable.

She had come back.

Lenia was about to go to her when a man appeared behind her, chasing her as she began running down the stairs. For a moment Lenia froze, wondering what to do, and then she felt it, she understood that the man would not hurt Margrethe, that he was trying to protect her, that they were taking her away.

She stopped in the water. Watched Margrethe cry out to her, her voice ripping into her again as the man pulled her away. He put his arms around her and drew her next to him. Margrethe was freezing, the cold wracking her body. Lenia focused and saw, felt all of it, watched them until they disappeared. And she knew, then, she would not see Margrethe again.

The shore was desolate now, and bare. A grief broke open over Lenia, a feeling that was brand-new to her, raw and pulsing.

She pushed forward, through the water. In moments she was at the shore, feeling the rocks under her palm. They glittered where she touched them. She remembered the feel of the prince in her arms as she moved from the water onto the beach. He had lain right there. She had kissed him, felt his skin under her palms, her lips. Now, it was as if he had died, as if both of them had, and she felt real grief moving through her. She had not felt this way since her grandfather had turned to foam a few years before. Everyone had celebrated his passing. She alone had felt it was an irretrievable loss. *He is a part of the sea now,* they had said. But she had watched his body disintegrate, disappear into the water. Become nothing at all.

Margrethe's voice rang in her ears. The longing inside of her.

And the thought came to Lenia, as it had repeatedly since the day after her birthday, when her sisters had given her the necklace she was wearing now.

She could go to the sea witch, Sybil.

She shook her head. She should go home, forget this world, mate with Falke, who was the best of the mermen, as Thilla had said, and lay her eggs. Spend the rest of her three hundred years with her sisters and her children, her sisters' children, all of them together. And she could tell the children stories about souls as they laughed and played, imagining what it would be like to have webs of light living inside them. Why did she have to long for more than that?

But the thought kept lingering, still.

FROM AS FAR back as she could remember, Lenia had heard tales about the sea witch, and her great powers. They all knew that the witch had once been favored by Lenia's great-grandmother, the former queen, and that the two had fallen out spectacularly when the queen issued the royal decree forbidding interaction with humans. Some said that Sybil had argued vehemently against the decree and openly defied it, others that the disagreement was of a more personal, scandalous nature. Whatever the case, the queen had banished Sybil to a cave at the outskirts of the central kingdom. Where, the story went, she'd been practicing magic ever since.

Lenia had always heard rumors of mermaids consulting her for love potions and spells, for charms to ensure the healthy hatchings of their children, and now she'd learned that her own sister had gone to see Sybil, too. All of this was strictly forbidden, of course, but for some, magic had its own allure, stronger than a royal decree.

Ever since Vela had mentioned Sybil, Lenia could not stop

thinking of her—and what she might know of the prince, whether or not Lenia could see him again.

She would do anything, she thought, to see him one more time.

ᦂ

THAT NIGHT, AFTER the thought had lingered long enough to turn into a possibility, a shining hope, Lenia made a decision. She would visit the sea witch, just to see. It would not have to mean anything at all, but it would do no harm just to see.

And then she could go to Falke, she decided. This was just one last thing to take care of before she started her new life, as an adult and as a mother. One last adventure.

She left the palace quietly, when she was sure no one was watching. She let her heart guide her as she swam past the mountain range that cast shadows over the palace and into the vast sea, passing caverns and volcanoes and streams of glowing fish, drifting underwater stars, all manner of shell and pearl and coral. After a long while, the contours of the sea began to change. The luminous green seaweed and glowing bulbs disappeared, and the terrain turned dark, limned with black, starry rock. The water shifted, sparkled, grew dark and dense; a strange sort of electricity moved through the ocean, and she knew she'd entered the realm of the sea witch.

It was unmistakable: the cavern gleamed in front of her like a black star. Outside stood the figure of a witch built from twigs and grass and leaves from the upper world. Materials so out of place in the deep ocean that they had taken on their own magic.

Lenia swam through the huge, gaping opening and into the cavern. The walls seemed to be made from glittering black jewel, with huge red flowers blooming out of it. Winged white fish fluttered around, moving in and out of view, illuminating the surroundings.

"Sybil?" she called. To her surprise, her voice rumbled in her throat, the way it had above the surface of the water, in the air. She looked about, disoriented, but she was still at the bottom of the sea. Surrounded by black jewel walls. Nothing had changed.

There was no answer. Across the room was an archway, and she moved through it, into a second room, filled with strange plants that grew so thickly she had to weave through them. Even as Lenia approached, they grew and changed color right before her eyes.

She pushed through and came upon a mermaid busy tending a batch of flowering vines climbing up one of the cavern walls. The mermaid had a tail like melted pearl, wild pink-silver hair streaming to her waist.

"Hello?" Lenia whispered, suddenly afraid. It couldn't possibly be her, she thought. Sybil had to be near three hundred years old by now.

Lenia started when the mermaid turned and looked at her. Her eyes were the strangest, palest gold, the kind of eyes you could feel yourself sinking into. They pulled her in like two arms, and Lenia immediately looked down at the floor, which was a black, glowing sand, scattered through with silver rocks.

"Hello?" the mermaid said, approaching her. Her voice was so lovely, and it seemed to take on a life of its own as it left her mouth, entwining itself in Lenia's hair.

"Are you Sybil?"

"I was expecting you."

"You were?"

"These plants," Sybil said, pointing. "I can see bits of the future in the vines." She plucked a flower and then opened it, let the petals collapse until only the thick center shot up. "Can you see?"

"See what?" Lenia could not see anything but the heart of the flower in Sybil's hand. Suddenly, for just a flash, it took on the shape of a mermaid—of Lenia herself—and then it fell back and became, once more, the center of the flower. "Oh." She looked up at Sybil, who smiled, dropping the flower onto the sea floor. Instantly, it shot up again to its full height.

"You need something?"

"Yes," Lenia stammered. "I wanted to—"

Sybil put her hand on Lenia's shoulder. "It is all right. Tell me."

"On my eighteenth birthday, I saved a human man who was drowning, and I love him. I want to find him again." It seemed to come out in one long breath.

Sybil did not even blink with surprise. "You have not fallen in love with just *any* human. He is a prince, is he not?"

"A prince?" Lenia said. "How do you know that?"

"My dear," Sybil said, ignoring her question. "It's best to accept your own nature, rather than try to be something you're not."

Lenia spoke the next words carefully, slowly. "But is it possible? To become something you're not?"

Around them, the vines twisted and untwisted, sprouted leaves and flowers that grew and died in an instant. The black gem walls seemed to fade to silver, then grow dark again. Suddenly Lenia could see the witch's years. She was as smooth and beautiful as before, but there was a deep sadness in her, a weariness that spoke of infinite loss.

"Yes," Sybil said, finally. "But the cost is great. That is the thing about magic. There is always a cost."

"What is it?" Lenia whispered. And everything shifted then, became serious, sacred. The cavern seemed unbearably quiet.

Sybil looked at her and cocked her head. "It has been a long time since any merperson asked this of me," she said.

"It has happened before? Others have asked this?"

"Yes," Sybil said. "You're not the first mermaid to love a human. This has happened for as long as our worlds have been separated. It is one reason we have all these rules now, why they try so hard to keep us away. You, my dear, might simply have more human left in you than most. Maybe that's what makes you long for their world."

"Yes," Lenia said. For the first time, someone understood. The witch knew what she felt. Others of her kind had felt this way before. *Yes.* "Please, tell me what the price is. What I can do."

Sybil looked at her sympathetically. "I can give you a potion," she said, "that will split your tail into legs."

"A potion," Lenia breathed. "It is that simple?"

"It is very, very painful. When your tail splits, it feels as if you're being slashed by a huge sword, and it continues to feel that way. Though you keep your grace and ease of movement, you feel as if you're walking on knife blades with every step, even when every human who sees you is struck by your uncommon elegance. Would you be willing to suffer all that? For a mere human?"

Lenia could not even imagine such pain, but she felt she could bear anything to see him again. How could she think that she could return to the palace and mate with Falke? "I think so," she said.

"You cannot be a mermaid again, once you take on human form. You cannot visit your parents or your sisters. You cannot watch their children grow. You have to abandon everything of the life you've known, everyone you've loved. Could you do that?"

Sybil paused, waiting for her response.

"Yes," Lenia said, but her voice was trembling.

"And furthermore, you must win the prince's love. Win it so completely that he is willing to marry you, and a priest must cleave his soul to you. That is the only way for you to gain a human soul, Lenia."

"He will love me," Lenia whispered, nodding. "I know he will love me."

"If he marries someone else, the next morning at dawn your heart will break, and you will turn to foam. If he does not marry at all, you will live as a regular human does, and die, but without a precious soul. Here, in the sea, you have hundreds of years left to live, as long as you stay away from humans. But in the upper world, you can die at any moment. Your body will be fragile, and there is danger everywhere there. And when you die, you will turn to foam."

"Unless he marries me."

"Yes. Unless he marries you."

"And if he marries me, I can live forever, right? It is true?"

Sybil nodded. "You can gain a human soul, and a human soul lives forever, in heaven. But do not forget that we, too, continue to exist, as part of the sea."

"But we turn to foam. We disappear."

"Yes."

"It is not the same."

Lenia thought of her mother and father, her sisters and their children, their gleaming eggs. The sea. All that she loved of the ocean. The power of her own body as she glided through the depths, the water streaming on all sides of her and the glow of fish and octopi and starfish all around.

But what were the riches of her own world compared to everything that would come after death? Even the bonds of family would disappear, eventually—and then all that would remain would be memories, memories and foam, and eventually all those who remembered her would become foam as well. Their palaces would crumble, their stories be forgotten. Until there was nothing, no trace, left. She thought of all those who had come before her. With their loves and pains, their vicious battles, their children, their passions. All those sea folk who'd reveled in the feel of the water, who'd loved the ocean, who'd lived amid the coral. What were they now? What was left of them?

And then she thought of the brightness of the upper world, the sun streaming down, the infinite variety of sounds. The men falling from the ship, dying, screaming for life. And his lips under her own, the softness. She imagined herself with two legs, walking to him. His soul, already inside her—she knew it—joining with hers.

A holy man marrying them, fusing their souls so that they would be together forever. She thought of Margrethe praying in the convent on the cliff. In the sea, Lenia would die, turn to foam, become nothing. All of this now would end. But with the prince, she could live in heaven forever.

"There is one more thing," Sybil said.

"What else?"

"The price. It is how magic works, Lenia. What you are asking for is so great, you must also give up your greatest asset in exchange. Every merperson who asked this before you has had to do it. The potion will not work without it."

"But what else do I have to give, if I'm willing to give up my place, my family, the sea?"

"Your voice."

She clutched her throat automatically. "My voice?"

"Your beautiful voice."

"But . . . how can you take that?"

Sybil looked pained as she spoke. "To do this, my child, I would have to cut out your tongue."

"My tongue?"

"Yes. You would not be able to sing, or to speak."

"My tongue," Lenia repeated. "How could I make him love me, if I'm unable to speak to him?"

"You would have your form, your beautiful movements, your expressive eyes. You have more gifts than you realize. And in the upper world, they would be that much stronger. Humans can sense that there is something special about a merperson, though of course they do not know what it is they are sensing."

Lenia's mind was spinning. What would it be like to have no voice? Her voice was so much a part of her, who she was. Her singing, which could so easily move her fellow creatures to despair or laughter. It was a gift, simply, something she'd been born with. Not something that had ever mattered much to her, but even so, she could not imagine herself without it. Maybe it was for this, though, that she'd been given it. To have this.

Sybil leaned forward, taking Lenia's hand into her own. "This is not a decision you can reverse. Do not make it lightly. Take some time to think about what it will mean."

Lenia nodded. "And if I decide to do this, you will prepare a potion for me?"

"Yes. I can prepare a potion for you, and then take your payment. That is the last part of the spell."

"And afterward, I could go to him? Right away?"

"Yes."

Lenia was wild with excitement, possibility. Could she really leave everything, all she'd ever known, give up her voice? For him? All of that for him?

She thought of the prince so soft and warm in her arms. A web of light moving from him into her, expanding, filling her. Everything she'd ever wanted, right within her grasp.

CHAPTER NINE

The Princess

THEY RODE ALL DAY AND THROUGH THE NIGHT, THE steady, heavy rhythm of hoofbeats carrying them forward. They passed through pristine forests of giant snow-laced pine trees. They galloped through villages and walled cities. They raced across long stretches of countryside scattered with huts and farms, all of them iced over now, glittering under the winter sun.

In village after village, peasants and merchants appeared in windows and at doorsteps to catch sight of the king, his royal guard, and the rescued princess. The story had spread like fire: that the enemy prince had stolen into a convent where the princess had been in hiding, that he'd gone there to murder her, and that the king had arrived just in time to save her. All over the kingdom, people were enraged. The king's coat of arms was displayed in windows and on shop doors. People stood in the streets and screamed for blood. Peacetime was over.

To go to war was one thing. To steal into a place of God with the intention of killing a young princess was another altogether.

All Margrethe could do was sit back in horror and watch it unfold. The anger of the people. The villages that had been devastated by years of war, where houses and shops still lay in ruins and the suffering was so obvious she could nearly taste and smell it. News of the prince's stay at the convent had only strengthened her father's hatred for the Southern kingdom and increased the blood-lust of his men, and now she herself was the wound around which they all rallied. She did not know where it came from, this hatred, this conviction that the land belonged to them and their bloodline. *Her* bloodline. That the Southern king and his predecessors were pretenders to a false throne. All this hatred and rage, extending so far back—it was like a great ocean wave she was powerless against.

She was riding sidesaddle, Edele was on a horse behind. They were both still in their novices' habits, though Margrethe could easily have changed back into the dress she'd worn those few months before, the day she was first brought to the convent. But her father had wanted the country to see her and her lady wearing the holy garb, to know that all the rumors were true, and she had not dared to defy him. She needed to pick her battles now.

Pieter sat behind her with the reins in his hands, his arms around her, holding her in place. She knew that her father had chosen Pieter as her rider because he was the strongest of the group, and the most adept horseman, but she also knew that he was one of the main champions of the war effort, the one arguing it was time to deal the crushing blow. Not long ago she had thought she could marry someone like him. Now it felt strange and wrong, being pressed up against him, when she could still feel the prince's lips on her hand.

The prince, the one they were all shouting against . . . For the first time, despite everything, she felt an opening. There had been a new beauty in that convent garden, standing over the mysterious, unfathomable sea, the possibility for a new kind of world. Where was he now? she wondered. Did he remember? Did he know who she was? And now, as they flew through the countryside, the horse under her, the cold against her face, the sacred garments protecting her, the memory of the mermaid so vivid in her mind, she was beginning to feel reborn, ready to fulfill a great destiny.

THEY ARRIVED AT the Northern castle after a full night and day of riding, just as the sun was beginning to set.

The gates opened, and they entered to cheers and waving banners. Hundreds of people had gathered to celebrate the princess's safe return.

The riders slowed, and the people rushed up to Margrethe, bowing in front of her as she passed, reaching up to touch her habit, and then bowing to the king, who had so selflessly put his duties aside to rescue his daughter.

Margrethe had never been so exhausted. Her body ached from sitting in one position for so long. Finally one of the guards helped her down, and her feet touched ground again. The stablemen ran out to take the horses, and she rushed up the steps, through the front door, and into the haven of the castle.

Her father remained outside, and the others stayed with him as he began to address the people. Behind her, Margrethe heard shouting and cheers, her father calling for blood and retribution. She paused in dismay to listen. Lens appeared at her side and gently took her arm. "To war!" the people shouted as her father railed against the young prince and reminded them all that Margrethe would one day, according to prophecy, bring forth a great ruler for the land.

She leaned against the wall, catching her breath.

Lens stood back, watching her carefully. "You have had a long journey, Your Highness," he said. "Perhaps you would like to rest?"

She nodded, grateful.

As they made their way into the great hall, it seemed the whole court was there, waiting to greet her. All the highest nobles, all the members of the royal council, the ladies who'd once been friends with her mother and who now vied for her father's heart, not realizing that their charms were lost on him, that his heart had turned to stone the moment his wife died. Now all the courtiers turned to welcome Margrethe, bowing and kissing her hand as she walked past.

She knew she cut a ragged figure in her habit, her hair tangled, coming loose from the riding. She wanted to scream out to them: *I am perfectly well! I was never in danger from that gentle man, you fools!*

But instead she smiled gracefully as they all filed past, blessing her. She'd had years of practice at denying herself, stifling her very nature.

Finally, she was able to retreat to her own rooms. A fire was waiting for her, full of burning pinecones, and a hot bath was being prepared. It seemed like unbelievable luxury now. The smell of pine and wood and perfume from the bath, the sumptuous fabrics on the bed and furniture, the tapestries hanging from the walls. Her ladies waiting for her in exquisite dresses, their faces painted and hair strategically arranged. After so long in the convent, it seemed almost shocking, all that beautiful display, yet at the same time her whole physical being responded with relief.

She was home.

Gently, her ladies stripped her of her habit, took down her hair. In the midst of everything, Margrethe was almost surprised to see that Lenia's shimmer was still there, on her forearm.

"Do you see that?" she asked Josephine, the lady, after Edele, of whom she was most fond.

"See what?" Josephine asked.

"A sort of . . . sparkle, on my skin. Do you see?"

"No."

"How strange," she said, stepping into the bath. As they helped her sit in the warm water, another servant poured in fresh hot water from a kettle that had been heating over the fire, and Josephine began sprinkling dried herbs in the water from baskets she had set nearby. Margrethe sat and let the warmth envelop her. Her arm shimmered faintly from under the water. She watched it for a moment and then closed her eyes, breathing in the steaming herbal scent.

Her other lady-in-waiting, Laura, knelt down behind her. She gathered up Margrethe's thick hair and began to wash it thoroughly, rubbing it with herbs and powders.

"We are so glad you are safe," Laura said. "How terrifying, to think the enemy was so close to you."

"It was not so bad," Margrethe murmured. "He was . . . not so bad." Despite herself—her exhaustion, her natural pride—she could feel a flush coming over her, a smile playing at the corners of her lips.

"Oh! You . . . liked him?" Laura said, widening her eyes. "You did! And he our enemy! Is it true? We do hear he is a very handsome man."

"Oh, he is," Margrethe said, no longer able to keep herself from breaking into a smile. "He is larger than life. Edele will tell you, too. He's like something from a story."

The two ladies gave each other knowing looks as they lifted Margrethe's arms on either side, dipping pieces of cloth into the water and then squeezing them over her shoulders.

"There has been much talk of him here," Laura said. "They say he's a great warrior. They say he was sent to kill you. But it sounds like you were in a different kind of danger."

"I am sure he was not sent to kill me," Margrethe said. *I met a mermaid*, she wanted to say. *We sat on the beach together.* "As for the danger you're referring to, I'm not sure I know what you mean."

She gave Laura a sly look then, and the girl burst out laughing.

"But he was . . . He came to the convent where you were staying," Josephine said. "Why else would he be sent there?"

"He was not sent there," Margrethe said. "There was a terrible, terrible storm. He was not supposed to be there at all. He . . .

swam to shore. I was the one who found him on the beach, nearly drowned."

"Nearly drowned?" Josephine asked. "They said he appeared on his horse, with a gleaming sword at his side."

"No," Margrethe said, shaking her head. "He washed up on the shore one day, soaked through and shivering. If I hadn't come upon him when I did, he would have died. He was alone. Does that sound like a man sent to kill me?"

"You know how they all like to tell such stories here," Josephine said. "They've talked of little else."

"I know," Margrethe said. "But it was not like that. It was . . ." Her mind spun as she tried to reach back to those moments on the beach, in the infirmary and the garden. "He thought I was a novice, you know. He had no idea who I was. I was the girl who found him on the beach. He thanked me over and over."

"It was a coincidence, then?" Laura asked.

"No," Margrethe answered. "Fate."

"Fate," Laura repeated, sighing. "That's so romantic."

"Imagine if he knew who you were," Josephine said. "Do you think he knows by now?"

"Maybe," Margrethe said, her heart sinking. She had avoided the thought: Christopher, learning that the young novice was actually a princess, the daughter of his father's enemy. How would he react to that news?

She had no idea what he would think. She had no idea what would happen to any of them now.

Slowly, she stood from the bath. "I need to sleep," she said.

She remained silent as they dried her off and dressed her in her nightgown. Then she dismissed them and curled up on her bed, falling asleep almost instantly.

SHE WOKE TO a hushed, dark world, wondering, once again, if she had dreamed everything. If it was months earlier, when her biggest decisions had been what to wear that day, what manuscript to read, what delightful pastimes to partake in. Back then, the world had seemed so safe. There were enemies in the South, evil and ferocious, but the bravest men of her land were ready to fight them, and she had no doubt that, when the time came, they would be victorious, loved as they were by God.

She held up her arm, and it was still there, the shimmer across her skin in the sunken firelight.

Edele was sitting near the fire. Margrethe stood up, groggy from sleep, and walked over to her, put her hand on her friend's shoulder.

"Have you recovered?" Margrethe asked.

Edele looked up, surprised, then broke into a smile. Margrethe was struck for a moment by the girl's vibrant beauty: her elaborate brocaded green dress that dipped down in the front, revealing her pale skin and ample cleavage, her mass of red curls and open, freckled face. Back to normal, as if the last months had never happened at all. The fire reflecting against her skin, making it glow.

"I feel like I slept for days," Edele said, standing. "I'm a new woman. And you? You must be dying to get into some civilized clothes again." She walked to the wardrobe against the wall, began rifling through the rich gowns hanging in it.

Margrethe laughed. "It is strange to be back, isn't it?"

"Yes. But I am so relieved. I missed it here. I do not like being in a world without men." She turned back to Margrethe and winked.

"Edele! There are other things in the world besides men."

"Not anything of importance, m'lady."

"You are terrible. Did you really hate it so much?"

"Yes! What was there not to hate? Rising at all hours of the night, never getting a proper rest, wearing those awful habits, all those hours ruining our hands at the loom, the terrible food. Worst of all, no men but that mean old bishop and the son of our greatest enemy." Edele pulled out a pale blue silk gown. "This one," she said, turning to Margrethe with the dress in hand. "Did you not hate it as well? All that time, and not once being able to speak as openly and loudly as we are now!"

"I think I found some beauty there."

"Well. That you did."

There was a knock on the door, and a servant entered, followed by Josephine and Laura, announcing that the king expected Margrethe at dinner.

"I will be there shortly," Margrethe said, nodding, as Edele embraced the others and started regaling them with tales of the convent's horrors.

They all bustled around Margrethe, dressing her in the gown Edele had selected, combing out her long hair and piling it on her head, perfuming her with exotic oils. Margrethe closed her eyes. She could not help but savor the feeling of being stylishly clothed again after months of dressing plainly. Having her dark hair out and in full view, elaborately adorned. She moved to the glass and peered at herself, spread her palms on the silk of her dress, admiring how it cinched her waist. How splendid her dark hair looked against the pale blue. She found herself imagining, for a moment, Prince Christopher standing before her, seeing her like this.

"You are back in the world now, too, my princess," Edele said. "I know there are many gentlemanly eyes that have missed the sight of you."

Margrethe started, embarrassed, as if Edele had been reading her thoughts. "I hardly care about such things," she said, lifting her head and turning to all three ladies. "I am ready now."

They led her down the austere old halls, lined with portraits of the past kings. The smell of roast pheasant wafted from the banquet hall, making her mouth water. The sound of voices drunk with wine. The stomping of feet on the old wooden floors. The pleasures of court life.

"It smells like heaven," Edele said. "I wish I'd made my dress looser . . ." She put her palms at her waist and grimaced.

They all laughed, then quieted as they approached the door. The ladies stood back, according to custom, and Margrethe entered the banquet hall before them. The entire room broke out in cheers, and she smiled, nodded serenely, immediately slipping into the courtly style. She was a princess. This was what she knew how to do. Her father sat at the head of the table, with Pieter and Gregor flanking him, dressed in fur capes, while the rest of the court sat down the length of the table covered with platters of roast pheasant and soup and bread. Along the walls bright torches burned, reflecting in the silver and gold that decorated each place setting.

Immediately the king stood and raised his glass, and everyone else followed suit.

"To war!" he called out, his voice booming.

"To Margrethe!"

She curtsied the way she had since she was a girl, accepting the court's toast with a princess's grace. But a sick feeling moved through her. She remembered the boy drawing a mermaid with a stick in the ground, living in squalor while here there was such abundance. How much worse would it get for him? How many more children were there spread throughout her father's land, *her* land, like him? Suddenly the smell of meat suffocated her.

"Welcome home, my daughter," the king said, as the room quieted. "We all thank the glory of God for your safe return."

"Thank you, Father," she said. She walked up to the platform and took her seat, which Gregor quickly exchanged for the next chair down, beside her father. Calm and elegant, though every part of her wanted to stand up and shout what she had seen, what she knew.

In front of her, a servant spread a lavish meal: roasted meat, spiced rice, thick bread. Just a few months ago, she would have been content to sit here and dine on pheasant and cake, accept the young courtiers' attentions, clap as the court musicians played. The talk of war would have made her feel safe and strong.

When I rule this kingdom, she thought now, her heart hammering in her chest, *a great change will come.*

She pushed her plate away as the king continued. "It is only through God's glory and His love for us, His people, that no harm came to my daughter, though she was within the enemy's grasp. We will not let the South make fools of us. We will not let the prince's disrespect for the North go unpunished."

All the nobles in the room raised their glasses and cheered as the servants scurried in and out, bringing more wine, more meat.

"To war!"

Margrethe forced herself not to flinch, not to show any emotion, when all she wanted to do was stand up and scream at all of them.

The men stomped their feet and clanged their silverware against their plates.

"Marte," Gregor said softly, using his old nickname for her and taking her hand in his.

She turned to him, grasping his hand gratefully, and felt comforted, instantly, by his touch. He was a brilliant man, learned in the ways of the skies and stars, the ocean and earth, literature and the arts. He'd been schooled, long ago, in the East, and brought from one of the universities to teach her father when he was a boy. When her father became a young king, he kept his old tutor close at hand and often turned to him for advice. It was the late queen who had insisted that Gregor school Margrethe, and, because of the prophecy made at her birth, her father had agreed. Margrethe's happiest memories were of sitting with Gregor in the library, reading the poetry of the troubadours, stories from the ancients. When

her mother died, all the times her father had gone off to war . . .
she had always had the library to escape to.

Gregor was like an anchor for her in the midst of all this confusion. Aside from Edele, he was the person she trusted most in the
world.

"I have missed you greatly," she whispered. She clutched her
old tutor's hand, feeling close to tears. Next to her, she could sense
her father's anger as if it were a stone wall.

"Let us eat!" the king said as the room erupted once more into
cheers and stomping. All along the table, members of the court
picked up their utensils and resumed eating. The musicians started
playing a well-loved song, walking up and down the room. From
the kitchen, the servants brought plates piled with cakes.

"You are not eating, child?" her father asked after a few minutes, turning to her.

She was surprised to see that, despite everything, he looked
happier, more handsome even, than he had in ages. Since before
her mother died, maybe. His dark eyes were bright, he was suddenly smiling and relaxed, where a minute ago he'd seemed overcome with rage. *He likes this,* she realized. *He thrives on it.*

And then she felt guilt and love flow through her, too. It had
been too long since she'd seen him look happy.

"I am not feeling well, Father," she said. "I'm still tired from
the journey."

"It is no wonder," he said.

And her father reached out his large, ringed hand and touched her
face tenderly, the way he'd done when she was a little girl. It took
her by surprise, this gesture, and for a moment she again felt close to
tears.

She sat quietly through the rest of the meal, pushing her meat
around her plate, forcing herself to take a few bites of bread. The
music became more boisterous, and some courtiers began to sing

along. She watched Edele, sitting with a group of young noble men and women, laughing with her head back, her hair tumbling down her shoulders. She wished she could sit with them, carefree.

"Margrethe, would you accompany your old teacher on a walk in the garden?" Gregor asked as the servants cleared their plates.

"Of course," she said.

He rose and gestured to the king, who nodded. Margrethe followed Gregor out of the hall, and through the doors that led into the heated, glass-walled garden, a project of her mother's last years.

"Everything you have been through, it must have been very traumatic," he said, taking her arm in his. They began walking along one of the pathways that wound past exotic trees that had come on ships from the southern part of the world. "I am so relieved, Marte, that you are safe. But I can see something is troubling you." He looked at her carefully. "What is it?"

She looked at him, wondering how he always knew what she was feeling, and then, unbidden, the tears came, streaming down her cheeks. Sparkling like crystals in the night air. Above them, the moon was full and bright through the glass.

"What is it?" he asked, stopping and turning to her. "Did he hurt you? Is there something you're not saying? When we received a report that Prince Christopher had been not only nearby but within the same walls . . . Oh, your father! That he had been right next to you, down the hall—it was unimaginable, what might have happened."

"No, no," she said. "That's just it. I tried to tell my father this, Gregor, when he came to the convent that day. That he has it completely wrong. They all do. But he wouldn't listen to me, and now there's this talk of war, and it's wrong, Gregor, all of it. He was not there to kill me."

"What are you saying? Why else would he have been there?"

"He was not there to hurt me at all. I talked to him, to the prince. In the convent infirmary, I spoke to him, alone."

"Just you and him? Did he know who you were?"

"No! He did not know anything. And he was kind to me. He believes that he owes his life to me. Well, not to me exactly, to the novice he thought I was. All this talk of retribution, it's based on a coincidence. A stroke of fate. It is wrong."

She was relieved to see the concern on Gregor's face. Despite their closeness, she'd half expected him to dismiss her as her father had.

"You need to talk to your father," he said gently. "When he left to get you . . . He was out of his mind. Terrified he could have lost you, the way he lost your mother. Now you are safe and home, and he may be able to listen."

"Gregor, my father stopped listening to me a while ago." The idea of going back to her father made her feel sick. She had never before stood up to him aside from those few moments in the chaos of the convent. But she had never before had a reason like she did now.

"You need to try. It's too important. Too many lives are at stake."

She cocked her head, studying her tutor's weathered face, which she loved so much, with its high cheekbones and deep crevices. "You are not as in love with war as my father is, are you?"

"No," he said. "Many of us are not."

She nodded slowly. "I did not think of it much before. I just figured it was how things were, the way they were supposed to be."

"You have seen something of the world now."

"I will try to speak with him," she said, looping her arm through his. And then they continued along the path, past trees bursting with fruit and flowers while snow drifted silently to the ground outside the glass walls. In front of them, an ornate fountain, with water trickling down, shone icy in the moonlight.

❧

MARGRETHE WAITED TO go to her father until the next morning, when she knew he'd be in the best spirits, right after morning Mass and before the midday meal.

She stood up straight, lifted her chin, and nodded for the guards to open the door. She was reminded of a night not long before when she'd stood outside the convent infirmary and been just as nervous as she was now.

The guards announced her presence and led her to her father, who stood by the window, looking out over the grounds.

He turned to her, and she could see that he was in a somber, melancholy mood.

"Father," she said, curtsying before him.

"Margrethe," he said. "Come to me, child." She walked over to him awkwardly, let him pull her to him. He was such a large man, she felt enveloped by him. As a child, she had loved climbing over him as he lay on the floor, her mother laughing nearby, loved when he lifted her on his legs and swung her back and forth in the air. It was impossible to imagine this aged man ever behaving like that now.

"I am sorry you were so worried for me, Father," she said. "And I thank you for rushing to help me."

"Of course," he said, stepping back and looking at her. "You know there is nothing I would not do to protect you. I am only sorry I sent you into that den of vipers."

"Father," she said, "it was not like that. Those women there, they are holy and good. The abbess was a friend to me."

He smiled slightly, gestured for her to sit on a couch nearby, and then sat down beside her. "You think well of those who do not deserve it, Margrethe. You are a gentle soul, but you will have to learn hardness, too, before you are queen."

"It is not weakness that makes me say this," she said. "Not about the women I knew there, and not about"—she hesitated and then forced herself forward—"Prince Christopher."

"What about Prince Christopher?"

"Father," she said, taking a deep breath and turning to face him. "You cannot go back to war over this. You cannot break the peace agreement because of what happened. There has been a terrible misunderstanding. The prince was not there to hurt me. I promise you that. But even if he *had* been . . . the cost of war is too great."

She watched his face harden. "You do not know enough of the world yet, Daughter," he said, "to speak of these matters."

"I believe the prince was sent there for a greater purpose. He washed to shore, bruised and battered, nearly dead, and *I* was the one who saw him, who made sure he lived. How can you explain that, except as a sign from God?"

"You must not let yourself be fooled by Southern tricks," he said. "Remember the horse the Greeks used to win the Trojan War. I would hope your studies could serve you better than this."

She was startled by her father's reference to the old tale and could not help raising her voice. "*I* am the one who found him. He was not tricking me by dying! I should never have been standing there watching the sea in the first place. At any other time, he would have just died there, on the rocks. How else can you explain what happened?"

To her surprise, her father's face softened, and his eyes filled with tears. She almost gasped, it was so unexpected. For a moment she thought she'd convinced him.

"Sometimes you are so like your mother," he said.

"I am?" She was shocked to hear him speak of her.

He smiled, and looked far away, remembering. "She was always passionate. Never afraid to speak her mind to me, even when almost no one else would. It is why I trust Gregor. I know he is never afraid to say the truth."

She smiled at his memory. Her mother had been strong, though it was a quiet strength she'd had. It had made her a good match for him. "I can only hope to become as brave as she was," she said.

"I have no doubt. Bravery and passion, these are not things you lack, Margrethe."

"Thank you," she said, feeling her own eyes fill with tears. "I miss her so much."

"I miss her, too," he said. "And it is for her that we must defeat the South, our enemy."

"Wait. I don't understand."

"You remember when your mother fell ill? She insisted on visiting her cousin in the South. When she came back, the sickness had entered her. *That* was a sign from God. That land is ours, Margrethe. We should never have been divided."

"But it happened so long ago, Father. Why can't we just live peacefully, side by side?"

He raised his hand. "Enough, Margrethe. We are not a weak kingdom. I will not stand by and watch my enemy kill my queen, and attempt to kill my daughter."

"But so many people will die!"

"They will die for their kingdom. It is the best reason to die."

CHAPTER TEN

The Mermaid

*L*ENIA TOOK HER TIME SWIMMING BACK TO THE PALACE, letting the water soothe her. A school of tiny, translucent fish drifted past, and she watched them, how the light from a nearby medusa caught them, making them flare up like stars in the night sky. Like tiny souls. Euphoria moved to sadness, and then back again. She didn't know how she could leave her family, her world, her very own body, and yet, at the same time, how could she say no to what had now been offered to her? She wished she could bring her sisters with her, and her parents, and her sisters' children. She wished she could bring everyone with her, every single creature in the sea, and they could all have souls that would shine together eternally.

When she returned to the palace, all the others were sleeping, tucked against rocks, inside giant shells, and among the lush sea plants that flourished at the bottom of the ocean. She swam to the royal chamber and peered in at her mother and father, twisted together upon their bed of pearls, a gift from her grandfather to her grandmother many years before. Her mother's hair was long and white now, but she was every bit as beautiful as she'd been when Lenia's grandmother had stepped down from the throne, as Lenia's mother would do one day soon so that Thilla could take her place. And her father, the king: as she watched him sleep, she thought about all the swims he had taken her on when she was a child, the two of them holding hands, the way he'd tossed her through the water and then swooped down to catch her, how he'd shown her the wonders of the ocean while her mother stayed in the palace and dealt with the court.

She had already made her decision, she realized. Of course she had, the moment Sybil told her that everything she'd ever wanted was possible.

She left her parents' doorway and drifted back through the great hall, where the mussel shells opened and closed, where all kinds of luminous sea life swam through the dark. She had never had this feeling before: of being fully present in a place she might never see again. She tried to memorize every detail. She would remember all of it in the future, she thought, and in that way it would never die. If she left, if she let Sybil take her tongue and give her a potion to split her tail into legs, she would carry all of this with her into heaven. Even the mussel shells with the pearls inside, the tiny fish scurrying through when the shells flapped open.

Slowly, she floated through the palace and the palace gardens and watched each of her sisters as they slept. She touched the eggs in which Thilla's children were developing, glittering things hidden among the rocks and plants, and she whispered advice to them, for when they were grown, for when they left their shells and entered the sea.

∿

THE NEXT DAY, at the palace feast, Lenia sang for her family and the court. Her voice echoed through the waves until every kind of creature appeared. The most wondrous fish, like nothing that could be imagined in the world above. Her sisters watched her, mesmerized, not one of them suspecting what was in her heart, that this would be the last time they would hear the voice that made them feel things they would never have felt otherwise, see the necklace they had found for her sparkling on her neck. Her beautiful sisters with their shining faces, like blooming flowers. Pearls fell from the ceilings, the mussel shells flapped open and shut, and the glow of a thousand ocean creatures glimmered from beyond the amber walls.

Her last hours seemed unbearable. Already she was seeing everything through the haze of time. As if she was already married to the prince, there was a web of light pulsing inside of her, and she had long forgotten how to swim and breathe through gills. She thought about how, when she was an old woman in the upper world, she would remember the other world she'd had once—the coral palace and her sisters with their shining skin and beautiful, long hair that spread about them like wild clouds in the water, the gangly, glowing creatures that had never left the very bottom of the sea. The shells and pearls and bones and brambles of sea plants that spread along the caverns and jutting rocks. How wonderful it would all seem then, to her.

～

AND THEN, FINALLY, she returned to the sea witch. She shot through the water, flexing her tail behind her, trying to ignore the lurching of her heart. Past the leaf statue outside, and into the witch's cavern. Past the gem-black walls with the red flowers bursting from them, into the room full of twisting plants and vines.

Sybil was waiting. She had a large, smoking cauldron in front of her. When she looked up at Lenia, her face was even more heavy and sad than it had been the day before. Her long lashes drooped down to her cheeks. Her eyes sparkled as if they held tears. "You have made your decision," she said.

"Yes," Lenia said, nodding. "I am ready."

"You do not need to do this today, you know," Sybil said. "You can take more time. This is not a decision to be made lightly."

"I know," Lenia whispered, fear coursing through her. "But I am ready."

"Very well," Sybil said, sighing, swimming out from behind the cauldron to where Lenia was floating.

"So what will I do . . . after?"

"You will go to the southernmost part of the land. There you will find the castle where he lives. You will feel him. Go there, and when you get to land, wait till nighttime, when no one is about. Then leave the water. Be sure that no one sees you. And then, only then, drink this potion. If you grow legs while you are in the water, you will not be able to swim, and you will drown the way a human drowns. As I warned, it will hurt, your tail transforming to legs, but when it is done you will be as they are, and no one will know otherwise."

Lenia nodded, unable to speak. Inside of her, deep down, there was a faint voice, a tiny niggling feeling that she should leave, now, go back to the palace, go to Falke, her sisters, forget all of this. She closed her eyes and willed the voice silent. She wished she could skip over what would happen next, blink and wake up in his arms.

"I am ready," she said, more loudly now, trying to keep her voice from quivering. The thought shocked her that these could be the last words she would ever speak.

"Then I must take your payment now."

"Wait!"

Sybil's eyes widened, hopeful.

"Can you tell my sisters what I did? They will come here, at least Vela will. Tell her, please, that I chose this, and that I am happy."

Sybil nodded. "Of course."

"And that I love them all. Please."

"Yes."

"I am ready." Lenia swallowed and made herself very still. Sybil reached out to the plant next to her and withdrew a long silver knife. Lenia opened her mouth. Involuntarily, she cried out. She was shaking, she realized.

"You are sure?" Sybil whispered.

Lenia nodded. Closed her eyes and imagined webs of light.

Sybil's voice was gentle, loving, like a hand stroking her hair. "Open your mouth as wide as you can."

Lenia opened her mouth, keeping her eyes closed, every part of her body tensing in anticipation. And then she felt Sybil's fingers clutching her tongue, moving her head back farther, and Lenia could feel all the witch's sadness, as if it were that grief and not the knife about to slice into her. But as she felt the sharpness of the blade, Lenia thought only of the man's soft skin, his heart beating under her palm, the heaven they would go to after death.

She felt pain, real, searing, physical pain, in a way she never had before, as the blade sliced through her tongue. She clenched her fists and screamed, yanking her head back involuntarily, but Sybil kept hold of her tongue, and then, a moment later, Lenia was free, falling back in the water, opening her eyes to see Sybil floating there with a bloody tongue in her hand. Lenia reeled with pain, falling until she hit the black wall. She could feel the pain all the way down her spine, to the tips of her tail. Her mouth became a wound, and she clamped her lips shut, swallowed blood. Pressing herself against the wall as if she could disappear into it.

The walls changed to a deep, smoky gray. As if from a great distance, through slitted eyes, Lenia watched Sybil take the tongue—red, like a bleeding, pulpy fish—and drop it into the cauldron. After, Sybil took the knife to her own palm and cut into it, squeezing her own blood into the pot.

"What are you—?" Lenia began to ask, but no sound came out. She clamped a hand over her mouth, then pulled it away, saw it was covered in blood.

Sybil looked at her. "It always costs me something as well. But my blood is the least of it."

Lenia knew then—she was not sure how—that Sybil had once been in the upper world, and that it had brought her only pain and grief. Somehow, in the magic between them, their mingled blood, she could see it. But Sybil had not fallen in love with the prince, she thought, had not saved him in the middle of a nighttime storm and brought him to land. It would be different for her.

Sybil brought out a small bottle and dipped it into the cauldron, filling it with potion. Small bubbles swirled up from the bottle, through the water. As Lenia watched her, the pain began to lessen, mute down to a throbbing ache.

She could do this, she thought.

"I hope you find what you are looking for," Sybil said, capping the bottle and handing it to Lenia. Lenia took it, and the witch leaned forward and touched Lenia's face, her eyes brimming with feeling. "Remember everything I've told you."

Lenia nodded, swallowing blood. It was all starting. There was no way to go back now.

"Now go," Sybil said, "to the other world, to him."

CLUTCHING THE BOTTLE in her hand, Lenia left the sea witch's cavern and began to swim. The pain made her numb, and she just flexed her body, racing through the water, trying not to think or feel anything at all.

She had a long way to go, and eventually, as her body calmed, she let herself relax into it. She knew more what to expect now, the pain she would have to endure. Soon her legs would hurt her the way her mouth did, but right now, at this moment, her body was strong, perfect. She stretched her tail behind her, held out her arms, and brushed past fish and whales and sharks, squid and manta rays.

This was the last time she would ever swim like this. She reveled in the power of her tail, the ease with which she moved through the water, the pleasure that came from deep inside of her, despite the pain in her mouth.

As she traveled south, the waters began to change, become more green than blue. She swam up from the deep and stayed near the surface now, so that she could watch, fascinated, as the landscape went from icy white to brown to a deep, lush green. Even with her thick skin and scales, she could sense how the air was changing, going from cold to warm. She'd become accustomed to thinking of the upper world as white and gray and silver, all ice and snow, but here, now, it was as bright and lush as the ocean. The flowers were as varied as they were in the sea, the grass and water and beaches the colors of deepwater fish. And the sun! It poured down, full and complete, soaking everything in a light so rich she was surprised the world was not in flames.

She snacked on fish, reaching out to grab one or two as whole schools of them swept by. Small ones that she could push down her throat, in an attempt to avoid irritating her healing mouth. But eating made the pain flare back to life. A few times she wanted to rest, to swim down to a coral reef or a cave and curl into herself. But she forced herself to keep going. She did not like this in-between state, the unbearable loneliness of it. No longer part of the sea and yet still immersed in it, not yet fit for land. She clutched the potion in her palm, terrified to lose it and be stuck in this state forever.

She could sense him, as Sybil had said she would—the prince, his soul. That she was drawing closer to him.

And then, finally, after two days and nights had passed, she reached the castle of the Southern king.

It loomed in front of her, above the water, at the end of pathways that ran from the harbor. Jutting up into the sky, a mass of stone whirls and towers. It looked like something from the deepest sea, a structure carved from rock and water over thousands of years. Green and gold flags waved over it. Great big flowers burst from the windows, above golden railings and trees heavy with fruit. Ships and boats hovered in the harbor, like giant whales come to the surface of the ocean. And all of it, so alive and bright with color, laid out before her like a great feast.

She forgot all her pain.

Slowly, she swam toward shore, keeping her head and body under the surface. Watching the castle through the water. As the waves rushed forward, she gathered the sea foam and veiled her face with it. She was careful to stay out of view as she pushed her head above the water.

People strolled about, up and down the beach. Soldiers were on patrol, coming on and off one great ship at rest, its prow rising into the air like it was about to take flight. Men hauled nets full of gleaming fish from small boats tethered to the docks. A few groups sat around tables. There was music, sounds she'd never heard before splitting the air. Above, soaring in the sky, was a white bird with wide-spanning wings.

The sun was only just starting to drop, and she knew she must wait until nightfall to leave the water. She lifted the potion to the light, watched as it turned a strange reddish hue, watched as the sun reflected against her own skin. She closed her eyes, trying to remember this feeling, right now, at the end of one world and the beginning of another. Her last moments in this mermaid body, with this tail that stretched out behind her, ready to propel her to the bottom of the sea. Would she one day remember these moments and regret what came next? It was impossible to know what the future held for her here the way she knew it in the sea.

She turned back and watched the humans as they went about their work and pleasures. Soon she would walk among them, on legs of her own. Maybe she would know that woman there, with hair piled about her head and strung through with flowers, standing by a group of soldiers with her hands on her hips. Lenia watched as the woman stood on her toes and whispered in one of the men's ears, almost letting her cheek and bare neck graze against his. She imagined herself, standing like that, dressed as these woman were dressed, her own wild, wet hair dried out and twisted atop her head.

What if they rejected her? How would she live, then? What if she couldn't get near the prince? Lenia touched the necklace around her neck as if it were a talisman as she searched the faces of those standing before her, trying to focus and imagine what it would be like to be one of them. She would know soon enough.

She tried to see past the harbor, past the gates, into the castle. He was there. She could feel it. And from behind the windows, she could see lights coming on one by one, illuminating the life inside. She had never before seen fire except in the sky, and now there were small blazes everywhere, and the people were illuminated by them as they laughed and moved.

Such beautiful ladies and men she saw, or imagined she could see, within. Like something in a story she might have heard once, from her grandmother. Behind some of the windows, she was sure she saw dancing. Men twirling women around, pulling the women close and then releasing them. Would she dance like that? Would she be one of those ladies, smiling, stepping forward and back, forward and back, across the floor, in and out of her beloved's arms?

She held on to the potion, closed her eyes, and tried, for the first time, to pray.

LATE THAT NIGHT, when the harbor was almost empty and the lights from within the castle had gone out, she pulled herself onto the shore. Away from the docks, farther from the castle, where a clutch of trees swayed in the light wind. Just shielding her from the guards who stood by the castle gates.

Above, a giant moon shone down, and the sky sparkled and glittered, completely clear. She lay back and watched. Let the breeze ripple through her, over her hair. It carried a faint tinge of flowers, though she did not yet recognize what it was. Scent. Strange and wonderful.

She stared up at the stars. Here she was, above the water, and then there, above her, was someplace else still.

She set the potion on the ground beside her.

This was it. She took a deep breath. This was, she knew, the most important moment of her life. The moment when she made a choice. All her life she'd been Lenia, the daughter of the sea queen. She had a beautiful tail, a beautiful voice, hair the color of the moon . . . She looked at her tail, watched the scales gleam and glitter in the moonlight. Stretched out her arm and looked at her own skin. Like diamonds.

Yet she was choosing something else. How many of us can choose to leave one self, one world, behind and embrace another, better one?

She clutched the sand on either side of her, let it sift through her fingers. It was gritty, unlike the sand on the ocean floor. She liked the feel of it.

I choose this, she thought.

She took one more look at the sea. Quiet now, all of its secrets hidden. And then she sat up, carefully picked up the potion, and uncapped it.

Smoke streamed from the bottle, sharp and pungent. She coughed.

Please, love me, she breathed into air.

And then she took a deep breath, exhaled, and drank.

It was like drinking fire. Worse than the amber liquid she'd found in the shipwreck. Worse than anything she'd ever consumed or felt, even the pain of her tongue being sliced out of her mouth. The potion burned down her throat, through her body, and down the length of her tail.

She screamed, but no sound came from her.

She felt a terrible burning from her tail, and then a ripping that seared through her. It was so fast! She clutched down, grabbed hold of her tail as it was rent apart. Under her palms, she could feel her body splitting. It was the most horrible pain she'd ever felt. She could not possibly feel more pain than this, she thought. Her scales were crackling, dissolving, her tail being split in half. She cried and writhed on the earth. And then, all over her body, her skin began to come apart. There was nothing she could do, no position she could twist into to lessen the pain, and all she could think was that Sybil had tricked her, the potion was poison, punishment, that this was as close as she would get to the earth, and she was sure that, among the sounds of tearing and ripping, she could hear her heart breaking, every hope she'd had crumbling to dust and foam.

Visions flickered before her eyes, all of them blurring together: Thilla's silver arms, the prince's heart beating under her own, the snow melting as it hit the water, the dark sky strewn with bits of starry fire, the human girl's skin turning to jewels under her own hand. All the visions she'd seen, the emotions she'd felt, every second of her life coiled into the great pain that was consuming her, searing up and down her body.

And just when she thought it was more than she could bear, the world, mercifully and suddenly, turned dark.

CHAPTER ELEVEN

The Princess

OVER THE NEXT DAYS, THE ARMY ASSEMBLED. ALL THE warrior nobles who'd stayed home during the last months, waiting, tending to their estates, knowing the king was preparing to call them to arms, began heading to the castle. Roads throughout the kingdom became thick with travelers. Pigeons flew overhead carrying coded messages. More and more nobles gathered in the castle while their servants crowded the fields around the city walls and messengers raced between estates. An entire tented city rose from the lands surrounding the castle in a matter of days. There was excitement everywhere, a feeling that something new, something better, was about to come into being.

Margrethe paced her room, crazy with frustration. She heard the whispers going through the castle: that the Southern prince had enchanted the young princess, used the black arts to put her under his spell.

She hated to be thought of as a fool. And, further, to know that anything she said—talk of mermaids, enemy princes with open hearts, suffering peasants, and the possibility for peace, real peace—would convince them all the more. She tried to keep to her room as much as possible, sitting alone with the pinecone fire blazing. But every night she went to the great hall, which became more crowded and rowdy with each passing day. New tables were set out, not only in the great hall but in the smaller one next to it, which was emptied of its usual furnishings. Her ladies were mad with excitement, and she relieved them of their duties to her so that they could flirt with the handsome young soldiers bravely offering themselves to their king.

And so that she could be alone, to think.

Over and over she saw the same images: the sick children, the figure in the dirt, the devastated villages, and the mermaid offering up to her the enemy prince.

Save him. You, come now.

There had to be something she could do. Some meaning to everything that had happened.

Save him.

Her father was going to war, there was nothing she could do to sway him, and he was using what had happened to rally the strongest men in the kingdom. She knew how they spoke of her, imagined how close to danger she'd been, the beautiful princess upon whom all their fates rested, dressed in a novice's robes, while the treacherous enemy prince stalked the convent, a gleaming sword at his side. It was too seductive a story for anyone to care about the truth.

This was not her fate. Not this.

Whenever she shut her eyes, he was there. His curving shoulders, his eyes the color of weeds, the way he'd stood in the garden, waiting for her. The first time she'd seen him: splayed out on the beach, nearly drowned, with the mermaid leaning over him, her lips on his forehead. Her wet hair that snaked over her bare arms and breasts and belly. These images haunted Margrethe's dreams, made her wake with the sheets twisted around her, aching, unable to slip back to sleep.

One night, a week after arriving back at the castle, she woke up with the feel of the prince's lips on her own. It was so real she had to look about the room to make sure he hadn't slipped from her dream and into the bed next to her. She was shaking, her whole body flushed and loose. What was wrong with her? She tossed in the bed and then, frustrated, threw off the furs and went to sit by the waning fire.

She was staring into the flames when it came to her that she knew what to do. It was the only thing she *could* do as a woman, even as the daughter of the king.

Marry him.

⟅

THE NEXT MORNING she sent a message to Gregor, asking him to meet her in the library that afternoon, while the king and a group of soldiers went out to hunt.

She washed in the basin by the fire and dressed carefully, Laura lacing her into one of her finest gowns. Then she hurried to the library.

She had decided to tell him everything and prayed that he would help her. She knew her father was planning an invasion soon. Pieter rarely left his side, and they were often joined by the kingdom's greatest warriors—preparing for battle.

Gregor was waiting for her at the table where they'd met for her studies, behind a shelf of precious manuscripts.

"Marte," he said, standing. "How are you?"

"I am well, friend," she said, smiling warmly at him. She remembered the countless hours she'd spent right here, bent over manuscripts of Greek and Latin, old tales of traveling warriors and angry gods, young girls turning to trees and doves and spiders.

"I understand that your talk with your father did not go as you had wished. I was sorry to hear it."

"Thank you," she said, nodding. She leaned forward. "Is it safe to speak openly here, Gregor?"

His face became serious, and he got up and locked the door.

"We will say we are having a lesson," he said, "to refresh your Greek, if anyone asks."

"Yes, good," she said. "I need your help."

"Of course."

"First . . . I have to tell you, there is something else, something that I have not told anyone. That I *can't* tell anyone, not even Edele. I know her too well, and she could not keep this to herself. You are the only one I trust with this information."

"What is it, Marte?"

"The prince, he did not just wash up to shore. He was brought there. I saw it. I was standing in the garden, looking out over the sea, when I saw a creature from myth. A mermaid. Carrying him in her arms."

"A mermaid?" he repeated.

"Yes. She saved him when his ship was caught in a terrible storm. He was unconscious, nearly drowned. I'd never . . ." She choked up with feeling, and tears came to her eyes. "It was the most beautiful thing. Standing there, on a cliff, everything ice and gray and empty, and then she appeared, with him in her arms. I had no idea who he was. You should have seen her face, the way she looked at him. It was rapture. *That* is how I know he was not there to hurt me. She brought him to me. *To me.* For a reason."

To her surprise, he wasn't laughing at her; her words seemed to be moving him. "A mermaid," he whispered. "Astonishing."

"Yes. This is why I am so sure that my father is wrong. But I could never tell him this. I can't tell anyone but you."

"You're right," he said. "We have lost these beliefs. Your father will find you mad."

"And you?"

Her face betrayed how much she needed his affirmation, needed him to believe that what she was saying was true.

Suddenly his face seemed to cave in, and he brought his hands to his eyes, covering them.

"Gregor? What is it?" She jumped up with alarm. Never, in all these years, had she seen the old man like this. "Gregor!"

He pulled his hands away from his face. He, too, had tears in his eyes. They were red and watering, his mouth was open, and for a moment she thought he was having some kind of an attack. "Please sit down," he said, his voice hoarse, strange. "It's just . . . Fate, my dear, is a very funny thing."

"I don't understand."

"Let me tell you a story," he said. He took a long breath and waited for her to sit again. And then he spoke slowly, remembering. "When I was a very small child, my parents took me to the ocean for the first time. Down south, just a few years before the old king died and our kingdom split in two. I wandered off by myself, out of my mother's sight, collecting shells. My mother was not paying attention. I walked into the water, lured by the sight of a jellyfish. The tide was coming in more heavily, and I slipped somehow, and the sea pulled me into itself. I fell into the water. I could not swim. I would have drowned but for the woman who came to me then. She appeared from nowhere and carried me in her arms, singing to me all the while. Later, my parents found me soaked through to my bones but sleeping peaceably on the beach, curled into a snug formation of rock, protected from the bite of the wind. I think of it more and more often as I get older. It was the most extraordinary moment of my life."

"She was a mermaid?"

He nodded. "Later, I found out that there had been many mermaid sightings in that area. The locals told stories about her, this beautiful woman with pink hair who emerged from the sea. But she never, as far as I know, saved anyone else the way she saved me. No one ever even claimed to see her up close, the way I did."

"Did she . . . did she mark you in any way?" she asked.

"It has always made me feel like I had a special purpose," he said. "Always. The way you feel now."

"I mean, on your skin. Like this."

She lifted the sleeve of her dress and held her forearm up to catch the light. As she twisted her wrist back and forth, her arm shimmered—though more faintly now, she thought, than before.

He smiled, his face open, his eyes bright. "Yes! Of course. For a long time, yes, my skin had this sheen to it, where she had held me. It is in the old lore, that the touch of the mermaid changes us. Not everyone can see it, you know."

She nodded excitedly. "I thought that. My ladies, they could not see. He had the shimmer on him, too, Gregor. The prince. The three of us, we have all been touched."

Her old tutor was watching her as if he hadn't quite seen her before. Margrethe had never seen the expression on his face that was there now, as if he were years younger, full of childlike wonder and awe. He looked from her face to her arm, then reached up and traced the skin Lenia had touched.

"I know she brought him to me for a reason, Gregor. I know she's not an angel, but I felt that God was working *through* her. I did not know who the man was, I had no idea he was Prince Christopher, and he did not know who I was, I promise you. He said he was forever in my debt, for saving him. He believes *I* am the one who carried him to shore."

"How wonderful," he said, "to see your destiny begin to unfold. To see my own unfold, after all these years."

She smiled, wiping her eyes. She hadn't realized until now how much she needed to share this with someone, someone who would take her seriously. She felt reconnected, suddenly, to that world of magic, as if it was tangible again, now that she'd shared it with him.

She took a deep breath. "Gregor, I know what my destiny is now. I know what I need to do."

He nodded, waiting. She could hear her own breathing, her own heart.

"My father is intent on fighting. I know I cannot convince him otherwise. And I know it is wrong. Even though he is my father and my king, he is wrong. This isn't God's way, this suffering, this violence."

Gregor nodded. "I hoped you would be able to convince him, but your father does not care what is true and what is not true. He wants only war. War is how your father exorcises his own demons, his grief. It is how he has always been. It made him a great warrior once." He paused, became wistful. "You know, there was a time when we all lived in peace together, when we were all brothers and sisters, shared the same blood. But when the old king died . . ."

"I know," she said. "It is strange, Gregor. The mermaid . . . she, too, spoke about how we were all unified once, but she was talking about humans and merpeople. How there was a time when all of us lived in the sea."

"It is a never-ending dream for everyone, it seems, to find again what was precious and has been lost. There is a group of us who have been arguing for peace for a very, very long time. We even succeeded a few times." He smiled, yet his face was more grave than she'd ever seen it. "Your father was ready to fight when your mother died, but I was able to reason with him. But the king is less and less willing to listen to those of us who caution him; he listens more and more to Pieter and his men. They've been replenishing the army for a long time, Marte, and now there is the excuse they have all been waiting for. Soon we will be back in battle. Maybe even within a fortnight, from the looks of it."

"Gregor, I know what to do. There is not much I can do in this world, even as daughter of the king. But I can marry. *That* is what I can do."

"I do not follow."

She swallowed. "I want to marry the prince."

"The prince?"

"I want to marry Prince Christopher." She watched his surprise, and rushed on. "My father is planning war on the South for a crime they did not commit. The North and South have a peace treaty now. Which the South has honored, yes? Despite all the rumors that they were planning an attack?"

"Yes," he said, nodding slowly. "Yes. The South is tired of war. Many of us doubt the legitimacy of those rumors that the South was preparing for battle. But even I believed that the prince's arrival at the convent proved them to be true."

"They're not true," she said. "It will be my father's excuse, and they're not true."

"Yes."

"But what if I offered to go there? What if I went there and married the prince? My father would have to acknowledge the marriage and agree to maintain peace, or else he would have to forsake me. Right?"

"Yes," Gregor said once more, staring at her as if antlers were sprouting from her head. "It has even been mentioned before. A marriage alliance, to make our blood one again. But no one has ever dared suggest such a thing in earnest. There is too much hatred. And you are too important, Marte. You are this kingdom's future."

"But what do you think my father would do, if I defied him?"

"Your father loves you, more than you even know, and he believes in the prophecy. It is hard for me to think he would abandon you to the South. It is passion and grief that drive him to keep fighting. It may be that his love for you will make him stop."

She nodded. "He would see it as a great betrayal, but . . ."

"It would be a great risk, Marte. There is no doubt. Even talking of this, as we are now, is high treason. Your father has put many people to death for less."

"But it is right. You know that it is right."

He watched her, refusing to answer. She could see his heart twisting inside of him. To her, it seemed simple. She was one girl. How could she weigh her own life against the lives of all her people? She knew what she meant to Gregor, to all of them, and she loved him for it. But it was this importance she carried, the meaning that was placed upon her at her birth, that made her the only person in the kingdom who could do what she was proposing now.

And beyond all of this, of course, she loved him. Christopher.

"Can we do this, Gregor? Can we send a message to the Southern king? Can you help me? We can make this offer, and, if the South agrees, I will go."

"You are a brave girl, my dear," he said, shaking his head. But she knew he agreed with her.

"You would do the same thing if you were me."

"You realize that your father must approve of this marriage before it takes place. You would have to put yourself under the South's protection. If your father chose to forsake you, and continue the war, there would be no telling what the Southern king might do to you. You would be in his castle, his ward. I hate to think of what could happen to you if he decided to withdraw that protection. He would have the perfect way to attack your father, through you."

She shrugged. "That is the risk, Gregor."

He sighed. "I wish I could turn back time, Marte, back to when your mother was alive, when we were all happy. I wish I could force you to stay here, live the life you were supposed to live. A good marriage to an important man. Children, a home. You and your children heirs to one of the greatest and oldest kingdoms in the world."

"But if I could choose my own path, thinking only of myself, I would never choose such a life."

She smiled at him. She loved his old face in this soft light. As vibrant as court life could be, with the music and dancing, the great feasts, her happiest moments had always been with him, learning of all the different ways there were to live in the world. The others at court never seemed to think of anything beyond the castle, building their lives around the whims of the king and his favorites.

"What is it that you would want, Margrethe?"

She thought for a moment. "I would like to read, and to study, the way we always did. I'd like to be a scholar. But I know my place is in the world. Imagine what our kingdom might be, if we succeed, if I could unite the North and South again. I can do that. I have the power to do that, to make peace among us."

He sat back, and she could see that she had moved him to hope for something he'd not dared to hope for before. "You are not unconvincing," he said. "I regret now teaching you rhetoric."

"So we must write a letter to the Southern king and wait for his response. Yes?"

"Yes."

"You can send a messenger, can't you? Someone you trust?"

He nodded. "Yes, I can arrange that without too much problem. What will be trickier is getting you there safely."

"I will be fine," she said, with a bit of false bravado, spurred by her excitement. "I can ride a horse and wear a disguise as well as anyone."

He laughed. "You are so young, and so confident." And she detected a hint of nostalgia, even envy in his voice. "I remember having that kind of confidence, when I was a young man."

"Maybe this will give you a reason to be confident again, Gregor," she said.

"I hope so, dear girl."

She smiled, and a new kind of energy coursed through her. For the first time, the prophecy surrounding her birth felt like something that was a part of her.

Who she was.

ᐤ

MARGRETHE FELT LIKE a new person as she stepped into the hallway, overwhelmed by what she had just decided.

She would go to the Southern kingdom to marry Prince Christopher. Her father would acknowledge the union, and there would be peace. One kingdom. An end to this war.

She was woozy suddenly, and she stopped, leaned against the wall.

She felt so strongly that this was meant to be, it was as if she and he were already married. The prophecies, the mermaid, Gregor's own past, the convent, the prince arriving battered and nearly drowned on the shore, there at the end of the world, the way he'd looked at her as they stood together in the garden . . . all of it came together then, so perfectly, and she knew that her life had a purpose beyond herself.

It was what the nuns felt, as they rose in the middle of the night for Matins.

Just then, Pieter turned the corner, having come from the banquet hall. He was with Lens and another guardsman.

"Margrethe?" he asked, rushing to her side. "Are you feeling unwell?"

"No," she said. She cleared her throat and tried to collect herself.

"You are so flushed."

"I am just a bit tired, Pieter. I was going to get some air."

"You were with Gregor, yes?" he said, and his look was not friendly, she realized.

"Yes," she said. "We were just going over some Greek."

Pieter gave her a tight smile. "I have not known any other lady to be so schooled."

She stared at him, astonished at his insolence.

"It was my mother's wish," she said. "As you well know."

"Forgive me, my lady," he said, bowing. "I mean you no dishonor."

She swept past him, down the corridor, her heart racing in her chest.

She thought of her mother—pictured her, dark-haired, smiling, soft. Rarely did Margrethe allow herself the luxury of thinking about her mother anymore, but now a feeling of longing passed over her, and she missed her with all the rawness she'd felt at the time of her death.

She stopped in the corridor, overcome. She'd stopped visiting her mother's quarters shortly after her death, two years earlier, around the time the king had banned all mention or memory of the queen in the castle, except for her perfectly maintained chambers, which no one but the maids were supposed to enter. It had been easier for everyone that way.

Now, steeled by her new sense of purpose, she found a torch and walked determinedly to the former queen's apartments: through the great hall, past guardsmen who watched her and turned to whisper as she went by, past her father's offices, into the south wing, quiet as a grave. She walked more slowly, remembering rumors that the south wing was haunted, and then she shook them away. These were the rooms of her beloved mother, that was all. But when she caught a glimpse of her reflection in some polished wood, she started and cried out. The tall, slim woman with long dark hair, her skin pale in the flickering light of her torch. It was herself, of course, but she had not realized how much she'd become the image of her mother.

She paused to calm her racing heart before pushing open the heavy door and entering the outer chamber of her mother's rooms, the parlor where the queen's friends used to spend hours talking together, listening to her stories, working on embroidery, playing games, and drinking wine. Now Margrethe walked the length of the parlor, smiling as she remembered all the time she'd spent here as a child, sitting at her mother's side and watching her laughing face, her graceful hands punctuating her speech or deftly moving a needle through fabric. Her hands had seemed magical to Margrethe then, able to conjure whole scenes out of almost nothing at all.

As she walked through to her mother's private bedroom, it was as if a veil of grief dropped down over Margrethe, and she remembered the morning her mother refused to wake up. She walked to that ancient bed now, touching the same linens her mother had slept on that last day, the same pillow her mother's head had rested on. Remembering how, after hearing her own nurse whispering to another servant, she'd run through the castle and into the queen's bedroom, where the king stood over her and the physician was packing up his bags and there was her mother, never more beautiful, her dark hair spread across the pillow, peacefully asleep in her bed. Margrethe had never before seen her father overcome by grief, and that had made everything even more terrible. The thought that this impermeable man could be brought down by a simple stroke of fate. No one had ever known the cause of death. And to this day Margrethe did not understand why everyone—her nurse, her father, the servants—had made her leave the room before she could reach her mother's bed to say good-bye. She felt a fresh stab of grief as she remembered.

She stretched out on the bed, in the last place she'd seen her mother, imagining she could still feel the indent of her mother's body. Closing her eyes, feeling an exhaustion move through her, she drifted to sleep and dreamed of her mother deep in the sea, her skin covered with diamonds and her legs curving together into one long silver tail. Waiting, like an angel, for Margrethe to join her.

⟋

"Are you feeling better, Margrethe?" her father asked as she entered the great hall that evening.

"Yes, Sire," she said, curtsying to him.

The king stood and raised a glass to her. Her heart broke a bit as she sat next to him, and she prayed that her plan would work, that he would, in the end, agree with her and think she had been right.

She looked at Gregor, sitting next to another of her father's close advisers, who was also watching her intently and talking quietly to her old tutor. Pieter was standing off to the side, looking from her to Gregor. She breathed in sharply. So much was going on, under the surface, that she'd never seen before.

After the meal, the court musicians played, and some of the men and women rose to dance. Gregor came and sat next to her as she watched.

"I have something for you," she said, smiling over at him as if they were speaking of the day's hunt.

"Already?"

She pulled a folded letter from her sleeve and casually dropped it into his lap. "Yes," she said. "If you think it looks appropriate, maybe we can send it right away."

"Wonderful," he said. "We must be very careful in these next days to act as if nothing out of the ordinary is happening."

"Oh, Gregor, I am well used to that, as you know."

He smiled. "Good. It is in God's hands now."

BACK IN THE silence of her room, late that night, Margrethe sent her ladies away. She wanted to savor this moment, the way she felt now. If her plan failed, she might never feel this full of possibility again. But right now, anything at all could happen. She walked to the window, threw it open, stared out at the snow and the stars. Wondered if he was staring at the same stars right then. Thinking of her.

She lay back on her bed. She closed her eyes and tried to conjure him up before her. The dark room in the convent where he lay wounded. His skin shimmering in the pale firelight. His yellow-brown eyes, like weeds.

She sighed, relaxed into the mattress.

She imagined him in the garden, kissing not only her hand but her hair, her eyelids, her cheeks. His lips pressing against her, the snow falling around them. The two of them slipping into the water. Her legs covered in scales, her perfect breasts exposed to the air as she leaned over him.

An ache moved through her. The idea was shocking, exciting.

Being in the water wearing nothing but a long, sleek silver tail that flared from her lower belly and curved down to a fin. Holding him in her arms, his skin against her skin, his mouth open and warm and soft.

She turned onto her belly, pushed herself into the bed. She could smell the sea, his skin, feel his palm sliding down her back. Keeping her legs pressed together, she rubbed against the sheets. A deep ache extended from the center of her body. Until she broke open and everything seemed to slip into dream.

She sat up then, covered her mouth. Horrified at what she had done. And then she knelt down by the side of the bed and prayed for forgiveness.

CHAPTER TWELVE

The Mermaid

WHEN LENIA OPENED HER EYES, AN OLD WOMAN stood over her, peering down. The sun was bright behind the woman's wrinkled face.

"Are you hurt?" the woman asked. "Can you sit up?"

Lenia opened her mouth to speak, but she had no words, no tongue. Under her back, she felt rocks cutting her skin. Was she dreaming? The air on her skin felt strange, like nothing she'd ever felt before. She was . . . cold. She had never been cold in her life.

"Are you from the court?"

Lenia just blinked up at the woman.

"Are you visiting here? Can you sit up?"

The woman leaned down and put her hand on Lenia's arm. It felt like an iron on her skin. Lenia sat up, automatically, backing away in pain. The sand seemed to move under her, scraping at her bare skin.

And then she felt the strangest thing—the sensation of rocks and earth at the end of her body, where her tail should be.

She looked down and gasped.

Legs. She had human legs.

Wildly, she looked back up at the woman, at the world around her, and everything hit her. Off to the side, leaning against a rock, was the bottle the potion had been in.

The sun was so bright. It had not been this bright before. It burned against her eyes, made everything seem like it could turn to flame at any minute.

From a distance came more voices, and the woman called to them. "Help us!" she said. "There is a woman here who's been hurt."

She looked back at Lenia. "Here, cover yourself, dear. They are soldiers from the king's castle." She took off the fabric wrapped around her shoulders and handed it to Lenia. After Lenia did not respond, the woman knelt down and carefully wrapped the shawl around Lenia's torso, tying it, to cover her breasts.

"What a strange necklace you have," she said. "It looks very rich."

To Lenia's surprise, the fabric felt soothing on her skin. She remembered how Margrethe had been covered in furs to ward off the cold.

"Can you stand up?"

Lenia looked from the woman to her own body.

She looked down again, at her legs. Her smooth, flat skin, her arched feet, her curved calves, her knees, and the thighs that met at the center of her body. Everything hurt. She felt everything. Her scales and skin had been stripped away, and now she was raw blood and bone. A clam or a mussel that had lost its shell.

"You're shaking," the woman said, crouching next to Lenia. "What happened to you?"

The woman was carrying a basket with bread in it. The smell of yeast, of egg, was so strong it almost made Lenia gag. She could smell the cloth of the woman's dress. The wet salt of the sea, the perfume of flowers in the breeze. The smells swirled around her, sliding in and out of each other. This new body was so weak, she could do nothing to stop the assault on it.

Footsteps were approaching. Two human men, dressed from head to toe in matching green and gold uniforms, appeared in front of her.

"I found her lying here," the woman explained. "She seems

confused. I think she might have wandered down from the castle. She must be wealthy—look at that necklace."

The men peered at her, nodding. "The king and queen have some visitors from the East. She might be one of them," the darker of the two men said. He spoke loudly to Lenia, overpronouncing every word. "Can you stand?"

"I'd love to have been at whatever party she was at last night," the other one said, more coarsely. His eyes swept up her legs, over her center, her torso. "My God, I've never seen a woman more beautiful."

The old woman coughed disapprovingly. "Perhaps you might lend her your jacket."

"Of course," the first soldier said, slipping off his jacket and handing it to the woman to hold. He turned to Lenia. "I'm just going to put my arm around you to help you up, okay?"

Lenia nodded.

"So you understand me but you cannot speak?" he asked.

She nodded again.

"I think she has been hurt," the old woman said. "I think something terrible has happened to this girl. You must get her to the castle so someone can tend to her."

"We will take her to the head of the king's household."

The two soldiers positioned themselves on either side of Lenia and lifted her from the ground. Her legs uncurled, stretched out, and it was as if blades were shooting through her. She tried moving one foot in front of the other and it was excruciating, just as the sea witch had promised.

Water dripped down her cheeks, and she realized she was crying. An image flashed before her through the haze of pain: Margrethe, with tears on her face as the two of them sat on the shore.

Slowly, the soldiers helped Lenia into the jacket, and they were surprised at how awkward she was, as if she did not understand where to put her arms. Then they half led and half carried her to the castle. She tried putting her feet down, stumbling and then walking as they moved alongside her, their hands under her arms. The sand cut into her bare feet. It was all a blur now—the pain, the smells, the blinding light, the sounds moving toward her from all directions. She concentrated on the movement of her own body, trying to get used to the feeling of being wide open, all blood and muscle and bone.

The castle was quiet now, and the paths leading up to it were empty. Just a few guards paced around in front.

"It is early. They might still be at Mass," the woman said.

Just then, a beautiful auburn-haired girl in a white dress stepped outside, holding a stringed, wooden instrument and a bow in one hand. She stopped and stared down at the scene in front of her. "And who is this?" she asked, in a high, lilting voice. Behind her, a few other girls hovered quietly, all also holding instruments.

The old woman bowed deeply to the girl.

"Princess Katrina," one of the soldiers said, also bowing. "We have come across this woman on the beach. We thought she might be a friend of your family's?"

"Why do you talk of her as if she is not there?"

"She doesn't seem to be able to speak, Your Highness. We think she is wounded."

"How strange," Katrina said, walking right up to Lenia and looking into her face. "You cannot speak?"

Lenia stared at the girl, frightened. She could see the prince in her features—the same lips and green-yellow eyes. She shook her head.

"Can you write?"

Lenia shook her head again.

Katrina's eyes dropped to Lenia's neck. She visibly started. "How—" Katrina reached out her hand and touched Lenia's necklace, her fingertips grazing Lenia's skin, tickling her. "Where did you get this necklace? I know it."

Lenia willed her thoughts into the air. *Because I was meant to be here, with him. Because I found your treasures at the bottom of the sea.*

Katrina looked back up at Lenia, and they stood like that, watching each other. For a moment, Lenia wondered if the girl had understood her.

"Do you know my family?" Katrina asked, finally. "Are you some relation? You look familiar somehow."

"She was not here with the other guests?" one of the soldiers asked.

"I have not seen her before," Katrina said. "Not here, anyway. I wonder if I have met her at another court, though. Does she not seem familiar?" She turned, asking the question of her three ladies standing behind her. At that cue, they streamed onto the steps, surrounding her.

"Oh yes, she does," one of them said. "I might have met her once. I'm quite sure I have, actually, when I was traveling in the East." She smiled at Katrina, blinking her long lashes.

Katrina reached out again to Lenia, running her fingertip along the gold of her necklace.

"Does she need help?" another lady asked.

"Yes," Katrina said, with a nod of her head. She turned and signaled to the servant. "Put her in the room next to mine. Pauline, you will need to take one of the outer apartments for now." The long-lashed girl sighed loudly as Katrina turned back to Lenia. "Now let's get you dressed properly, and maybe someone can figure out where you came from."

The old woman who'd found Lenia slipped away, bowing all the while.

"How interesting," Katrina said then, not acknowledging the old woman in any way but turning back to the door, "to have someone new here. Everything lately has been so boring."

∾

ONE OF THE ladies took Lenia's arm, steadying her, and they led her back to the princess's rooms, at the west end of the castle. As they walked, Lenia looked around in amazement: at the massive tapestries hanging from the stone walls, at the silver statues of gods and goddesses, the flickering torches. She recognized some of the objects from similar items in shipwrecks, though she'd seen such things only covered in the murk of sea and decay, and here everything was immaculate, almost unreal-seeming. And in each hallway and room she looked for the prince. They walked by men and women of all types, some smartly dressed and at leisure, others hard at work, cleaning or cooking or hauling in supplies, all of them eyeing Lenia and bowing to the princess, who had a habit of tilting her head and raising her thin red brows at the handsome men and ignoring almost everyone else. The other ladies followed suit.

Outside one room, Lenia stopped, almost gasped out loud when she saw the figure of a beautiful, bleeding man hanging from a cross on the wall. The same cross shape she'd seen above the building by the icy sea, where she'd met Margrethe. Who was this man?

"Did you want to see the priest?" Katrina asked, watching Lenia.

Lenia shook her head, embarrassed, and they continued through the corridors, up a set of winding stairs that led to a hallway with a series of rooms in it, and stopped in what was clearly the grandest of them all, a large room filled with feminine ephemera—long golden necklaces and rich powders and perfumes and headpieces scattered across the top of a bureau, jewel-studded dresses hanging in an open wardrobe with designs carved along its edges. In the center of the room was a large bed with dark silk curtains hanging down on all sides. Lenia had seen something like it before, though broken and rotted and cradling two decayed corpses.

"Sit here," Katrina said, leading Lenia to the bed, pulling back the shining curtain. She set down her instrument and bow on the mattress.

Lenia sank down onto the bed. She had never felt anything so supple and shivered with delight despite herself. She crossed her legs under her and, for the first time, found some relief.

"They are heating water for you," Katrina said. "So you can have a bath. You look like you have not been bathed in a while. After, it will be time to eat, which will also do you good."

"I wonder what happened to her clothes," one of the ladies said. "Surely she had beautiful clothes once. Imagine the dress you'd wear with a necklace like that."

"I know," Katrina said. "You'd think she was a queen." She picked up her instrument. "Shall we play?"

They all took up their instruments and sat prettily on the couches at the far end of the room.

The most strange and plaintive sounds moved through the air. Lenia's head shot up, and she watched the group of women pulling bows across the small instruments resting on their shoulders. She could feel every note vibrating in her, as if it were being played on her own body.

There was a knock on the door. "Her bath is ready, Your Highness," a servant said.

"Go," said Katrina, gesturing to Lenia and then to the servant. "Be sure to put her in something that will show off the necklace." She turned back to the ladies. "My mother will *love* her," she said, and something in her tone put Lenia on edge.

"I know who will love her more," another replied.

"Let's hope so."

Lenia heard the girls burst into giggles as the door clicked shut behind her. The servant led Lenia to a smaller room, where a large tub of steaming water was waiting, along with another female servant. At first Lenia just stared at the tub. She had never seen water before like this. Not seawater but dull water, without fish or salt or plants. Without even thinking, she backed away.

Gently, one of the servants removed Lenia's jacket and shawl, and motioned for her to step in. "We are only bathing you," the servant said. "Go on now."

Lenia took a breath. She stretched out her leg and was so dazzled by the sight of her bare foot she almost lost her balance, and had to grab the side of the tub to steady herself. She laughed at how ridiculous she was, and laughed harder when she looked up at the servants' confused faces.

Then she cleared her throat, steeled herself, and stepped in, submerging her foot in the bath. She was surprised at how warm it was, how lovely it felt. She wiggled her toes and moved her leg up and down. When the servant motioned to her, she stepped into the tub and sat in the water, letting it come up to her neck.

She was surprised by how much it soothed her. The muscles in her body loosened, blissfully, until her legs almost didn't hurt. She leaned her head back. It was not at all like being in the ocean. It was something entirely new, not unlike the feel of the fabric the old woman had placed on her. This new skin felt so much. Even her aching mouth was soothed by the steam rising up.

The servants washed her hair and her skin, giving each other confused looks as the beautiful, mute stranger reveled in every sensation. They did not know what to make of her. The way she laughed as the water splashed and the sound echoed against the walls. As if she had never before bathed, never heard bathwater splashing.

After, the servants dried her off, rubbed oil into her skin, and dressed her in a long ruby red dress that laced up the back. They combed her hair and dried it—she had never felt her hair dry before, moving her palms over its silken texture, running her fingers through the strands—and wove white flowers through it. Lenia remained still the whole time, letting every new sensation pass over her. Every touch and tug of hair, every bit of fabric that fell or rubbed against her skin. After a while, she was able to contain herself, at least so that the servants did not think she was entirely mad. *Perhaps only half mad*, Lenia thought and smiled to herself.

When they were finished, they led her over to the heavy glass that stood in the corner of the room.

She was shocked to see her own face staring back. She thought immediately of the glass in her mother's palace, and for a moment, a split second, her heart ached for home.

But as quickly as it had appeared, the feeling went away.

She looked . . . human, like a real human girl. She no longer looked like herself, though she had the same face, the same blue eyes and moon hair, twisted up now and hanging in shiny, bouncing tendrils down the sides of her face, but her skin was soft and blank, a sort of pale beige color. She looked just as she'd thought she might look the day after her eighteenth birthday. It suited her, this human skin. Would her sisters even recognize her, if they could see her now? She imagined Thilla with legs and human skin like this, and the thought made her gasp with amusement. No, she decided. They would recognize her only if they knew to look. If only she could see them once more, just to show them.

And what would they say about the red dress that covered her chest and arms, matching the necklace perfectly, causing the bright red stone to gleam, and flaring down to her pale, perfect feet? The servants had covered her feet in sandals that revealed her toes. Her toes! Which she could not help but stare at and wiggle.

And then her thoughts moved from her sisters to him, the prince, who was right now somewhere within these walls. What would *he* think when he saw her? For the first time she felt a twinge of nervousness. Would he find her beautiful in this human form? Would he remember her, love her?

When the confused servants finally returned Lenia to the princess and her ladies, Katrina clapped and squealed with glee. They were giddier now. "You were right about my brother," she said, turning to the others. "Maybe our new friend is just what he needs. I miss how he used to be. Nobody is fun around here anymore."

"We all miss him," one of the ladies said, pretending to swoon. "And everyone speaks of his great change."

"He's already had his fun with you, I'm afraid," Katrina said, and Lenia noticed the girl wincing slightly—she felt the sting of pain as if it were an arrow shooting through the room. "But *this* one, he will not be able to resist. Look at her."

"Why can't she speak, anyway?" one of the others asked.

"I would love to find out," Katrina said, her eyes sparkling as she looked at Lenia so long that Lenia looked away, feeling herself blush for the first time.

As they entered the dining hall for the afternoon meal, all eyes turned to Lenia. For a moment, she panicked, her heart racing in her chest as if she were standing right there in front of all of them with her fish tail exposed. She glanced down at her hands, her skin, to reassure herself.

The king and queen and some other nobles were sitting at the head of the long room, on a raised platform. The rest of the tables extended the length of the hall and were nearly full.

Lenia had never seen so many humans all together, not since the shipwreck on the night of her birthday. Everyone was alive, beautiful, their skin glowing in the candlelight, and the faces that looked back at her were more interested than anything else. She scanned the room quickly for the prince, terrified, suddenly, she would not recognize him, though she had thought of him every day since her birthday a few weeks before.

Katrina gestured for her to sit with the others, while she took her place at the king's table. Lenia moved to one of the benches, surrounded by young men who stood and bowed.

The smell of the meat hit Lenia. She felt human hunger for

the first time, searing from her gut. The odor of cooking flesh re-pulsed her, but her body responded so strongly she almost lost her balance as she maneuvered herself onto the bench. What a strange thing this body was, shifting around every new taste and smell.

One day this will all be normal, she thought, *and the sea will seem as foreign as all these things do now.*

One servant set a plate of meat and bread in front of her, while another poured wine. She took a long sip, wincing when it hit her sore mouth. But as it went down her throat, she found she did not mind the sharpness of it, the way she could feel it move into the center of her body.

All around her, people talked and laughed. Musicians came into the room, and a cacophony of sound erupted from them. It was so much, all at once, she could not focus on anything but the wine, the meat, the strange, intense way this body experienced hunger, how she would be able to eat this food with no tongue. She watched as the others brought the meat to their mouths and chewed and she held a small piece to her own lips. The taste blocked out everything else. Both awful and delicious, she thought, letting her teeth sink into the meat. She chewed and had to use her fingers to help get the morsels down her throat.

Though she was focused on eating, adjusting to this mouth with no tongue, this cooked animal flesh, the moment the prince entered the hall, Lenia knew. All her fears had been unfounded. Every cell of her body felt him.

She looked up, and there he was, the same man she had seen drowning in the water, so helpless and afraid as his men died around him. But now he was strong, ferocious. He was tall, his body full and muscled, his skin and hair touched with sun gold. There was not an ounce of fear in him now, not an ounce of dying. He looked like the son of a king.

Any glimmer of the sea left in her, everything she was now and had ever been—all of it turned to him. *Do you remember me?* she thought. *In the water? Do you remember? It is me. I have come here for you.*

His eyes went to her immediately, and he stopped, stood frozen. He was dressed in hunting clothes, his hair disheveled. On his skin, she could see the shimmer she'd left. It was barely there, but she could see it. Where she'd kissed him, where she'd moved her palm over his skin.

Everyone turned to watch the prince as he stood unmoving. After a long moment, he seemed to become conscious, suddenly, of how awkward he looked and how much attention he was attracting.

He laughed it off. "And who is this mysterious new lady who has so bewitched me with one look?" he asked, addressing the room at large.

"Ah, Brother, I expected no less," Katrina said, leaving the king's table and marching down to meet him. "This is my new friend. She cannot speak, see. Which makes her perfect for one so rich in words as yourself."

The king laughed, and everyone followed suit. "It would seem your sister knows you and your needs better than the king and queen do," he said.

Lenia watched as Katrina took Christopher's arm and led him to her. "And this is . . . Well, since she cannot speak, she cannot tell us what her name is. If she has one at all. What shall we call her?"

Christopher laughed along with the others, good-naturedly. "It is as if you emerged from my deepest heart," he said to Lenia, in an exaggerated manner, going along with the game, as he neared her. "I am certain that I have dreamt you here."

Yes, Lenia thought. Hadn't he?

He looked at her, tilting his head. "Would you like me to name you, O fair-haired one?"

She smiled, nodded. *Yes.* Without thinking, she held out her hands to him, and he smiled, surprised at her forwardness, and took them, kneeling down beside the table.

"I say we call her Astrid," he said. "Because she is so fair, and beautiful."

"Perfect," Katrina said. "Astrid it is."

Astrid, she repeated to herself, turning the name over in her mind.

His skin on hers felt electric, magical, shrinking her body to the one place where they touched, then expanding it again as the feeling moved throughout. The rush of excitement and love. And through his playfulness, through the laughter surrounding them, through his own brilliant smile, she could see that he remembered. Maybe not consciously, but there was something inside of him, a knowledge that they'd met before.

Do you remember how I carried you through the sea? How strong I was then?

"Is it true you cannot speak?" he asked. His was voice soft now.

Lenia nodded, overcome. Even being in love felt different now. The sensation of his hands on hers . . . He was no longer overwhelmingly soft and warm and fragile. Now he was strong, beautiful, alive. She could smell him, feel him. Her body reacted to him the way it had to the dinner feast, with a need she could never have imagined in her mermaid form.

"Would you like to take a walk with me?" he asked. "I will cancel my hunt this afternoon and stay with you. Would you like that?"

She looked up, met the eyes of Katrina and some of the others. They were all smiling, listening intently, though by now some of the other diners had gone back to their meals and the king seemed to have forgotten them altogether.

"Go," Katrina said. "Do not feel obligated to remain with us. My brother will take good care of you."

Lenia smiled, ecstatic. She nodded. *Yes.* He was right there, next to her, looking at her in wonder and delight. It was as easy as she'd thought it would be. He was hers. His soul was her soul.

And this body! The feelings running through it. It was like lying in the water and watching the sky as the clouds moved across it, constantly shifting shape. Brewing storms, unleashing them on the earth, going calm as if nothing had happened at all.

Her body was breaking open now, and storms moved across it.

∾

WHEN THE MEAL was over and everyone dispersed, Christopher led Lenia up a winding staircase, into the recesses of the castle. Walking along the stone corridors lit dimly with torches, she felt as if she were swimming through sea caves. Her legs were almost numb by now, the pain a constant she was learning to ignore. The torches caused their shadows to flicker against the walls, like silent fish.

"I do feel I've seen you before," he said. "Yet I know I have never looked upon a woman like you."

He stopped and reached out to touch her face. He held her chin in his hand, stroking her with his palm.

She was at the mercy, now, of this strange body. Every touch made her want to disappear into him. Her breathing grew heavy, and she could not bear it when he pulled his hand away.

She took his hand and put it to her neck. He watched her, bewildered. "You like being touched," he whispered wonderingly, opening his palm slowly, softly, on her neck, moving it up to her chin, back down to her collarbone. Moving the chain of her necklace back and forth across her skin. "You are not afraid to let me see." His fingers pushed back, to her hair, and ran through it. It sent a shiver through her, his touch. It was wonderful. She moved into his hand, automatically.

Marry me, she thought.

He pressed his lips to hers, and she opened her mouth to let him move into her, fill her with his soul. He pulled away in surprise.

"You have no tongue." When she didn't answer, he asked, "Is that why you are silent?"

She nodded, running her hands along his chest and stretching them around to his back, his neck and hair. She could not stop herself, this new self that was a vessel for him now. There was nothing she could do. She had given up everything for him. She had been made anew for him, in every way possible.

She felt he wanted to ask more, but he was not able to focus any longer on his thoughts. "You are . . . ," he began. She could see she was shocking him, but she did not care. "Most women are not like you."

He put his arm around her waist and led her to the end of the corridor, past a group of guards, and finally into a large room with tall, diamond-shaped windows overlooking the sea.

He was flushed, his eyes dark now, as if he were drowning. He opened his mouth and ran his tongue over her lips, and she bent forward. His lips on her neck and his hand running over her chest, down to her breasts.

"You're a goddess," he said, over and over. "Your hair, your skin. I've never seen anyone like you."

She felt like her body was dropping open. His fingers in her mouth, feeling for her tongue. "Yes," he said. "Someone has taken your tongue." And then he kissed her more intensely, his mouth warm on her skin, sending shivers through her body.

His hands worked at the back of her dress, unlacing it, and as her dress came off she thought how delicious it was, shedding this unnecessary layer; she was happy she had skin and not scales, and even her soft, mussel-like body did not seem naked enough now. He shed his shirt and his pants, until all she could feel was his bare skin on hers as he held her, moved his hands over her, pulled her onto his bed until she was lying under him.

She had been reduced, all her power and beauty, to this one perfect human feeling, and she pushed herself to him, felt like she could not get close enough to him. She opened her strange legs, revealed her weakest spot, and then he was pushing inside of her, and a pain flashed through her, but all the pain that pierced her human body, her legs, was worth it, for him, for this, and she loved it then, all of it.

I love you I love you! was all she could think, *Your soul, my soul.*

⌇

THEY LAY BACK on the bed, and his body became a shell as he held her in his arms. She felt so warm, but it was lovely, that feeling, the thin sheen of sweat covering her, the feel of his wet body on hers. After a while, he kissed her cheek and forehead. "We must leave each other now," he said. "I have to meet with some of my father's advisers. I will have a servant take you back to your room."

She looked at him, worried, and though he smiled at her and stroked her hair, something did not feel right.

And the next thing she knew, she was walking back through the corridors in her disheveled dress, her body battered, every bit of her feeling bruised, cut. And in the center of her body, a terrible wound. Blood moving down her legs.

When she arrived in her own room and the servant had left her alone, she stood by the window and stared out at the sea. The sun had set while she was with the prince. She felt a pain inside her— not where he had touched her but somewhere else. Tears dripped down her face, coated her skin in salt.

She didn't understand why she felt so empty now. She should have felt full, fuller than she'd ever felt. This was everything she wanted. The prince was in love with her. She was human, and would have immortal life.

The moon beat down on the water, which shattered it into a thousand splinters of light.

CHAPTER THIRTEEN

The Princess

MARGRETHE WAITED BY THE WINDOW OF HER ROOM, wrapped in furs and in her warmest dress, left unlaced, with a pair of men's wool pants underneath. A small bag sat at her side. Edele stood next to her, dressed the same. Josephine and Laura paced in front of the fire. Almost six weeks had passed since she'd come back to her father's castle, and now, finally, everything had been arranged. Margrethe had spent the last days crazed with anticipation, as her father continued to ready his men for battle. Then, after what seemed like forever but was really only slightly longer than it took a messenger to travel to the South and back again, just under three weeks, the Southern king had agreed to marry his son, Christopher, to Margrethe in a new alliance. Margrethe and Edele would go together to the South, accompanied by two guards, who would be rewarded for their services. Margrethe and Gregor had planned out the route, and he'd arranged for them to stay with various sympathizers along the way. The king and his court would be diverted when they found a note from Margrethe explaining that she had fled back to the convent, having found her true calling there. The king would send men after her directly, there was no doubt, but she would most likely be under the Southern king's protection—or close enough to it—before they realized what had happened.

It was not very far from the truth, Margrethe thought, feeling guilty for lying to Josephine and Laura, who had been like sisters to her for as long as she could remember. But they could not be put in harm's way, subjected to her father's anger. As for Edele, Margrethe had been surprised at how quickly her friend had agreed to this new adventure. Of course, Edele was nothing if not high-spirited, but still. Margrethe had expected her friend at least to have some trepidation about committing high treason and risking her life.

Instead, now, she could see that Edele was struggling to remain calm, she was so excited.

And when she was honest with herself, Margrethe had to admit that for her, too, it was a grand adventure. The grandest adventure she'd ever had, and maybe ever would have.

Outside, the snow-covered landscape stretched off in every direction, endless, shining icily under the moon as if it had been sprayed with stars. Any minute the signal would come from below, and the horses would be waiting.

Her heart pounded in anticipation. In a way, it was as if she *were* returning to the convent. That she *had* heard her call. After all, she was returning to the magic and the beauty she'd discovered there, and she would be serving God by bringing peace back to her land.

She blinked away thoughts of the mermaid, the longing that seized up inside her. It might have been the happiest she'd ever felt, she realized. Sitting on the beach with the mermaid, realizing that there was such breathtaking beauty in the world.

There will be more, she thought. *If everything works as I hope it will, there will be more beauty everywhere.*

"I will pray for your safe journey," Josephine said.

"Thank you," Margrethe replied, taking a deep breath and turning from the window. "Remember, at Mass tomorrow, you are to say that I am ill. Later, you will be as surprised as everyone when they find my note and realize that we're gone."

"You have been back such a short time, my lady," Laura said. "I am sorry for you to leave so soon."

"Oh, but we are happy for you, too," Josephine said quickly. "It is a true gift, to hear such a call."

"But are you sure you'll be safe there?" Laura asked.

"I'll be fine," Margrethe said. She put her hand on Laura's shoulder. "Everything is fine. I will be well protected now."

"All I want is your happiness, my lady."

"I know. It's time for me to return. I belong there. My father will not understand now, but I hope that he will, with time. That he'll see my reasons were pure."

"He will be very proud of you, my lady."

"I hope he will be," she said. "Eventually."

A faint, low whistle sounded from below.

"We must go," Edele said, lifting her satchel. She reached for Margrethe's as well, but the princess stopped her.

"I will carry it," she said.

"Let me help you," Laura said, rushing forward.

"No. You are to stay here," Margrethe said, gently putting her hand on the girl's arm. "We cannot draw any extra attention to ourselves."

Laura nodded and stood back.

Margrethe and Edele said their good-byes, tearfully kissing and embracing their friends. Then they slipped the hoods of their cloaks over their heads and moved to the outer chamber, and into the corridor, down to the western part of the castle and the side door that led to the stables. It was late, and even most of the servants were sleeping. All the fires were out except a small one in the heart of the kitchen, which an old servant was tending. He did not even look up as the two figures slipped by like silent shadows against the wall.

As quietly as she could, Margrethe pressed open the outer door. Just beyond it, two guardsmen stood waiting with their horses standing calmly beside them, as still as trees.

The guards bowed and took their satchels, helped Margrethe and Edele mount the horses. Both girls lifted their skirts, revealing the men's pants underneath, and they sat the way men did, straddling the backs of the horses. Speed and safety were more important than decorum, Margrethe had believed, much to Edele's delight.

They walked their horses slowly across the lawn to the castle drawbridge, the two guards leading them quietly through the snow. Margrethe breathed in the night air, the smell of frost and smoke and wood. It felt fresh, bracing, a world cleaned out and about to be remade. A thrill shot through her as she thought of the grand adventure that awaited them, and she almost laughed out loud. The sky was as clear as she'd ever seen it. She looked back at the castle, where her father slept. The moon shone down on it, and on the drifts of snow all around. She looked at Edele, whose face was shining with anticipation. Margrethe smiled. She felt impossibly small, at that moment, swept away by the forces of history. It was all God's will, she thought. She would trust in Him.

When they had walked a good distance away, well past the drawbridge and completely out of sight and earshot, the two guardsmen mounted the horses behind the girls, reached around their bodies to take the reins, and began to ride. The four of them rushed into the night. The world sped up all around them. Adrenaline pumping through their veins.

They rode through the forest, surrounded by thick green pines that seemed as tall as the sky, like ancient monsters. It was so different from her last flight, Margrethe thought. This time she was like an arrow. She knew exactly where she was going and what for. This sense of purpose. Desire. Power over her own destiny.

❦

AS THEY'D PLANNED IT, the journey would last seven days. They rode all through the first night and the next day and night, stopping only for short breaks in the woods, and, almost thirty-six hours after stealing down to the castle lawn, they were met on the road by a lord and his servant, who ushered them into a large country estate.

Dawn was just breaking over the countryside as they rode up to the great stone manor.

Margrethe and Edele were taken through the kitchen, their heads covered, and put up in secret in a simple room away from the bustle of the great hall. The guards were housed nearby. The four travelers were given wine and hot meals—all by the same trustworthy servant—before being left alone to sleep through the day. No one else at the estate suspected who these guests were; most of the servants and knights and aristocratic guests didn't even realize the newcomers were there. The few servants who did notice the extra food leaving the kitchen, the extra linens sent to the laundry, or the extra horses being stabled and groomed, just assumed that the lord's errant son had returned from his recent bout of carousing, most likely with some hapless maidens in tow.

The next night Margrethe and her companions stole out again, their horses rested and fed and watered. She and Edele looked at each other, smiling with excitement, as the horses rushed forward, so fast that the world blurred around them, into a new life. It *was* a great adventure. No matter how exhausting, or how dangerous. And it did not hurt that Edele found her rider handsome enough to flirt with as she spent hours on end pressed against him.

They kept doing this—rushing through villages and forests until they came to an agreed-upon destination where servants or guardsmen appeared like specters, out of thin air, to lead them into a large manor, where a lord or lady waited, honored to help the princess and the Northern peace faction on such a worthy mission.

Margrethe was exhausted. No matter how well she slept, her body ached from the long nights spent on horseback, and more and more she just leaned against her guard as the horse raced forward, closed her eyes, and allowed herself to think about Christopher and what it would be like to see him again, how he would react when he saw her. She imagined that he would recognize her instantly, despite her great change in dress, and that his warrior face would soften as he walked toward her and took her in his arms. And as she slipped deeper into fantasy, her own skin took on the mermaid's sheen, her body was soaked through, and she was leaning over him, pressing her lips to his.

Always she stopped herself, berating herself for such thoughts, forcing herself to look back out at the world passing by her, the landscape slowly becoming more and more green as they approached the range of mountains that split her own kingdom from the Southern part of the land, that caught the cold somehow, trapping it in the North.

On the fourth night they began to ascend the mountains, and, as the sun was setting the next evening, they arrived at the estate of another noble family, nestled among fir trees high on a peak. Here a great feast awaited them. The lord himself rode out to meet them, dressed in rich velvet. He hopped off his steed and bowed deeply to them, kissing both women's hands.

"I am Lord Adeler, and I am humbly at your service," he said. "We cannot tell you, Your Highness, how grateful we are to you, for this. What you are doing for all of us."

"I hope to help bring a great change," Margrethe said, fumbling a bit for words, taken aback by the strength of his emotion.

"We have long wished for peace," he said. "I lived most of my childhood in the South. My mother used to tell stories about her childhood, what our kingdom was like years ago, before I was born. I have spent much of my life working to get that world back."

"It is my great wish, too," she said.

"It is an honor to have you in my home, and if you are not too tired, we have a feast waiting for you, which I hope will nourish you as you near the end of your long journey. I have guaranteed your safety to Gregor, my oldest friend, and you will come to no harm in my household."

"Thank you," she said. "That sounds wonderful."

Lord Adeler mounted his steed and led them to a small stone castle in the mountains, up a path lined by flourishing green trees and grass. Inside, a suite of rooms and warm baths were waiting for them, and Margrethe sank down into the water, letting the exhaustion slip out of her. After, she and Edele were dressed in gowns loaned to them by the lord's wife, then led to a small room full of flickering candlelight.

The lord stood and introduced Margrethe and Edele to his wife and two sons, both handsome, tall with light hair and strong faces. Margrethe could sense Edele shifting beside her and had to stop herself from smiling. Of course Edele would leap at the chance to flirt and find love, even in the midst of a dangerous journey like this one.

"I thought we would have a special dinner here rather than with my court, for safety reasons, as much as I love and trust my little estate. It is also so nice to get to know new friends in such intimate surroundings."

"Thank you," Margrethe said. "It is an honor to be your guest."

They all sat at the table, and the servants brought out platters of fish and pheasant, bowls of rice cooked with blueberries, everything heavily spiced.

"It looks delicious," Margrethe said.

"We are all praying for you, Your Highness, and for the happiness and security of your upcoming marriage."

"The prince is a splendid man," the eldest son, Rainer, added. "We schooled together, when I was a boy."

"Ah!" she said. "And what was he like?"

"Much as I understand he is like now. Quick, fearless."

"Beloved by women, even then, was he not?" the lady of the house asked, interrupting him.

"And that, yes." Rainer smiled.

"Well, we can all only hope that the princess is as swayed by his charms as your childhood friends were," Edele said, flirting with him. He responded with a sweet smile.

"We are right at the border," the lord explained. "More Southern than Northern. It has caused us much difficulty at times."

"You were friends with my father once, weren't you?" Margrethe asked.

"Yes. When I was a young man, I spent a lot of time at his court. I was at his wedding, at your mother's wedding."

Margrethe breathed in. "You were?"

"Oh yes."

"What was it like?" she asked. For a moment, she was like a small child about to open a gift, her dark eyes glowing, a small smile playing at her lips. "My mother, what was she like, then?"

"Your mother was astonishing. She was a bright woman, full of energy. She seemed to get along with everyone, no matter how base or dull. And that laugh she had! It could change the temperature of a room completely."

"No one is allowed to speak about her at the castle," she said. "It is like she was never there."

"Ah, well, it must have been hard for your father. He was very, very much in love with your mother, you know."

"I hope to be in love like that one day," Edele said.

Margrethe poked her under the table.

"I wish that for us all," Rainer said, smiling at Edele and raising his glass to the table. "And for you, Your Highness. I would be honored to attend your wedding to my old friend, Prince Christopher, and I hope your love will be as legendary as that of your mother and father."

"Thank you," Margrethe said, raising her glass, trying to hide the blush that was creeping into her cheeks.

CHAPTER FOURTEEN

The Mermaid

THE SUN STREAMED INTO THE ROOM, WARMING LENIA'S skin. The waves crashing against the shore, lapping at the boats in dock, the faint sounds of voices, seagulls, footsteps in the corridor outside—all the sounds of the upper world rattled in her ears. She turned onto her side. Her mouth ached, and her body felt even more raw than it had before.

Painfully, she sat up, the sheets twisting around her. It was as if knives were being pressed into her calves and thighs.

Specks of dust floated through the air, illuminated by the sun. She observed them for a moment, fascinated, and then ran her hand through the air, watching them disperse.

She could still feel his mouth on her.

As she stood up, throwing off the sheets, she gasped in pain. It was as if the soles of her feet were open wounds. The day before they had begun to numb, and she had almost become accustomed to the pain, but now she had to acclimate to it all over again.

She took one step, and then two. Slowly, she walked over to the window, then peered at herself in the heavy glass next to it. To her surprise, she did not look at all as if she were in discomfort. She stepped away from the glass, then toward it again. Her body moved gracefully, perfectly, just as Sybil had said it would, despite the pain that shot through her with every step.

She opened her mouth, red and warm. The stump of her tongue was pink and flowerlike. The sight of it made her mouth ache even more than it did already, though she had barely thought of it until now, most likely because the pain in her legs was so much more vivid. Her eyes dropped to her breasts, the patch of hair between her legs, the dried blood on her thighs, her long, curving legs and arching feet.

In a way, this body was horrifying. Without thinking, she ran her left palm across the edge of the glass, and watched the blood drip from the thin wound down her wrist. Her skin was flat and so soft. She ran her fingers over the wound, rubbed the wet blood between her fingers and let the sting of it move through her.

Outside her door she heard voices. She stood still, her head cocked, hoping to hear his among them. But it was Katrina's voice, and others she did not recognize.

Awkwardly she reached for one of the dresses Katrina had had sent to her. She stepped into it, tried to pull it up over herself, and was dismayed to see blood dripping onto it.

There was a knock on her door then, and she jumped, frightened by the sound. A moment later, a servant entered.

"Let me help you get into that," she said, moving behind Lenia to lace her dress up the back. "The princess wants you to join her on the hunt today."

Lenia nodded as the girl pulled the dress in tightly around her torso. She placed her palms against her sides, feeling the way the dress pinched in her waist. When she took her hands away, her dress was stained with blood.

"You're hurt!" the girl exclaimed.

Lenia looked at the red mark on her dress in horror.

"Is something wrong?" another servant asked, appearing at the door.

"Yes, she's bleeding."

The servant bowed and rushed away as Katrina entered the room, splendidly dressed in a pink gown, with pink jewels hanging from her neck.

"What has happened?" she asked and then saw the blood before her lady could respond. "Oh!" She turned away, her hand on her head. "Have you called for the doctor?"

"Yes," the lady said. "He is on his way."

"Good," she said, heading back out the door. "I need to lie down now."

"She cannot stand blood," the lady whispered to Lenia after the princess left.

A few minutes later, a man came in, very official-looking and holding a bag, followed by several servants, who helped Lenia onto the bed.

"She is cut," he said, examining her hand. "It is not serious. It just needs to be bandaged." He paused, pressing on her abdomen. Lenia opened her mouth, as if to cry out in pain. The center of her body raw and searing. "Ah," he said. "There is bleeding here, too. This seems to be . . . a feminine matter."

"Shall I call for the healer woman?" one of the ladies asked.

"Yes, I think she will be of more help here," he said and nodded shortly. Then he left as a servant came back with strips of cloth and began bandaging Lenia's left hand.

A while later, there was another knock on the door. An older woman, short and bulky, with wide, rounded hips, came in. She had long, dark silver hair, pale eyes, and a loose skirt. Bracelets jingled from her wrists.

She focused on Lenia straightaway. "Leave us now," she said, gesturing to the servants and ladies who remained in the room. Her voice was soft, a voice used to being around sickness, and her movements were surprisingly graceful.

Quietly, the servants stole out of the room. The woman walked right up to the bed, peering into Lenia. A strange, herbal scent came from the basket she was carrying, covered with cloth. Immediately Lenia thought of Sybil.

"They say that someone found you, on the beach," she said. "That you can't speak. Is that right?"

Lenia nodded.

"And you can't write?"

No.

"Will you open your mouth for me?" the woman asked gently, nodding.

Lenia opened her mouth and let the woman peer in, watched the look of surprise that came over her face.

"Someone removed your tongue."

Lenia nodded.

"You must have had something to say in your time, didn't you? You poor girl. Someone wanted to hurt you, didn't they?"

Lenia shook her head no, focused on the woman. *I chose this,* she thought. *It was the price I paid to come here. I came here to be with him and to live forever.*

To her surprise, the woman reared back and stared at her with wide eyes. "Did you say something?" she asked. She examined Lenia for a moment, then picked up Lenia's right hand and turned it over, staring at her palm.

"What a strange creature you are," she said. "I have never seen a palm with a life line like yours. You have the life line of a child."

Lenia pulled her hand away, embarrassed.

The woman looked at her. "I only mean that I can see you are very special," she said. "Forgive me. My name is Agnes. I am a friend."

She took Lenia's other hand and carefully unwrapped the bandages, then rubbed a salve over the palm, closing Lenia's fingers around it.

She lifted Lenia's dress and placed her palm against Lenia's abdomen, felt between her legs. "Relax," she said. "I will not hurt you."

Lenia closed her eyes, wincing with pain. How strange to have a body that could be forced open like this. It was so different from when she'd been with the prince, when her body had opened naturally.

"Ah, you are fine," Agnes said, removing her hand, which was streaked with blood, and pulling Lenia's dress back down. "You have had your womanhood broken. Yes?"

Broken.

"It is painful business, lying with men," she said. "Do not let yourself be abused. Do you understand me?"

Lenia nodded.

I need him to fall in love with me. Please help me.

"You cannot make it too easy for a man like him. Do you know that? If you want him to love you."

Lenia just looked back at her. Agnes dropped her eyes, shaking her head slightly and letting out a small laugh. "I've become a mind reader, it seems," she said.

Yes.

Agnes wrinkled her forehead. "Now, I will arrange for you to be washed. If you need anything, I live close to the castle, in a small house across from the church. You can recognize my house by the dried yarrow on the door. Call for me or come to me, any time. I will just leave you with this salve made from bark. You can use it to ease aches and pains."

For my legs, my feet.

"Yes," Agnes said. She stared at Lenia again, into her eyes. "You are trying to say something to me, aren't you?"

Lenia nodded, pointed to her legs.

Agnes smiled. "The salve. It will help the pain in your legs."

Thank you.

Agnes cocked her head, as if trying to hear Lenia, then reached out and touched Lenia's hand. "What a strange one you are. Be careful here."

Lenia nodded and watched her go. Then she looked down at her injured palm, which was smooth and perfect now. As pale as a pearl.

❧

LATER, KATRINA CAME in and sat on the bed next to her.

"I think perhaps . . . you lay with my brother yesterday?" she said as she stroked Lenia's hair. "I thought he would find you pleasing. No one has caught his fancy since he returned from his last exploit. It was very out of character. I don't like it when people change like that."

Katrina's hand was soft against her, and the princess smelled of flowers. A pleasant smell. Lenia stared at her, trying to read her mind. Could Katrina tell that something was strange about her? That she had come from the sea?

Help me, she thought.

"There is a hunt today," Katrina said brightly. "Will you come, Astrid? It will be wonderful."

Lenia looked at her, liking the sound of the name he'd given her. She nodded.

"My brother loves to hunt."

❧

THAT AFTERNOON, THERE was great excitement around the castle. Noble men and women, and the king and queen themselves, gathered on the greens, where horses were being brought around and the dogs and huntsmen were assembling.

Lenia stared, shocked. These huge black creatures with long, thin necks, faces bobbing up and down as if they were floating on water. Their black eyes on the sides of their heads, staring. *Like fish,* she thought, breathing in. She watched as a stableman lifted Katrina up onto one of the beasts, as she settled in and grabbed the reins, her delicate heels resting along its glistening, muscled side. On the other side of the field, closer to the forest, Lenia could see the prince ready for the hunt, consulting with other men and nobles, all of them with horns and weapons strapped to their sides. A swarm of dogs crowded at their feet, howling. The forest wavered in the distance, as one by one the huntsmen began to disappear inside it.

A stableman brought one of the horses to her. It towered over her, then bent its long head to her neck. She could feel its breath, her skin prickling where it nuzzled her. And then its long lashes were right next to her face, grazing her cheeks.

She put her palm on its neck, stared up at it in amazement. For a moment, she forgot the prince, the long dress, which felt awkward and heavy on her body, the pain slicing through her legs, forgot everything but the warm creature in front of her, whose heart seemed to beat into her fingertips, move through her own skin.

"Let me help you up, my lady," the stableman said, and she did not resist as he helped her step into the stirrups and position herself on the horse, both her legs pushed to one side, the way she saw the other women mounted. She teetered, felt herself slipping, and then the horse shifted with her and she was steady.

It was strange, looking down at how far she could drop to the ground in this fragile human body.

"How is she?" Katrina called.

Lenia looked up, saw Katrina and several other ladies smiling over at her, the sun lighting them from behind. All of them so pretty. The grass so green, the sun so bright behind them.

They started moving toward the forest that spread out like water, the sea bordering the castle's other side.

Lenia swayed on top of the animal, grasping the reins. She could feel the blood moving through the horse, its pounding heart. With each step she felt more in line with its body.

The dogs were released, a pack of animals bolting out ahead of them, and the group of them followed. Lenia's horse began to gallop, and she was not afraid but felt a part of it. She leaned into her steed, shifted her body so that they moved faster and faster. And she was laughing, soundlessly, as the hounds rushed ahead and the horse raced to follow. The wind streamed against her skin like water. In front of her the men charged forward, and the prince was before all of them, lifting his weapon.

She tore into the wind, faster than anyone else. It was wonderful, the feel of this powerful beast under her, moving her through the forest as if she were swimming, as if she were being propelled by her powerful tail. She felt less awkward, freer on this animal. She hadn't realized how much it was a part of her, that power that had come from living in her mermaid's body, having that strong tail that pushed her through the water. Here, now, she almost had it back. Almost, but not quite. And for a moment, she *missed it*, that freedom and power she'd had once, with every fiber of her being.

The scent of the forest, the dank and the rot, was overwhelming, but she accepted it now. She was almost becoming used to being assaulted by scent, though she did not always like it. In the distance, she caught sight of an animal with huge, sleek antlers, bounding in and out of the light that filtered through the trees.

The dogs ran and bayed in front of them.

And then she was riding up alongside the prince. His head was bent forward, his hair slightly too long, his red cape flying out behind him in the wind. She turned to him, euphoric, and he was riding next to her, staring ahead, leaning into his sleek black horse, focused on the animal running in front of them, in the distance. Then he glanced to the side and saw her.

He laughed out loud in surprise.

His concentration broken, he fell behind. One of the other noblemen raced forward, and as the animal disappeared and then came back into view, there was a loud *whoosh*, an arrow whizzing through the air.

The prince slowed down and watched as the arrow hit the animal.

He looked over at her, shouted: "I've never seen a woman ride like that! I thought you were flying."

She looked around and realized she was surrounded by men. All the ladies were far behind, riding daintily through the woods, making their way to the scene of the kill. She felt self-conscious suddenly, stabbed by a pang of fear. Had she given herself away?

She looked back at him, but he was riding ahead now, to where the animal was staggering in a small clearing, the men gathering around it. It was so light, she saw, much lighter than the beasts they were riding on.

Everyone was clapping, laughing, as the creature fell, the sunlight pouring over it like butter. It cried out with a terrible bleating noise, looking around with terrified black eyes, and the forest smelled of blood and dying. She remembered, suddenly, her birthday, all the human men screaming, crying as the ship split apart, the men in the water clawing to get back to the surface.

She looked over and saw that Christopher was watching her. He was no longer on his horse. Keeping his eyes on hers, he walked to her, exuberant, bright, as full of life as the animal was full of dying, and she felt exhilarated and horrified by all of it, all at once.

This is why I'm here, she thought. *Him.*

She focused on him, on his weed-colored eyes, and it all slipped away, the smell of blood and death and fear, the loud celebration.

He reached out his hand and helped her off her horse.

"You do not like to see the animal dying, do you?" he asked.

She shook her head. This was not at all like the ocean, where there was not this hunting, these wounds, this slow, bloody dying. The animal seemed nearly human.

"I have been raised around these woods. I've lived here my entire life. I wish you could tell me where you came from, where you are not used to such things."

He nodded to a guard, who nodded back, and then he was leading her away from the hunt and into the forest. Suddenly everyone
else was gone. The leaves and brush crunched under their feet.

After a short walk, they came to a river. She rushed forward
and peered in, looking for fish, for mermaids, for shells and pearls.
A tiny ocean, she thought. Exhilarated, she kicked off her shoes,
picked up the hem of her dress, and walked in. The water was cold,
freezing, but she reveled in the feel of her feet sinking into the
muck, the muddy water, the tiny fish snaking past. She laughed,
soundlessly, and reached out, caught a tiny fish in her fingers and
nearly popped it in her mouth before catching herself. She opened
her hand and released it.

A breeze ruffled by, and birds swooped down from overhead,
their wings spread on either side. She watched, tears coming down
her face. The birds were like fish, and if she closed her eyes she
could believe she was on the ocean floor, fish swooping down from
overhead, the feel of the sand under her.

All these emotions arose in her at once, until she felt crushed by
them, and he was there watching, taking her in.

His eyes hooked into hers, and she stepped out of the water and
went to him. He turned her around, toward the water again, and
began unlacing her dress. His mouth pressed against the back of
her neck, sending shivers through her entire body.

He loves me, he loves me.

He pulled her down into the grass, and she pressed her hand on
his heart as she slipped out of her dress. She luxuriated in this, this
human feeling. Being this soft, this sensitive, naked in the grass,
with the breeze flitting over her skin, his fingers pressing into her.
The things this skin could feel!

And then he was crushing her in his arms until she couldn't feel
anything except his mouth and that need, a pain that wasn't a pain,
from the center of her body, a place she had never felt before coming to this world, warm and aching, wet, pressing against him, and

then he was turning her over, on top of her, moving into her, filling her, and her body seemed to dissolve, what little body she had left, until it was just him filling her, and from the depths of her body a screaming came, a strangled cry, and it was warmth and water. And she was, she was certain, healed.

She was shaking, her body red, warm, she had never been so warm. Her body itself like the ocean now.

And for a moment she felt a great, blissful nothingness.

He lay next to her, stroking her hair. "You remind me of someone," he said. "You seem so familiar to me. I know I've said this before, but I can't shake this strange feeling I have with you."

She looked up at him, shining.

He leaned forward, opened her mouth. "You're so perfect, so beautiful, and yet you have no tongue. You're like a dream creature, sent here just for me. Aren't you? I can tell you anything, and you just look at me with those beautiful eyes, like you understand everything."

She reached out her hand and stroked his face.

"I have felt so strange lately," he said.

My soul, she thought. *Tell me everything.*

He lay back, pulling her in next to him. "I almost died," he said, "not too long ago. I saw all my men die, my friends. It was terrible. I used to love the sea, but she took everything away. The sea, I mean."

Tell me.

"We were on a sailing expedition, me and a crew of men. I wanted to see the end of the world. They say there is an end, past the ice and snow, where the world just stops. Past the Northern islands, they say, though no one knows for sure if they are really there. Can you understand that? Wanting to see the end of the world?"

She nodded. *Yes.* Something in his voice, some softness, something unbearably sweet, made her want to hold him in her arms and stroke his hair, kiss his forehead over and over.

"I haven't been able to tell anyone else about this, what happened to me. What I saw."

My soul. Tell me.

She was so open. Just a vessel to hold him.

"My men thought I was crazy, but I convinced them that it would bring all of us much honor, and that I would reward them with jewels and gold. I want to explore, see the world. This kingdom is so small, but I look up at the sky and out at the water, and they are endless and vast. So we set off, my men and I, with a chest of treasures, prepared for whatever we might find. Your necklace, actually"—he moved his hand over the red stone that dangled from around her neck, falling to his chest—"it reminds me of the jewels we brought."

She smiled into his shirt as he continued.

"Then one night we were caught in a storm, and my men died. I should have died with them, but I had a vision, the most beautiful vision, an angel in the water."

She sat up, staring at him with wide eyes. He barely noticed, lost in the memory he was describing. His hands were automatically tracing the line of her spine.

"She was calling to me, lifting me from the wreckage and carrying me to shore. I just have the faintest memory of this, staring up at the sky, which I'd never seen so clear."

He remembered! Surely, he knew who she was. Surely that was why he had led her out here.

"And she was singing, and this voice! This voice. I have never heard anything like it."

She smiled and stroked his face, tears coming to her eyes. His hand, on her skin, his palm. The grass under her legs. The breeze over her. All this feeling, from the center of her body. Her powerful tail vanished and in its place these fragile legs, this great wound, and this most wonderful feeling, because *he knew.*

It was as if he had to wrest out every word. "I can't describe what I felt. How astonishing it was. I thought I had died, that the sea had taken me, too, and God had sent an angel to me, to take me home, and I thought, I didn't know that dying could be so beautiful as this, and I thought of my family, my friends, and I knew it would all be all right, no matter what happened.

"And the next thing I knew, I was on a beach, bitter cold, and I opened my eyes and she was kneeling over me, this creature. She was so beautiful. My God. Her dark hair and eyes, her white skin. And I was finally able to focus in on her face."

The breeze shifted and felt cold suddenly against Lenia's bare skin. *Wait. It was me. It was me.*

"But this woman . . . Can I tell you this? I see I can tell you anything. This woman, I have no idea who she was. She could be any woman, from any place, who gave herself to God. A woman of God. Married to Him. And I felt that, spilling over to me."

No, it was not her. I saved you. I chose you. She shook her head, gesturing *No!* her heart twisting inside her. *It was not her, it was me. I am the one you must love.*

He went on, oblivious. "It was a miracle, the way she appeared to me in the water. There is no other way to explain it. A miracle from God. He sent her out to me."

He sat up then, next to her, and looked at her with a face full of love and wistfulness. "You remind me of her, Astrid. You're so beautiful, like an angel. Like her."

CHAPTER FIFTEEN

The Princess

THE CASTLE FLARED UP, GLEAMING IN THE DISTANCE. They could see turrets, towers, the pennants of the South, the shimmering gold and green, colors of the old king. Under it, tiny black figures moved about. Around it, the earth was lush and green, like a bright, wet emerald, and beyond all of it was the sea, a shining blue sea sprinkled with diamonds and glass.

They stood in a clearing in the forest, at the top of a hill. "This is where they are to meet us," one of the guards said. "This is where we wait."

Margrethe looked down, her whole future laid out before them, filled with secrets and mystery. She turned to Edele, whose freckled face was lit up with excitement. In the sunlight her hair was practically orange. What a strange girl her friend was, Margrethe thought, filled with a sudden affection. She did not know how she could have made this journey without Edele.

"Finally!" Edele exclaimed. "We can rest."

"Yes," Margrethe said, slumping against her own rider, who laughed uneasily. She was exhausted to her bones. The guard dismounted and helped her down to the grass. She was unsteady on her feet after nearly seven straight days of riding. Her legs felt numb, her back sore. It would be so good to get to him, to this new life, and to rest. After she reached her goal, Margrethe told herself, she could sleep for days and days.

Edele was still radiant, too, from her time with Rainer, who had promised to see her at Margrethe and Christopher's wedding, when it would be safe again for everyone to cross from north to south. She ran about picking flowers and humming. Margrethe smiled sleepily at her as she leaned back against a tree.

"Do you need anything, Your Highness?" one of the guards asked, despite his own exhaustion.

"I'm fine. Thank you."

Already she was falling asleep. She half heard Edele's humming, her chattering and laughing with the guards, the low tones of their voices as they responded.

She might have dozed off for minutes or hours, when suddenly the pounding of hooves crackled through the forest, into the clearing. A group of soldiers rushed out of the trees, in armor, wearing green and gold. Quickly, Margrethe counted ten of them.

Her two guards automatically lifted their bows, and for a moment it seemed that anything could happen.

"We are here to take charge of Princess Margrethe, on orders of the king," one of the Southern soldiers said.

"Let us see proof," Margrethe said, standing up straight, striding toward the soldier. She could feel her hands trembling and quickly put them to her sides.

For some reason, she had expected Christopher to greet her, sweep her up in his touch and gaze into her eyes, the way he had in the garden. These men, here, were warriors, for an enemy king, and they knew exactly who she was.

The lead soldier dismounted his horse and bowed, handing Margrethe a sealed letter.

"From the king," he said.

She opened the letter and looked it over carefully. The king sent his greetings and extended his hospitality, guaranteeing their safe passage to his castle and during their stay inside it.

"You are in good hands," the Southern soldier said. "We are all willing to lay down our lives to ensure your safety."

She studied the Southern soldiers, the hard looks mixed in with more welcoming ones. She had the clear sense that not all of these men had positive feelings about taking charge of the Northern princess. Surely they all knew now that the North was planning to launch new attacks at any moment—there were too many spies about for such grand staging as her father's to go unreported—and it was clear that these soldiers didn't entirely trust the new arrivals.

She nodded, swallowing hard. "We are ready," she said haughtily, determined not to betray her uneasiness. At her command, the two riders transferred the girls' satchels and furs from their own horses to the horses the Southern soldiers had brought.

"Thank you," Margrethe said to the guards who had traveled so far with them, "for all you have done. May God be with you."

The two men would come into rich rewards for their service. They could not go back to the North, where they would be killed for their betrayal of the king. So Margrethe had arranged for them to receive a hefty payment, the last and biggest portion of which would come to them now that she and Edele had been delivered safely, that would set them up for life in the South.

Margrethe envied them as she watched them go, free to start their lives anew.

The Southern soldiers helped Margrethe and Edele onto the two horses—sidesaddle now, like ladies, which felt strange after so many days of riding like men. Margrethe grasped the reins, and they began to ride. Her heart was pounding as they moved from the clearing into the woods.

The sun streamed around them, through the leaves. Big bright green leaves shaped like hearts spilled from the trees. Birds squawked overhead, and they could smell the sea, hear it in the distance.

The short ride to the castle seemed endless. Margrethe and Edele rode hand in hand, the men silent around them. Margrethe concentrated on the seal she'd seen with her own eyes, reminding herself that they were safe. Even if some men in the group around them would have liked to see them dead, what mattered was the king and his wishes.

Still, it was not exactly the greeting she had hoped for.

They approached the castle gates. Outside people were selling wares, gathering to look at bowls and clothing and fish. A small band was playing, a troubadour standing in front singing a song about love.

The castle was bigger, more elaborate than any she had seen. It seemed at least twice the size of her father's castle, which was thick and close to protect its occupants from cold.

People stared up at them curiously, these two ragged noble-women surrounded by the king's soldiers, as they rode through the gates.

At the orders of the head soldier, most of the others split away, having performed their duty, a few of them bowing their heads or in some way paying respect to the foreign princess.

The remaining soldiers took Margrethe and Edele to a tower, where they were met by a guard and a servant.

The head soldier turned to the two women. "The king feels you will be safest here, in the tower. You will be well protected."

"We have tried to make it comfortable for you, Your Highness," the servant said, stepping forward.

The guard took their things and led Margrethe and Edele inside and up a long stairway. At the top, they came upon a wooden door that opened into a large bedroom. The servant followed behind.

They walked in. There were shining silk curtains hanging about the bed. A window that looked out over the sea. A small fireplace, unlit, a wardrobe, and a table with chairs. A large chest at the foot of the bed.

The servant began unpacking their satchels, putting everything in its place. A woman walked in with a jug of wine and two glasses, a plate of bread and fish.

"The king has said you are to rest," the guard said, "and then someone will be back to take you to him. I will be outside your door for the entirety of your stay, should you need anything."

"Thank you," Margrethe said, and then she and Edele were alone.

"It is like a prison here," Edele said, flopping on the bed, "a beautiful one, but a prison nonetheless."

Margrethe sat next to her, resisting the urge to cry.

"Let us rest, my friend," Edele said, putting her arm around Margrethe's shoulders. "This will all seem better once we are rested."

Margrethe nodded. "This isn't what I was expecting. But I was probably naïve to expect anything different. This is war, and I am the daughter of the enemy king."

"You expected him to be here waiting for you."

"Yes."

"I know, I did as well." Edele sighed and stood up, pacing the room. "The water is beautiful, though. Much more beautiful than at that horrible, gloomy convent."

Margrethe smiled. "I told you, I liked it there."

Edele shivered. "Maybe if I had met Rainer there, I would have liked it better, and be mooning about it now the way you are."

"I am not mooning about it."

"You're so mad about this prince you can't see straight. You're risking everything to be with him. It's like you think you're in some ancient poem."

"Edele, you know what is at stake here, for our kingdom. That is what I care about."

"Yes, I know what it is you say," Edele said, making a silly face, then reaching over to poke Margrethe's side. "But I also know your heart, my friend."

Margrethe sighed and lay back. "I am tired of arguing with you, Edele. You are even worse when you're in love, you know that? I think we ought to get some rest. Especially you. I'm not sure you've slept at all the past two days."

"These Southerners are incredibly good-looking," Edele said, still at the window.

"I can't believe you," Margrethe said. "Madly in love and we're here only two minutes before you start eyeing other men."

"It's not a man. A woman, walking by the water. Her hair is so blond it's practically white."

"Go to sleep," Margrethe said, rolling her eyes. "You exhaust me."

A FEW HOURS later, there was a tap on the door. Servants shuffled in, to bathe Margrethe and Edele in warm, perfumed water and dress them in splendid silk gowns. By the time the guard led them down the stairway to meet the king and queen, Margrethe was trembling with anxiety, but she held her head high. They walked past several rooms, through the great hall, and up another staircase, to where the king and queen sat on their thrones to hear matters of the kingdom. Outside the door, a throng of people waited to gain audience with the king. The room itself was filled with benches and guards.

Margrethe looked around for the prince the moment they set foot in the room. When she saw he was not there, she tried to hide her disappointment before turning all her attention to the king and queen, smiling in her most gracious manner.

The king was old but much more kindly seeming than her own father. Even in his elaborate crown, holding his jeweled scepter, he seemed more grandfatherly than regal, with his long, gray beard and hair. Next to him, the queen was far grander, striking, with her hair that had been dyed a deep black, her red lips and bright purple robes. She was dripping in jewels, from her forehead to her ears to her neck.

The king's eyes immediately went to Margrethe, and the room was cleared, seemingly in seconds, with one nod of his head.

"Princess Margrethe," he said. She was surprised by the warmth of his reception. "You are every bit as beautiful as I have heard. And Lady Edele, it is a pleasure. You are a great friend to your mistress here, to accompany her on such an arduous journey, and for such a noble cause."

The queen looked them up and down as her husband spoke. Margrethe sensed in her the same uneasy feeling she'd gotten from some of the soldiers, and she saw right away that king and queen did not share the same mind.

"Thank you, Sire," she said, curtsying, Edele following suit next to her. "I am happy to be here."

"It was nothing less than divine providence that led you here. I have thought for a long time that God was speaking to me and wanted me to die with my heirs secured and my people content, not ravaged by war the way they have been. I have grown more philosophical with age, it seems."

She smiled. "I pray that my father will follow your lead," she said. "I am sorry I had to defy him by coming here."

He nodded. "You are a brave young lady."

"I thought that I might see your son here today," she said. "My betrothed."

The king looked to the queen and then back at Margrethe. "I am sorry he is not here to greet you. But . . . The truth is he does not yet know about our arrangement."

"He does not know anything about you at all," the queen said bluntly.

Margrethe felt her insides cave in.

"My son is a headstrong young man," the king said. "With his own ideas. It has been necessary to wait to introduce you to him until we could present you in person. To ensure both your safety and his cooperation."

She stopped, confused. He did not know she was coming?

"Do not worry," the king said. "You are safe here, among friends. The main thing now is to get word to your father. I understand he sent men up north to search for you, but they must have returned at least a few days ago now. I do not know if he yet suspects that you came here."

"Have you sent word to my father yet?" she asked.

"I have just dispatched my men," he said. "You must make yourself as comfortable as possible here in my land until everything has been arranged. Your father will not take kindly to an offer of peace, I suspect, but he will come around. It is best for all of us, and our heirs."

"Yes, Your Highness," she said, curtsying again, her heart in her throat.

It occurred to her, for the first time then, that the prince himself might not want her here. He might not want her at all.

CHAPTER SIXTEEN

The Mermaid

LENIA STOOD ON A SMALL STOOL IN THE MIDDLE OF HER room. The chair next to the window was covered in rich fabrics, each with a different feel and hue—the plush softness of velvet, the smooth wetness of silk, the swirling hardness of woven brocade. Lavenders next to pine greens next to the palest, most delicate yellows. She was draped in a gorgeous deep blue satin dotted with red roses. Two seamstresses knelt at her feet, talking between themselves and hemming the skirt that flowed around her.

"You will have the richest gowns of anyone in the castle," one of the seamstresses said, smiling up at her, "and be the most beautiful woman at court."

"Not if Princess Katrina can help it," the other said and then laughed.

Lenia smiled politely. She knew that the prince, and the rest of the court, would find her pleasing in these new dresses the prince was having made for her, but she was still not used to the feeling of fabric weighing down, cold and heavy against her skin. Her waist cinched in, her breasts confined and pushed up, the sleeves tight against her arms. Even under the flowing skirt, there were layers of lace that brushed against her legs and made them ache.

But she did not mind. She had been in the castle for nearly two months now, and she had no doubt that he loved her, even if he did not remember her. At meals he could barely take his eyes off her; he had even started leaving the king's table to sit next to her. Everyone was talking about the two of them—more than one man commented on the prince's great fortune, finding a woman as silent as she was beautiful—and throughout the court, rumors flew about her origins. Elaborate stories were made up about where she had come from. Some said she came from the mountains that split the North from the South, others that she'd come from a faraway land where the castles were made of ice and diamonds. Some of the more flirtatious young nobles claimed that she'd been dropped straight from heaven itself. But no one could have guessed the even more extraordinary truth.

Prince Christopher sent for Lenia every night, when her maids helped her out of her stiff layers and into a thin robe, and combed her long hair until it hung in a stream over her shoulders and down her back.

When she was not with him, she thought of him. Even now, she could not wait for the seamstresses to finish their task, leave her to prepare for dinner in the great hall, and him.

The sun was beginning to set, and the smell of the sea came in through the windows. Outside, its surface shone black, like oil, reflecting the sun above it, revealing nothing of what it contained. Lenia scanned the water, as had become her habit. She thought of her sisters, there, beneath those waters. What were they doing, right then? She tried to bring them to her mind—Thilla with her wise face, beautiful Nadine, the flame-haired twins Bolette and Regitta, Vela with her exotic sea creatures—but they seemed so far from her. Her heart ached as she imagined them searching for her, the panic they must have felt when they discovered her gone. She wondered how long it had taken one of them to go to Sybil, who would have told them about what she had done.

Would they understand, eventually, and forgive her?

She thought of the necklace they'd found for her, within the prince's wrecked ship, and about how she'd tossed it angrily back in the water after hearing the prince speak about the human princess Margrethe. The woman he thought had saved him. Had one of her sisters found it, and taken it as a message from her to them? *I love you, and I am well, here in the upper world.*

"Are you feeling all right, lady?" one of the women asked.

She was swaying, she realized, off balance. A strange feeling rose from her belly. She tried to steady herself.

She nodded, but then the feeling swept through her, like a giant wave, and it was as if her body were turning inside out, and she was falling from the stool and one of the seamstresses was catching her and the other running for the chamber pot, and then they were both helping her to the bed.

She opened her mouth, and her insides came out. A hot liquid, a terrible sensation, like her body was being flipped over, everything contained inside her skin being pushed out. She remembered the feeling of her tail turning to legs, and for a moment she felt sheer panic. What if the potion was wearing off? What if she were becoming something else, something between mermaid and human?

As quickly as it began, it passed. She sat breathing heavily, rocking back and forth, not sure what had just happened.

"Here," one of the women said, handing Lenia some water, which she drank gratefully.

And she saw that, rather than panicking, the two seamstresses gave each other an amused look before going back to their work.

SHE TOOK TO her bed for the rest of the evening, to recover from the sickness that had overcome her. Never, in the sea, had she felt anything so awful and unnerving.

She lay alone and naked on the soft bed, with the curtain closed around her, clutching this strange torso she had, this curving belly.

Slipping in and out of sleep. Wishing there was a shell she could crawl into, the way ocean creatures did, burrowing into a smooth recess of pink.

Every smell suddenly bothered her, even more than before. The spice from the tea the servants brought. The lavender from the water that scented the fabrics. The vague odor of fowl coming from the castle kitchen.

She sobbed under the covers. Slick with sweat, with tears. She was like a raw, disgusting sea creature. A clam. A mussel.

Without him there, touching her, she was entirely alone. Abandoned, by everything. This, too, was a sickness.

Sybil, she thought, closing her eyes. *Help me.*

But she was so far away now. She pushed herself under the covers and listened to the hush of the castle. Her own breath, slightly ragged. The vague sound of the sea, breathing in and out, splashing against the shore. Horses clopping outside. Voices, laughter, the vielle. The occasional cough of the servant girl she knew was waiting on a chair outside her door.

Then, what seemed like minutes later, she could see, beyond the curtains, that there was movement at the door. And there was his voice.

She sat up.

The curtains moved back, and it was him, the prince, standing in front of her. He was wearing his hunting clothes—a big cloak, his riding cap, his carved ivory horn hanging from a strap around his neck—and he smelled of bark and forest. He breathed life into everything, she thought. Not only her. He was grass and dirt and sun and sky.

"Hello, my love," he said softly. "I was told you are not feeling well."

She smiled at him and stretched out her hand. Behind him, the servant girl bent her head and left the room.

"You are not well."

She shook her head, smiled at him.

I am more than well. I am perfect.

It was the first time he had come to her room rather than send for her. He slipped off the horn, his cap, his cloak, watching her with his strange, beautiful eyes. He was happy, she saw. She could feel it coming off him. Something had happened.

He slipped into bed next to her, under the covers, and pulled her to him, wrapped his arms around her slick waist. She smiled as he kissed her neck and jaw.

"Are you feeling better than you were earlier?" he asked.

She nodded, breathing in his scent. She could not get close enough to him. She wanted to disappear into him. There was nothing like this in her own world.

Can't you remember me?

"You're so sweet," he said, smiling at her. "So beautiful."

Love me.

"Your maids say you might be pregnant . . ."

She looked at him, confused. He was watching her tenderly. Tracing his warm hand from her neck to her chest to her belly, resting his palm there, causing another wave of sickness to move through her. From her belly to her throat and then down again.

Pregnant?

She shook her head, backed away from him.

"I was told that you had fallen ill, in the woman's way."

He put his hand on her belly. She looked down at her own soft, pale skin where before there had been scales, glittering and bright green-silver. Could a child be growing inside of her? What kind of child could she have, in this world?

She tried to ignore the intense feeling of disgust that passed through her.

He noticed her distress and grew worried. "Are you ill again?"

She shook her head, forced herself to smile.

He relaxed, reached out his arm, stroked her hair. His fingers ran over her neck and back, sending shivers up and down her skin. *He wants this*, she thought.

"My first child," he said, kissing her jaw. "A son. He will be beautiful, like his mother."

∽

DINNER THAT NIGHT was a splendid affair. The king and queen were dressed even more finely than usual, seated at the head table, and the service seemed especially extravagant, with elaborately dressed peacocks, their tails erupting at the ends of the silver platters, and pheasant and boar and lamb. Musicians played at the front of the hall, and jugglers made their rounds. Some nobles from a country estate were visiting, taking up one end of one of the long tables. The mood was firelit, jovial.

Though still recovering from her earlier sickness, Lenia was in high spirits. It seemed the whole world was celebrating her good news, though no one mentioned it outright. But Christopher sat next to her on the bench rather than at his father's table again, and Katrina kept looking over at them, a small smile on her face.

Halfway through dinner, the king stood up and signaled to the musicians to stop playing.

Christopher shrugged and raised an eyebrow at Lenia.

"We have an announcement to make," the king began, as a hush came over the hall. "We have been at war for a long time, and have lost many of our sons. Now we have peace, but the North, we have learned, is preparing a new set of attacks on the eastern coastline. We have already mobilized our soldiers, but our hope is that we can avoid more bloodshed. We have long desired a just and peaceful end to the fighting, as many of you know. We have long wished to restore our kingdom's glory of old, by joining the North and the South once more.

"This morning I dispatched a group of men to meet a new guest at our court. Princess Margrethe, daughter of the Northern king.

She comes to us by her own volition as part of a marriage alliance that will bring peace to our land for many years to come, should the North agree. This alliance will bring the bloodlines of our kingdom together, and make us whole once more. We have ensured her safety. Another set of men are now traveling to the North to lay out our terms to the king. Princess Margrethe will be a guest here at our court until we receive his response. If all goes as we hope, Princess Margrethe and Prince Christopher will be married, and we will have peace. Peace and the glory of the kingdom of old."

The king lifted his glass, and there was silence in the hall as his words soaked in.

Lenia looked over to Christopher wildly. He was livid. His face ashen, his jaw hard. She had never seen him look like that.

The king drank from his glass and set it down. "And now," he said, "I want to present to you my son's future bride, Princess Margrethe of the North."

Before anyone had time to react, a guard opened the side door to the hall, and a young woman in a bright blue gown, her black hair twisted elaborately under a gold headpiece, entered the room. She stepped forward regally and calmly, stopping to bow to the king. She looked over the court with her dark eyes.

Lenia stared. Her mouth dropped open. And for the first time she knew what it was to feel pure panic.

Margrethe.

She could see, just under the girl's sleeve, the diamonds on her skin where Lenia had touched her. The girl, Margrethe, had said she was the daughter of the Northern king. And Lenia, in this moment, understood what that meant. Understood what her lover's father had just explained.

No, she thought. *He must marry me.* Tears filled her eyes and dropped down her cheeks. As if her face were underwater.

In horror, she watched Margrethe's eyes searching the room before they stopped to rest on Christopher. She watched her soften and react to the sight of him, a slight blush coming to her face that only made her more beautiful.

But Christopher did not even seem to see Margrethe. His eyes flicked over her, his face a hard mask of fury.

The room erupted. Some clapped and cheered, others shouted in anger.

"Enough!" The king demanded silence with a gesture. "We have had enough fighting!"

The prince stood. "Father," he said, his voice shaking with rage. "I seem to have been mistaken in the assumption that my life was my own to lead."

Margrethe visibly blanched at this statement and then looked regal once more, transforming so quickly that anyone not watching carefully might have missed it altogether.

"Your task, my son," the king responded, "is to serve your kingdom."

The whole room was silent, steeled for what would happen next.

Several long moments passed as father and son faced each other, as if no one else were in the hall.

All the men braced themselves, their hands sliding toward their weapons. Each of them had sworn to protect the king at all costs, even from his own heir.

But Christopher surprised everyone. He turned to Lenia and extended his hand. She took it, her face burning, wet with tears.

"Come, my love," he said.

Tenderly he helped her from her seat, his back straight and head high, and, his hand in hers, quietly left the room.

As they walked out the door, Lenia glanced back once more at Margrethe, who stood awkwardly at the head of the room, looking as if a hundred men had, in fact, drawn their weapons, and pointed them all at her.

IT WAS PRINCESS KATRINA who approached Lenia that evening in the queen's outer chambers, after Lenia had spent over an hour trying to calm the prince, who insisted he would have no part in his father's plan.

"As my father said, she is the princess from the North," Katrina said. "They have arranged some sort of deal, to bring peace. And now my brother will be forced into this marriage." She spoke in a matter-of-fact fashion, as if Lenia's heart were not breaking in her chest. "You are crying! Why are you crying? Oh, sweetheart. Did you want to marry him? Even without this peace treaty, my brother could not marry you. He is a prince. He cannot choose his own wife."

Katrina sighed, then turned back to her ladies-in-waiting. "I would like never to marry, of course. I would like to play the vielle and write poems, and I would quite like to live like one of these court troubadours. Wouldn't that be lovely? Not be forced into some marriage to help the kingdom, as my brother will be. Most likely, though, I will be married off within the year."

"If we can find a man to have you," the queen said, making everyone laugh.

Everyone except Lenia, who sat stunned, watching her own tears falling on the crude embroidery in her hands.

CHAPTER SEVENTEEN

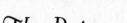

The Princess

MARGRETHE WOKE UP SLOWLY, TO THE FEEL OF A SEA breeze moving across her, dusting her with tiny, sparkling grains of salt. She'd dreamed all night of the sea. The mermaid's hand in hers, the two of them swimming together, gliding through the water like birds, deeper and deeper into the ocean, their arms spread on either side of them. She could feel the hard skin of the mermaid's hand, like soft metal, in her own. Somehow she knew that they were going somewhere spectacular, mysterious, as wonderful as the visions that the old nuns saw when they trembled with love. And the water turned to clouds, to stars, and the mermaid turned into her mother, leading her up . . . until she could no longer see, the light was so bright, the love moving through her.

She sat up, her heart sinking in her chest. Edele was awake, sitting by the window, staring out. Behind her, the sky was a dying smoky blue.

"You were dreaming," Edele said, turning to Margrethe.

"Yes." Slowly, Margrethe rose from the bed, her shift dropping in folds around her, and joined her friend by the window. "Edele, do you think I made a terrible mistake?"

Edele turned to her. "No," she said. "I think you've done the right thing. But anything could happen to us. I knew that, coming with you. The prince must not realize who you are, that he has met you before. And he was caught off guard. I mean, look how his father just humiliated him."

Margrethe nodded. "You saw?"

"Yes, I was seated with the princess's ladies. I thought you saw me."

"I could barely see anything, I was so frightened."

For a moment they were both silent, staring out at the beach from the tower, the guards stationed at the shore, the small boats rocking back and forth. Avoiding talking about the topic on both women's minds: the prince's lover. Astrid, they had called her.

"What did you dream about?" Edele asked, her voice falsely bright. "Tell me." She put her hand on Margrethe's, and Margrethe started, surprised, then relaxed into the gesture.

"Nothing, just silliness," she said, shaking her head. "I was swimming with a mermaid."

"A mermaid!"

"Yes." Margrethe smiled. "She was showing me all kinds of wonderful things, secret things in the ocean."

Edele sighed. "I wish I could dream about such fantasies. You looked so happy. In my dreams, I find a bit of thread or an earring I thought I'd lost. It is quite a letdown when I wake up."

Margrethe smiled. "It was nice being somewhere else. People don't like that we're here, Edele. *He* doesn't like that we're here. I don't know if this will work, if I've put us both in grave danger for nothing. Prince Christopher . . . He didn't even *look* at me. It has been so little time, really, since I was with him, and already he loves someone else."

"He was upset at his father, Margrethe, not you. He just needs time. You know he cannot marry that woman."

Margrethe shook her head. "If he does not marry me . . . I can't even think of it. None of this will work if the marriage does not take place. We are in this enemy stronghold, alone, and the king will have no reason to protect us."

"We have many allies here, and the king, he is friendly to us. Please, my lady. My dear friend. Do not despair."

Margrethe could not help having them, these feelings of doom and foreboding. Nothing was as she'd envisioned. The reality of being here, in this enemy castle, the way things had gone last night. The feeling had been so strong before, that sense of purpose and knowing. Never in her life had she felt so confident, and it had all been because of that mermaid. But now that mermaid was just a dream, slowly vanishing.

It hit her then: how much this Astrid woman had reminded her of Lenia.

Exasperated, Margrethe stood and walked to the window, and then her heart sank even more in her chest. "Look," she said.

Edele looked out to where Margrethe was pointing. "What?"

"Here, move closer to me. Look. Down there."

It was the prince, walking by the water. Walking arm in arm with Astrid.

Silent, they pressed against the window and watched.

"They look happy, don't they?" Margrethe asked.

"Yes," Edele whispered, putting her arm around Margrethe's shoulders. "But just give it time. He is a man, after all."

Margrethe hadn't seen such radiance between a man and woman since that day at the beach, since it had been the mermaid looking at Christopher like that. She shook the memory away. This was a real woman now—no matter how much she resembled a creature from myth—and the prince, whole and healthy again, was looking back at her with the same devotion.

"I feel sick."

"Shhh," Edele comforted.

"I don't know what this means. I thought . . . those moments with him, between us . . . I thought they were special, that they would sustain us, I thought they might be the seeds of love. Now I'm not so sure. Is he so fickle that he's forgotten me completely?"

"It doesn't matter, Margrethe. It only matters that you marry, and bring our two kingdoms together."

Margrethe took a deep breath and nodded. "You're right. That's true."

Below them, the prince wrapped the woman in his arms.

THE NEXT MORNING, Margrethe and Edele attended Mass in the queen's chapel. Quietly, with bowed heads, they entered and sat together in the last pew. Margrethe tried to focus on the priest's words, but she found herself watching as Astrid took communion with her eyes closed, her mouth gaping open. When she and Edele moved to the communion rail, Margrethe felt the eyes of the queen, the Southern princess, and the prince's lover burning into her back.

She shook her head, forced herself not to think of them, to focus on the communion and her prayers as she returned to the back pew, but inside she burned with shame. No one, not even her future husband, wanted her there. She had risked everything to come here, to marry a man who did not want her.

Margrethe asked for her lunch and dinner in her room for the next several days, claiming she was still exhausted by the journey.

"Let them get used to the idea of us, without the pressure of our constant presence," she told Edele, who did not argue.

THEY HAD BEEN there just over a week when they were invited to visit the queen's apartment, and Margrethe felt they had little choice but to go.

They walked into a large, richly decorated room, where the walls were hung with bright tapestries threaded through with a lacy gold. Margrethe could not help but think of the place where her own mother had hosted her friends, how much warmer it was in comparison. This queen was austere and grand, and her rooms reflected that coldness.

The queen wore a red dress, and her black hair was pulled back. She was as striking as her son, Margrethe thought, with the same golden green eyes. Combined with her dramatic coloring, those eyes gave her an animal look. She was playing cards with one of her ladies, and she looked up and nodded when Margrethe and Edele entered.

A dozen other women sat playing games, reading, and sewing, scattered about the room like place settings for a feast.

Margrethe met the eyes of Astrid and stared, despite herself. Up close, she was even more stunning. There was something mesmerizing about her, almost familiar. Like someone she'd met in a dream. Her mind flashed again to Lenia. The unbearable beauty of the mermaid glimmering on the beach, the prince dying beneath her. The thought came to her again: she was beautiful like *that*, and Margrethe's heart ached with the most terrible loss. A sense that she would never find such beauty again, in all the world. This girl had a hint of that same beauty to her. How could she, Margrethe, compete with such a woman?

"Welcome," the queen said, and Margrethe tore her eyes away, hoping her face had not betrayed her.

She bowed. "Thank you," she said. "We appreciate your hospitality, and I hope to return it one day."

The queen nodded. "Join us, please." She looked around at the women in the room. "We need to welcome my son's betrothed." She smiled at Margrethe then, but it was not the kind of smile that would make anyone feel warm inside.

Margrethe and Edele sat, awkwardly, a little away from the others, on chairs by a large window hung with colored glass. They picked up a deck of cards nearby and began to play.

The other women were talking, laughing. Margrethe noticed that Astrid did not say a word but seemed anxious. She was sewing, but fumblingly. Her hands were so perfectly formed and elegant, yet her movements were those of a child.

Edele, under her breath, said, "She is watching you."

"Really?"

She looked at Astrid, straight on, and their eyes met. The girl's burning blue eyes on her own. Margrethe looked away immediately, nervously. There had been something strange and pained in the girl's expression.

"Well, I *am* here to marry her lover," Margrethe said, surprised at the sense of triumph she felt saying the words. She had never had such a feeling before, tucked away in the study with Gregor, surrounded by books, in a castle where everyone adored her.

A viciousness rose in her. She needed this, she realized. Not only for her kingdom but for herself. She wanted to walk with him by the sea, bend over him the way the mermaid had done, her lips on his forehead. She wanted his heart as well as his hand in marriage, and she knew that, if he remembered her, just thought about her and those moments by the sea, he would forget anyone else. People said that Astrid couldn't even *speak*. Despite the girl's beauty, how could the prince love a woman who could not speak, who couldn't laugh with him or challenge him, who couldn't sing lullabies to the children she'd bear him? There she was, sitting at the queen's feet, not saying one word, as the others chattered around her.

Margrethe hated the prince's lover. The feeling flashed through her, nearly pushing her to her feet. She could have screamed with it.

"Do not let her fluster you, my friend," Edele whispered.

Margrethe started, felt the color rise in her neck.

"Don't be absurd," she whispered.

Edele met her eyes. "Perhaps you should pay the prince a visit. That's all he needs, you know. Go talk to him."

Margrethe nodded.

A moment later, she stood. "I am feeling tired," she said. "My lady and I will retire for the night."

"As you wish," the queen said, nodding.

To Margrethe's annoyance, she thought she detected a smirk on the woman's face, but she did not have time now to worry about the prince's mother. Not until she had won him over.

~

AS SOON AS they left the queen's wing, Margrethe turned to Edele, bursting with feeling.

"I'm going to him," she said. "Now. You're right. I will talk to him."

"Good," Edele said, placing her hands on her friend's shoulders. "Remember: you are a princess, the most beautiful woman in the Northern kingdom. And slightly intelligent, too, even."

Margrethe laughed, grateful at how Edele could always make her relax.

"He loves you," Edele said, lowering her voice as a guard turned the corner and entered the corridor. "Now go!"

Margrethe turned, in her most regal manner, to the guard approaching them. "Where is the prince?" she asked. "I must speak to him at once."

"I believe he is with the king, madam."

"Take me to him."

"As you wish," he said, nervous but unwilling to disobey a princess.

She followed the guard down a corridor that led to the king's chamber, thinking about what she would say to the prince. *You know me*, she wanted to shout. *You kissed my hand at the end of the world! I saved your life, remember? You called me an angel. Don't you remember? You would have died without me.* She did not care if it was true. *I carried you through the water!*

As they approached the king's chamber, the door was suddenly flung open, and the prince himself stormed out.

He brushed past them, his face flashing with anger.

"Christopher," she said.

He turned, ferocious.

"You," he said.

Her heart was pounding. "Yes." She shrank back.

He stalked toward her, and she watched him with wide, terrified eyes. "You. You made a fool of me. I thought you were a woman of God, and you were . . . You're . . ." He gestured at her in frustration.

"But I . . . ," she began. No one had ever spoken to her this way. Tears sprang to her eyes, to her horror. She wiped them away angrily. "I did not know who you were, either!"

"You tricked me! You let me stand there and practically profess my love for you, Margrethe." He emphasized her name angrily. "Like a fool."

"But I was in hiding," she said. "Nobody knew who I was there. I was not supposed to tell anyone. I don't understand what you think I should have done!"

"You should have told me your name. Who you were. I was nearly dead, what do you think I would have done to you? We were in a house of God!"

She gaped at him. The strength of his anger confused her. "What do you mean?" she said. "You . . . were my enemy!"

"Exactly," he said, quietly, and for the first time she saw the hurt in his eyes. He thought she had betrayed him. Had she? It made no sense to her. None of this did.

"I'm sorry," she whispered.

For a moment, his face relaxed, and she saw a glimmer of the man she'd met by the sea.

Just then, a guard appeared from the king's chamber. "May I be of any assistance, Your Highness?" he asked, and Margrethe and Christopher both turned to him at once.

He had been talking to the prince, who nodded. "I am just going back to my rooms," Christopher said.

"You know me," she whispered, trying to get the moment back.

He looked at her coldly. "I knew a holy woman. I do not know the daughter of the Northern king." He nearly spat the words before storming off, leaving her there alone with the guard, who was gentlemanly enough to pretend not to have seen anything that had just happened.

CHAPTER EIGHTEEN

The Mermaid

WITHIN DAYS OF MARGRETHE'S ARRIVAL AT THE castle, the healer woman, Agnes, visited Lenia and confirmed that she was indeed pregnant with the prince's baby, that he had filled her with his seed and that the seed would become a child. His child. Her child. Agnes had told Lenia that the baby was growing at an unusual rate, that she'd never seen anything like it.

"I can feel its heart," Agnes had told her, and Lenia had had to swallow to keep the sickness down. "I would've thought you'd arrived here already pregnant if I hadn't seen for myself that you were a virgin. I don't understand it, but you and the baby seem healthy enough."

Now, more than two months after drinking Sybil's potion and coming to the upper world, Lenia stood by the sea, staring out at the water, remembering the witch's words: *If he marries someone else, the next morning at dawn your heart will break, and you will turn to foam.*

The waves crashed, rising and cascading down into foam, and then turned to nothing, as if they were never there at all. All her life, in the sea, she had dreamed of this, the world above. And now that she was here, she yearned instead for the sea and for all she'd left behind. Would it always be like this for her?

She spoke to her child in her mind. *This is the sea, where your aunts live, and your grandmother and grandfather, your cousins . . .*

She was sick, clutching her swollen stomach. Her body was changing, and she felt as if a fish were trapped inside her. Her stomach seized up right then, and she bent over and vomited into the sea.

What was this inside of her? What would it become?

She was terrified that she would give birth to some kind of mutant, part merperson and part human, a child who would not be accepted in either world. There was nothing she could do now but wait.

All the grace she'd had in her old life, in her former body, seemed to be gone forever. She wanted only to eat, and sleep, and be with him. The prince visited or sent for her frequently still, but he seemed afraid to do anything but hold Lenia, as if she would break.

"I will not do it," he vowed, running his hands through her hair, feeling the slope of her belly. "*You* are my true wife, no matter what."

She spent more and more time in the chapel or by the sea when everyone else was out enjoying the seemingly endless amusements of the court. She knew that everything depended now on the Northern king. If the king allowed it, Christopher and Margrethe would marry, the North and South would make peace, and Lenia would die. If the king did not allow it, legally Christopher and Margrethe could not marry. And then, only then, would the prince be free to marry her. Despite what Katrina said, he would marry her if he could, Lenia was sure of it. The way he looked at her when they were alone . . . the way he touched her hair and whispered into her ear and her belly left her little doubt.

It had been over a fortnight since the king had sent messengers to the North. Any day now they would receive King Erik's response.

She prayed to the human God, to Christ and to Mary. She stared up at the crucifix in the chapel, at the suffering man with blood dripping down his face and a crown of thorns on his head. Sent to earth by his father to die for the sins of humans. His beautiful face, turned to the side in suffering. His wracked body, which she longed to touch.

Please let him marry me, she prayed, but she was not sure that the humans' gods would listen to her. *Help me and my child.*

Because even if her child was deformed and monstrous, as hideous a creature as the land and sea had ever seen, Lenia loved it. No matter what it was, it was *her child,* her child and the prince's child, something they had made together. She would die a hundred times over so that their child might live.

All Lenia could do was pray and wait, pray and wait, as word came trickling down from the North that the king was very likely to relent.

CHAPTER NINETEEN

The Princess

MARGRETHE LAY IN BED, UNABLE TO SLEEP. SHE HAD never felt this way about someone before. Never hated anyone. But now she hated the prince's lover. *Astrid.* Wanted desperately for her to just disappear. She was sure she could kill her with her bare hands if given the chance, and was tortured with dreams of her kissing the prince, of her bending over him on the rocks instead of the mermaid, her breasts against his bare skin.

She learned about the prince's lover from Princess Katrina's handmaidens: how Astrid had shown up at the castle one day wearing nothing but an astonishing, priceless necklace, how she was unable to speak, how she spent most of her time in her own room or walking by the sea when she was not keeping company with the prince. How strange she was. She learned that Katrina was the one who'd initially shown her kindness, but that the prince had been immediately smitten and still was, to the surprise of all the ladies, who thought Astrid was actually quite boring.

"It's the baby," one of the ladies said. "He is a good man, the prince, and that conniver managed to get herself pregnant the moment she arrived."

When she was alone, Margrethe stared at herself in the mirror, criticizing every flaw. Was she not beautiful enough? Did he not desire her? She stared at her long black hair and brown eyes, her pale skin and angular features. She had an intelligent look to her, people said, just like her mother. Before, Margrethe had always thought this was a compliment. Now she imagined herself as dull and dour, a woman suited more to convent life than to the love of a man. She didn't have the lushness or curves of Astrid, and she began to hate herself for that.

Of course, it was easier to believe that it was her dark hair or slenderness that was at fault, rather than the truth. Christopher felt she had betrayed him. And Christopher was in love with someone else.

Edele tried to comfort her and remind her why she was there. But she spent too much time crying about Rainer, whom she missed terribly, to be of much actual comfort.

The whole castle was on edge, all of them for their own reasons. Waiting to see what King Erik would do. Whether it was to launch a new attack or attend the marriage of his daughter, he would be coming to the Southern kingdom soon.

Margrethe's only consolation was reading, the way it had been since she was a child. Opening a manuscript and getting lost in the world inside of it. The clean precision of the Greek letters, like hands soothing her.

One afternoon she sat reading an old manuscript when she heard someone entering the library. She looked up, startled, her mind still swimming in the world of the book, and found herself staring straight into the face of Prince Christopher.

For a minute she thought he was going to turn around and leave. But his curiosity seemed to get the better of him.

"What are you reading?" he asked.

Her heart raced in her chest. The moment felt fragile, like a glass balanced on wire. She was almost afraid to breathe.

"*The Odyssey,*" she said.

"*The Odyssey*? You are able to read Greek?" He stepped forward and looked down at the page in front of her.

"Yes. My mother insisted that I be educated. My father's old tutor schooled me. I took to it."

He looked at her, impressed, trying to hide his surprise.

"We have spoken of this book before, you and I," she said. "The men with eyes in their foreheads, women with snakes for hair. The enchantress who put you under a spell." She waited for his reaction, expecting the worst.

He smiled. "We modern heroes can have adventures, too, you know."

"I do not doubt it," she said.

"Do you mind if I sit down?"

"No," she said, gesturing across the table. "Please."

He sat down and faced her. She breathed in. He was so handsome. In this light, his eyes were more green than gold. His body seemed too big for the table. She was used to sitting in rooms like this with Gregor, who was tall and lanky, not the warrior in front of her. Christopher looked like he should be in the sun at all times, shooting arrows at towers, chasing stags with a spear poised above his head.

He was the first one to speak. "I want to apologize to you, for how angry I've been. I have blamed you too much, Margrethe." He smiled wryly. "It feels strange, calling you that."

"I am sorry, too," she said. She lifted her hands. "For all of this. The position you are in now."

He nodded. "When I met you, it was wonderful." His face filled with emotion. "It was . . . otherworldly there, and then you, like an angel. You carried me through the water. I remembered it. You stood by my bedside dressed all in white. It changed me. For the first time in my life, I felt pure. Untainted. I was near death, my men were all lost, and then this angel appeared to me. . . . Discovering that the woman I had met was Princess Margrethe . . ." He shook his head. "I feel like I've been cheated out of something. And now you coming here, my father arranging this marriage without my knowledge . . ."

"And you have someone," she said, her voice quavering.

He nodded slowly, looking away. "I thought about you. You had been out of my reach entirely, a woman of God. I still hear your voice. I dream of it."

"My voice?"

"When you carried me through the water. You sang to me."

Her smiled wavered. For a moment, she froze.

But the mermaid was lost forever, deep in the mysterious, impossible sea.

"Yes," she said.

His face shifted. "This marriage, Margrethe. It would bring much good to both of our kingdoms. We could be one kingdom again, as we were under the old king. I know what it means, that you came here. I would be fighting now if you had not. The North would be outside our doors now, and we'd be at war. Losing our friends and brothers. I am like my father. Tired of fighting. Yet not willing to hand over our land to your father and become his slaves."

She nodded, close to tears. This was why she had come.

"We shall have his answer soon," she said, looking down. And then back up at him. "And it will be for you to decide then."

He smiled sadly and reached out his hand to her.

Nervous, she placed her hand in his, watched as he leaned forward and lifted her hand to his lips, the way he had in the garden. She shivered as his mouth pressed against her skin.

"This is not how I envisioned my life, Margrethe. It is a strange journey that has brought us here, to this moment. Don't you agree?"

She nodded, not trusting herself to speak.

MARGRETHE WOKE UP the next morning feeling lighter than she had in days. He had not made any promises or declared his love, yet there was an opening.

A chance.

Margrethe berated herself for being so selfish. This was not about her happiness but about the good of the kingdom. She could do so little in the world, and yet she had done this.

But still. He had not forgotten her.

She lay back and allowed herself this moment, this one moment to luxuriate in that feeling.

Margrethe looked over at Edele, who was asleep beside her. It was early. Outside, the sun simmered across the water, casting a sweet light over the darkness. There was an ache inside her. Suddenly she wanted to see him again. There was so much more she wanted to say to him.

She dressed carefully, then left the room and told the guard outside where she wanted to go.

"I am not sure that is safe for you, Your Highness," he said.

"Oh yes," she said. "It is fine now. Take me there."

Reluctantly, he led her down the spiraling staircase, through the corridor, past the great hall, and up to the prince's chamber.

The door opened just as she approached, and Astrid walked out of the room, her hair loose and falling past her shoulders, and just the barest hint of shimmer on her skin.

Margrethe stopped in her tracks. Their eyes met. Not knowing what else to do, Margrethe turned to the wall, her face burning, as the prince's lover rushed past her.

She stood with her forehead against the wall, her heart racing.

And then she turned and ran through the corridors. All her high-minded ideals, and it had come down to this. This: that the prince was in love with *her*. Someone else. Someone more beautiful.

Margrethe ignored the faces she passed as she ran back to the tower, and, when she reached the top of the stairway, she wanted to cry out with relief. She passed the guard and entered.

Edele had just awakened and was sitting, sleepily, by the window. There was a fire crackling in the hearth. Outside, the sea was calm and clear.

"Where were you?" Edele asked.

"Just taking a walk," Margrethe said, not meeting her eyes.

"I asked for some wine, for us," Edele said, "and cakes. I was not sure how you would be feeling."

"I don't know," Margrethe said. "I . . ." She shook her head, then burst into tears. Great, wracking sobs as the words tumbled out of her. "Yesterday, we talked. Finally. Talked. He remembered me, he did not forget me. He feels something still, I saw it. This morning I went to his chamber, I wanted to talk more, and then I saw *her* leaving. He spent the night with her, Edele."

"But, wait," her friend said, wrinkling her brow. "That is not anything new. Right?" When Margrethe didn't respond, she went on. "It will be different when you are married."

"I know."

"And it will happen. Everyone says so. That is the only reason your father is taking so long to respond. It will happen. And then you can be rid of her."

"I know," Margrethe said. "It's just hard. It's just . . ."

"It would be hard for any woman," Edele said gently.

"That woman," Margrethe said. "She cannot even speak. She gazes up at him with those eyes, adoring, like a puppy. That is all she does, and he loves her for that."

"You will teach him."

"He seemed different, when I met him. But he was wounded, and afraid. He was not himself."

"But it shows what he might be, does it not?"

There was a rap on the door then, and one of the servant girls walked in, carrying a jug of wine and a small platter of treats.

"This will make you feel better," Edele said. "Wine and sweets. And we can play cards. Yes?"

"Yes." Margrethe nodded. But she had no appetite, no desire for anything in the world except to be as far away from this place, from the prince and that woman, as she could.

The servant girl lingered at the door nervously.

"That is all," Edele said, waving her hand, and the girl ducked out.

Edele lifted a piece of cake and held it out to Margrethe. "Some sweets?"

Margrethe shook her head. "No. Maybe I'll have some wine later."

"All right," Edele said, pouring a large glass for herself.

Margrethe watched her, jealous of her happiness. She was loved. Loved. Edele. To some people, it came so easily. That day with the prince in the garden, she had thought that she, too, was one of them. The kind of girl men fell in love with and desired.

Edele was choking. Margrethe snapped out of her reverie and looked at her friend in shock. Edele clutched her throat. Her face was turning red. She gasped out Margrethe's name as she fell to the floor.

"Edele!" Margrethe cried, leaping up and running to the door. The girl was waiting outside. "Get help, now!" she screamed.

The servant ran to the top of the stairs, calling down to the two guards at the bottom. "Get the doctor!"

And then there was commotion, men running into the room, a doctor, who ran to Edele and took her in his arms.

CHAPTER TWENTY

The Mermaid

THE ASSASSINATION ATTEMPT ON MARGRETHE AND HER lady altered the whole mood of the castle. All the tensions flowing under the surface were brought into relief at once. The king ordered that anyone involved in the crime be hanged immediately. Edele survived, but she had to stay in the infirmary for a few days, recovering from the poison. The servant girl who'd served the wine quickly confessed her involvement and named the noble who'd engaged her, and, in the end, four nobles and two servants were hanged behind the castle.

Lenia watched with the other ladies-in-waiting as the criminals were led to the scaffold, their faces covered in hoods. She watched as the executioner came out and slipped the nooses around their necks, and as the trap door opened and the criminals dropped. The sharp *crack* of their necks, their swinging bodies—she took all of it in, watching for their souls. Like in a shipwreck at the bottom of the sea.

Before, the king had been content to allow Margrethe to stay in the tower, waiting for the decision of the Northern king. Now he made a great show of including her in activities, and Margrethe watched from his side as the traitors swung from the scaffold.

And more reports were coming in, every day, that the Northern king was relenting, and that the details of the marriage alliance were being discussed.

Lenia could walk only with great effort by now. Her body was heavy, unbearable.

It was monstrous, this fish growing inside her, flopping and twisting in her womb. Her legs, already so painful, were heavy and awkward, and she dreamed every night of the sea, thought longingly of the days when she'd had no legs and no womb, just her powerful, sleek, perfect tail pushing her through the water, the thick skin that never felt pain. Her sister's eggs glittering from the rocks, whole and perfect.

One afternoon, as Lenia lay resting, the curtains drawn about her bed, there was a knock on the door. One of the servants answered, then came back and drew the curtain.

"It is the prince, my lady."

He walked in and made his way to the bed. She watched him as if he were a stranger, someone she'd heard about in a song. He was as handsome as ever. Strong. It seemed unbelievable that this was the man she'd seen dying in the water, that she'd carried for countless miles in her arms. Her body had been indestructible then.

Now she could barely move. Christopher stood over her, the torch lights burning behind him, magnificent.

He would be a hero in his world, she saw, a great leader.

"My love," he said, sitting on the bed beside her, pressing his palm to her face. She moved into it, that warm skin. Even now she could feel his hot blood. "Are you well?"

She nodded.

He stroked her face. "And our child? The healer says this baby has grown more quickly than any child she's ever seen. A warrior, he will be."

She smiled, gesturing that the baby was kicking her, and he placed his palm on her belly to feel.

"But, Astrid," he began, sighing, and, despite the shift in his voice, she thrilled to hear him use the name he'd given her, "I fear that I will not have a choice about this marriage."

It was as if he'd put his hands around her throat. As if her heart was splitting—as her tail had split, and as her tongue had been cut out of her mouth, leaving a bloody pulp. She had never known so clearly how words could be like swords, slicing through this fragile skin, yet still he sat next to her, with his beautiful face, those eyes staring into her, full of sweetness and despair.

"My father has just received word from the North. It is a happy day for this land, my love, but for me it is bittersweet. I would have liked to have married you."

She nodded, barely able to breathe.

How could this have happened?

How could she convince him to marry her and not Margrethe, when she had no voice?

"You understand what is at stake here. Many lives, the peace and security of our land. Margrethe was brave to come here. And she is . . ."

He paused, and Lenia knew he wanted to protect her from the other truth: that Margrethe was the woman he'd told her about.

That he thought it was Margrethe who had saved him.

That he loved *her*, too.

She wanted to scream.

"I will take care of you," he said. "I will make sure our child is well provided for . . . You will have a good life here."

THE OFFICIAL ANNOUNCEMENT of Princess Margrethe and Prince Christopher's marriage came a few days later. The marriage would take place without delay, in five days, just after the signing of a formal peace treaty between the Northern and Southern kingdoms. No one wanted to risk waiting any longer than necessary, given what some perceived as the extreme tenuousness of the alliance.

King Erik was on his way from the North, along with a party from the Northern court. There would be a great celebration.

～

LENIA WAS SITTING in the chapel when the official announcement of the wedding was made. The cheers coming from the great hall below told her all she needed to know.

It is time, she said, feeling her great belly.

The moment for tears had passed. She knew she was caught now in the sweep of history, and it was only she who could save the child growing inside her. In six days, she would turn to foam. The morning after Margrethe and Christopher were married, Lenia's heart would break and she would become foam at sunrise, and return to the sea.

Her heart, she was sure, had already broken.

But this body, this child—maybe there was still some hope, for her child. She knew she had to save this child.

She went back to her room and pretended to be in great pain, writhing about in bed and gripping her belly. Agnes was sent for immediately, as Lenia knew she would be. When the old healer arrived, Lenia motioned for the servants to leave the room, which was normal enough during such an intimate examination. When they left, she grabbed Agnes's arm.

"Help me," she mouthed, rounding out the words with her lips, staring intently into the old woman's face.

"What is it? What is wrong?"

"I am dying," she mouthed. "I will die. Help me." She put all her energy and feeling into the thought: *I am dying. Help me save my baby.*

"Are you in pain?" Agnes asked, bending down, pressing her palm against Lenia's belly.

Lenia shook her head. She had to make her understand.

Agnes examined her and could not hide her surprise at the state of Lenia's body. "You seem to be doing fine, dear girl. I do not know how, but you are having the most rapid pregnancy I've ever seen. And you seem more than healthy. If I didn't know the facts, I'd think you were ready to give birth now."

Lenia nodded. She took Agnes's hand, pressed it on her belly, and then gestured down, to indicate the child leaving her body. Agnes's hand was hard and cold and small in her own.

If my child is not born before the dawn breaks on the morning after the prince's wedding night, it will turn to foam. Lenia shut her eyes, visualized it. Her own body dissolving, her baby dissolving with her, both of them becoming foam and drifting out to sea.

Help me. My child must live.

Agnes crossed herself then, her voice dropping to a whisper. "You want to get rid of it? My dear, it is much too late for that, and this is the prince's child."

Lenia shook her head.

She moved then, pushing Agnes aside, stood from the bed and went to the great jewel box on the table by the window. She opened it, and it gleamed with diamonds, rubies, and emeralds. All the prince's gifts to her, ancient family heirlooms mixed with pieces he'd had jewelers make especially for her, sapphires to match her eyes and rubies to match her lips.

Lenia scooped out a handful of them, then turned back to Agnes, opened her palms.

Agnes looked from Lenia's hands to her face, then back again. "I do not understand what you need. You are healthy."

Lenia dropped the jewels into Agnes's hands, closing her fingers over them and nodding. And then she pointed to her belly and made gestures with her hands and arms, showing her child being born and growing up to become strong and healthy, human.

Help me.

"Do you want . . . you want me to help you birth your child?"

Lenia nodded and pointed to the sun, holding up four fingers to indicate the number of days.

"You want to give birth to your child early?"

Lenia nodded again, tears flowing down her face now.

Please.

Agnes shook her head. "You want to give birth to your child before he marries the princess. That is it, isn't it? I hope you are not planning to do anything foolish, like harm yourself. I know that you love him, that it feels like the end of the world now, but I am an old woman, and I promise you: no man is worth taking your own life."

Lenia nodded. *Yes.* She focused every bit of feeling and power inside of her. *Please.* Something strange happened as she stared into Agnes's eyes. For a moment she was back again in Sybil's cave, holding up her face as Sybil floated next to her, bringing the knife down to her tongue.

Agnes looked at her strangely. "What is it?" she asked. "Do you see something?"

Lenia shook her head. Agnes stood in front of her, with her pale eyes and wise face. But for a moment, Lenia could have sworn she'd seen Sybil in her. The gleam of melted pearl, the shimmering pink of her hair. That same heavy sadness.

Was Agnes—had she been—one of them?

Lenia shook the thought away.

The moment passed, and Agnes let out a great sigh. "I don't understand why you think you must do this," she said, "and I don't recommend it. But somehow, you are far enough along. I don't know how, but you are. I think . . . I think you will be safe, and I trust you have your reasons." She opened her hands and placed the jewels back into the box by the window. "I will take one ring for this," she said, plucking up a ruby ring and placing it in her pocket. "Otherwise they will accuse me of robbing you."

Lenia smiled gratefully, as relief flooded through her, as intensely as any human emotion had since her arrival.

"Now," Agnes said, clasping her hands together, "I have herbs that you can take, to bring on labor."

She turned back to her bags and began collecting an assortment of herbs, which she then slowly ground together with a mortar and pestle as Lenia watched, fascinated.

When she finally approached Lenia, her face was dark. "I am giving you a powder," she said, "and you must take it every night for three nights, with your food. On the fourth night, your baby should come from your belly. It is not a guarantee. Your body knows when it is ready. To try to trick it . . . this is a risky thing. If there is any way you can wait, I would advise you to do so. I will pray for you."

"Thank you," Lenia mouthed, taking the packet from Agnes's hands.

After the old healer left, Lenia sat down on the bed, holding the powder with one hand and stroking her belly with the other.

Please, she thought, and then she made the thought a prayer and released it. *Please be safe, and whole.*

She closed her eyes and imagined: a child, her own child, with arms and legs and hair, soft human skin, a voice.

CHAPTER TWENTY-ONE

The Princess

THE CASTLE WAS IN AN UPROAR AS EVERY SERVANT AND every courtier prepared for the wedding of Prince Christopher to Princess Margrethe, and the arrival of King Erik and his court. Everyone seemed thrilled by the upcoming wedding—everyone, that is, except the bride herself.

Margrethe could not help but feel heavy of heart, even knowing that she had prevented enormous bloodshed and sorrow, even knowing that this was only the beginning of what she might be able to do in the world. She was more romantic than she'd realized she was, and she blamed Gregor and his stories. All those old Latin stories. If only he had limited her to the Greeks, she thought, she would have been far better off. But she wasn't: she wanted the prince to love her, passionately and truly. Not just marry her because he had no choice. Not marry her while being in love with someone else.

But she was ashamed of her selfishness. She *was* the future queen, after all, not a silly girl, and there was too much at stake to waste time mooning about.

She did not even let herself take private satisfaction in being able to prevent Astrid, the girl she'd come to think of as her nemesis—though such a designation was not entirely fair, she realized—from marrying the prince. It was an empty triumph, at best. Instead she forced herself, several times a day, to remember the boy who'd drawn a mermaid in the dirt, all the suffering of her people that she would prevent, now and in the future. If only she could make her heart understand that its own wants did not matter, not when there was an entire kingdom to take care of.

Edele had recovered quickly from the assassination attempt and had immediately occupied herself with Margrethe's wedding as well as the altering of her own entire wardrobe. The only real sign of what she'd been through was her newly svelte figure, a result of being unable to eat for days. For that, she confided to Margrethe one morning, it had nearly been worth it, especially with Rainer set to arrive at any moment to attend Margrethe and Christopher's wedding, just as he'd promised.

"I will remember that," Margrethe said, "the next time you complain about putting on a few pounds."

~

TWO DAYS BEFORE her wedding, Margrethe took a walk down to the water. It was so different here from the North. It was beautiful, of course, with its bright blue waters and gleaming golden sand, the scattered trees along the shore, the slew of boats tethered to the wooden docks, but she missed the gloomy beauty of the Northern sea. That endless expanse of rock and ice and silver sky. That sense of being at the end of the world.

As she walked along the shore, she thought about Lenia. What had it felt like for her? Saving the prince, carrying him through that storm—how far had she taken him? *I knew I should save him*, she'd said. *I couldn't let him die.* To think that there was such rich life under the sea. That a creature like that could come to earth, could be curious about their flatter, duller world.

Margrethe stopped now, knelt on the shoreline. She swept her fingers through the wet sand, watching the lines form behind her fingertips. And then, a moment later, a wave slid over all of it, the sand and her fingers, wiping the lines away.

And then, there. On the water. A fish's tail shooting out.

She shook her head. *Stop it,* she told herself. She stood up. *Time to go back inside,* she thought, before she went crazy altogether. Besides, she had a wedding to prepare for.

She glanced back at the water, and then she saw it, unmistakably: a glittering face, staring at her from the water. There for one second, and then gone.

A mermaid. She knew it, down to her bones.

She waded into the water, searching for another sign, walking slowly along the shoreline, until she came to a small group of trees and caught sight of something. A glittering stone. Not anything anyone else would notice, but she recognized that bit of shimmer, and what it meant. She picked up the stone in her hand, and decided to keep it as a talisman. Somewhere she had the oyster shell, too, didn't she? The one Lenia had left on the rocks after saving the prince.

Margrethe smiled, squeezing the stone for luck.

It was only late that night, as she went to her window for the hundredth time, searching again for the mermaid, that she realized, finally, who Astrid was.

CHAPTER TWENTY-TWO

The Mermaid

FOUR DAYS BEFORE THE WEDDING, LENIA SPRINKLED THE powder on her dinner, which the servants brought to her room. It was a warm broth filled with soft vegetables and meat. She watched the powder disappear into the liquid, like snow on the ocean's surface, and then she held the bowl to her mouth and drank.

Over the next days, Lenia dreamed again and again of her eighteenth birthday. She'd wake in the middle of the night clutching the air, afraid that she'd pulled Christopher underwater. If she'd just lost focus for a few minutes, let his mouth slip under the surface and water fill his lungs, he would have died right there in her arms, the way she'd watched the other men do. She would thrash about on the bed, searching desperately for his body, panicking, feeling the waves lapping over her, and then she would remember. Her own belly. The baby she was carrying now, trying to bring it to shore.

She stayed in bed for four days. Each night she roused herself from sleep and dreams and forced herself to eat the soup she was brought, sprinkled over with powder.

On the fourth night, a terrible cramping clutched at her insides.

When a servant came in to clear away the dishes, she took one look at Lenia and screamed, dropping the wineglass she was holding.

"Something is wrong!" she cried, running out of the room. "Fetch Agnes!"

Lenia was covered in sweat, clutching at the sheets. The pain ripping through her body had blotted out everything else.

This thing in her body, this baby. It was moving through her, making its way out, and she wanted to die, wished she could barrel through time, turn to foam at that instant. It would be a relief to die now, never again to feel like knives and swords were cutting through her, like her body was being ripped open from the inside and out at all times.

Just let this baby live, she prayed.

Soon she was surrounded by servants and women, all in a deep red blur of pain and longing.

"Push, breathe, take my hand . . ." Instructions came from all sides.

Her body opened and closed, opened and closed, and the thing inside of it pressed forward, and she was expanding, and all she could think was *Let my baby live*. This body, she realized, this frail human thing that could expire at any second, that was susceptible to cold and disease, to knives and sea, was stronger than she had ever imagined, to create this thing inside of it, to turn itself into a vessel through which a human child could come splashing into the world, whole and alive.

A miracle, if it could happen that way, for her.

Hours passed, and she moved in and out of consciousness. Through the haze of pain and voices she heard a name, her name.

"Lenia."

She was dreaming, she thought, back in the sea with her sisters around her. Vela was there holding one of the pulsing sea creatures she loved to collect, Regitta was there with her son shimmying beside her, his tiny tail a bright green by now, and her twin, Bolette, was beside her, and there was Thilla looking back at her through the water and, behind her, Nadine.

"Lenia! It *is* you!"

A terrible sound then, a deep scream that wasn't a scream, coming from her own body.

Her body ripping, the baby coming out of her, the cries and wails, and she opened her eyes.

"Lenia."

She looked up into Margrethe's face. Behind her, Agnes was holding her baby. Everyone else, other than a couple of servants, had left.

"It is a girl," Agnes said, turning to Lenia and Margrethe.

Lenia looked from her baby to Margrethe and back again.

"It's you, isn't it?" Margrethe said. "I don't know how it is possible, but it is. I know it is." Her eyes were full of tears. She was disheveled after what must have been hours of hovering over the birth table, but she was still every bit a princess in her purple gown, her long black hair piled elegantly on her head, a line of jewels running across it. "I am so sorry, for everything. I had no idea it was you. I'm sorry for everything that's happened."

Lenia nodded. She was too exhausted to think.

She reached up, mouthed "my baby," hungry to touch her, and Margrethe smiled and turned to Agnes, who was washing the child in a small bath the servants had brought in.

Moments later, Margrethe was placing the child in Lenia's arms. It was so tiny, the size of a lobster.

The baby stared up at Lenia with bright blue eyes.

"She is watching you," Margrethe said. "How strange."

Lenia stared down, terrified she would hurt the child, so light and tiny she was barely there at all.

She checked her daughter over, looking for a fin or a tail. The baby's skin was red and soft, and she had a thatch of white hair on her head, above her perfect, tiny face. She looked up at Lenia, out into the world, and she opened her rosebud mouth and let out a sharp cry.

"Your baby is perfect," Agnes said, walking over. "You are very lucky." She smiled, and it struck Lenia, right then, for certain: *She knows.*

But her baby was demanding her attention, twisting in her arms. The ferocity of the love that came over her then astonished Lenia. It eclipsed anything else she had ever felt. *My child*, she thought. Her human child, who could never survive under the water.

I am sorry I will not be able to care for you . . .

"Look at her!" Margrethe said.

The baby continued to stare up at Lenia, her skin glowing and sparkling, and then she kicked her tiny, perfect legs.

CHAPTER TWENTY-THREE

The Princess

MARGRETHE SAT AT LENIA'S SIDE, WATCHING HER hold her child. Both of them were sleeping now, the same perfect curving pout on each of their faces. The baby's shock of hair was the color of the moon. A wet nurse waited quietly on a chair on the other side of Lenia, careful not to meet the eyes of the foreign princess who had inexplicably spent hours attending the birth of her rival's child.

The room was dark but for a torch burning next to the mother and child.

Margrethe reached out and stroked the child's soft forehead, ran her fingers across her long white lashes. She watched the baby's glittering skin next to Lenia's clear paleness, which seemed so out of place and strange now.

Margrethe had known that there was something familiar about the girl. Her pale hair, her blue eyes, her otherworldly beauty. But never had it occurred to her that the girl might actually be the *mermaid* until the day she'd seen her leaving Christopher's room, her hair loose, the color of the moon, the faintest glow on her features. It might have been an illusion, the shimmer Margrethe thought she saw on her skin, but she had *seen* it. Before then she had not imagined that such a thing was even possible. How could it be? How had the mermaid been able to leave the water and come to the earth? It made no sense that the world could work that way. But then later, when she saw the second mermaid watching her from the water, all her doubts had evaporated.

"Why would you do this?" Margrethe whispered.

She knew that everyone would be looking for her, that she needed to prepare for the arrival of her father from the North, and the wedding that would follow. But all of that seemed less important now. Nothing in her life had been as beautiful as that instant when she looked down and saw the mermaid emerge from the sea.

She would give anything, she thought, to return to that moment.

There was a knock at the door, and, to Margrethe's surprise, Prince Christopher walked in, tentative and quiet. He stopped in shock when he saw Margrethe, and for a moment he seemed about to turn around and leave.

Margrethe gestured for him to come forward. She put her finger to her lips. "Shhhh," she whispered. "They are sleeping."

He walked toward her, watching her, and stepped into the dim light from the torch.

She nodded to him, pointing to the baby. "She is beautiful," she whispered.

Christopher hesitated, then turned and looked at Lenia with the child in her arms. Despite himself, despite the discomfort he felt under Margrethe's gaze, his whole face softened.

He looked back at Margrethe, radiant.

She watched him with a mixture of relief and sadness. "Go ahead," she whispered, and she saw that he was almost in tears.

He bent down and touched the baby's tiny hand, which automatically gripped his finger. Laughing, he leaned over and kissed her cheek, ran his fingers through the shock of pale hair.

He has no idea, Margrethe thought.

The baby opened her eyes then and looked up at Christopher. She let out a loud cry, and immediately Lenia was awake, sitting up and holding the baby to her.

The wet nurse stood and said, in a low voice, "I think she might be hungry, madam."

Lenia looked frightened but let the woman gently take her child from her arms. She looked up at Christopher and then to Margrethe, and back again, as the wet nurse quietly left the room.

"How do you feel?" he asked.

She nodded, attempting to smile.

"I thought . . . Would you like to call her Christina? It was the name of my grandmother."

She nodded again, smiling softly now, so dazzlingly Margrethe had to look away.

How could she have even thought she might compete with this creature?

"Christina," he repeated.

Margrethe watched the two of them, paralyzed by the intensity of the emotions moving through her. So much pain and euphoria, a sense that, even though her own heart was broken, the world could contain such beauty and magic she almost could not bear it. What did her own pain matter, in the face of that?

"I will let you rest now," he said to Lenia. "I will return later to look in on you and Christina. My daughter."

Lenia nodded, and, with an awkward smile at Margrethe, Christopher left the room.

They both watched him go, then turned to each other.

Margrethe felt tears beating at her eyes. The next thing she knew, she was crying, big, fat tears rolling down her face.

"I am so sorry," she said. She felt Lenia's hand on her own, saw her expression through the blur of tears. "I did not know it was you. It never occurred to me it could be you."

Lenia kept her hand on Margrethe's, moving her fingers back and forth.

"You brought him to me," Margrethe whispered.

Lenia shook her head, so faintly that at first Margrethe thought she imagined it.

"I thought you brought him to me," Margrethe said. "And that I was meant to love him."

Lenia just stared up at her with those blue eyes.

"Do you remember me? You brought him to me. We spoke on the beach. I would . . ." Her voice broke. "I would have given anything, to see your world. And then you . . . Now you're here. I don't understand."

Everything seemed to crumble, all around them. The sight of the mermaid, with her pale, wounded skin, bloody and tired from birth, made human, dulled down, broke Margrethe's heart completely.

"I believed in beauty, in magic, because of you . . . I thought . . ."

Margrethe remembered then, the way Lenia had looked at him that first day. The radiant love on her face. It was what Margrethe had wanted, too. To feel like that. The way the nuns felt, trembling with love.

"You saw him in the sea. You must have . . . loved him, to save him. You loved him. He is only alive because of you. And now I have . . . I just didn't understand. Is that why you cannot speak? They say you have no tongue. Is it . . . Is that how you were able to come here?"

Lenia nodded then, never taking her eyes off Margrethe's.

"You traded your voice, your tongue, and your tail, for human legs?"

Lenia nodded. She opened her mouth, and Margrethe saw the stump of her tongue. She winced at the sight of it.

Margrethe dropped her voice to a whisper. "Can you . . . Can you change back?"

Lenia shook her head, but she did not look sad.

"I am so sorry," Margrethe said.

Margrethe felt like she'd destroyed everything beautiful in the world. And at the same time, she loved the prince. She did. But she did not know how much she loved the mermaid, through him. Would she have felt the same way about him if she'd never seen Lenia bent over him on the beach, seen the shimmer she'd left on his skin?

In that bleak and windy place, once the mermaid had returned to the sea, Christopher had been the closest thing to magic left in the world.

"I have to marry him," Margrethe said, sitting down on the bed and putting her arm on Lenia's. "I would give him up, I would give up everything, for myself. I would die right now, to let you have him. But I must marry him. My father has agreed, he is on his way now, with the rest of the court; there will be peace, the two kings in the same room, breaking bread together, and we will be whole again, the way we were before. . . . So many people have died, have suffered, because of this war, and our union will end all of that suffering."

Lenia nodded slowly, and Margrethe could not read her expression. Numb. Resigned. Peaceful.

The wet nurse returned then, and both women looked up at the infant in her arms.

"Christina," Margrethe said. "She's so beautiful."

The nurse handed the child to Lenia, who clutched her in her arms. The baby seemed to melt into her. And then it was not numbness or resignation that Margrethe saw, but joy. Pure joy.

"I will do everything I can to give you and Christina the best life possible," she said. "Here, in the castle—"

But when Lenia looked back up at her, Margrethe stopped in midsentence, stunned into silence by the tears running down Lenia's cheeks, sparkling like tiny diamonds.

∽

THE NORTHERN KING and his court arrived that day with great ceremony. After days of frenzied preparation, the Southern court was ready for his arrival, and the two kings stood in the same hall for the first time in decades, shaking hands and vowing allegiance to a common goal, one united kingdom. Huge crowds gathered at the castle—some to protest but most to celebrate the ending of the war, the beginning of a new, better age. Armed guards were positioned everywhere.

Margrethe barely paid attention to any of it. While the castle filled with diplomats and aristocrats and visitors from the North and the Southern countryside, while great feasts were prepared and dances given and entertainments of all kinds brought out for the celebration, and while soldiers positioned themselves at every doorway, Margrethe spent every possible moment with Lenia.

Even on her wedding day, as the seamstresses frantically made last-minute adjustments to her gown, and as Edele rushed about helping with final details, Margrethe's heart was numb. All she could think of was Lenia and her child, trying to imagine what kind of world she would have come from, filled with mermaids, in the sea.

Margrethe's mind kept going back and back to those moments on the beach. To that image of Lenia bent over Christopher that first day, the look on her face as she kissed him. It had been that, hadn't it? That feeling that had made her leave her own world and come to him? Even a mermaid could want that, leave an unimaginably beautiful world behind, for a feeling like that.

She thought of the agony on Lenia's face as she lay contorted on the bed, unable to scream. It was unthinkable to Margrethe that a mermaid would suffer. That she herself could be so central to that suffering.

"Why are you crying?" Edele asked, motioning for the seamstresses to stop. "Do you need to rest?"

"No," Margrethe said, shaking her head. "I am just emotional, on such an important day. My wedding day." She paused and then asked, "Where is Astrid?"

Edele gave her a look. "My friend. This is your wedding day. You should not think of her now."

Margrethe nodded. She was numb with grief, and there was nothing she could do to lessen it. She could not forsake her kingdom for one girl, and yet. In her deepest heart, she felt there was nothing more important in the world than a mermaid who had come to earth.

"Why are you so upset? You are getting married!"

"This is not how I would have liked to be married."

"Forget her," Edele said. "I know it is hard, but he is a prince, it is his way. He loves life, and he was with her before you came, and it was you he chose, in the end."

"But he did not have a choice," Margrethe said. And then she turned to her friend. "Edele, I have something to tell you."

～

THE WEDDING WAS a splendid affair. Every man laid down his arms before entering the church. The two kings stood on either side of the altar. The priest, dressed in the finest sacramental vestments, spoke beautifully about the union of South and North, of husband and wife.

Margrethe and Christopher walked down the aisle together. Margrethe trailed a long silver lace veil behind her. When they reached the altar and turned to each other, Christopher lifted the veil from Margrethe's face.

She did not know what to feel as she looked at him, as he took her hand in his and slipped the ring on her finger. Her heart was in pieces. She loved him, and there was the chance, now, finally, for a new world. But the cost! One creature, and the possibility of everything beautiful crushed along with her.

"You are now man and wife," the priest said. "You share the same soul, the same blood."

The same soul, the same blood.

Christopher leaned over and kissed her. She closed her eyes and felt his lips press against hers, his warm mouth. Despite everything, the feel of his mouth on hers thrilled her. She imagined, for a moment, that they were back in the garden with snow falling all around, that he had been able to stay, to kiss her, that there had been no kings and kingdoms, but her heart was broken now and she could not pretend otherwise.

After the wedding and feasting, Prince Christopher and Princess Margrethe were escorted to the bridal chamber by a formal procession led by both kings and, in front of them, the priest.

And then, finally, they were alone.

She turned to face him. Her face was radiant with love, the way the mermaid's had been when she leaned over him. But she felt she was watching as if from a distance, as if she were an angel hovering in the corner of the room.

His voice was soft. "I am sorry for what you have had to endure here," he said. "But we will be happy. We will create a new world."

She turned around so he would not see the grief in her face, and he unlaced her dress, let it slip. "I love you," he said, whispering into her neck.

She closed her eyes, imagined she was underwater. Felt his hands move over her.

And she imagined it was her, swimming through the water, her skin as thick and beautiful as a gem, with his body in her arms.

∽

AFTER, SHE WATCHED him as he slept. Even through her sadness and guilt, she loved him. But she could not stop thinking of Lenia and Christina. She moved, gently lifting his arm from her shoulder and unwrapping it.

"I will be back," she whispered, kissing his cheek.

She pulled on a nightdress and took a small torch from the side of the bed, then slipped past the guards stationed outside the door.

"Princess Margrethe," one of them said, bowing. "It is not safe for you to go out right now. May I escort you somewhere?"

"Remain where you are," she said, pushing past them before they could protest.

She moved swiftly through the castle, to Lenia's room. The sound of Christina crying filled the corridor. She knocked on the door and pushed her way in.

The wet nurse sat with the baby at her breast. Trying, without success, to comfort her. Lenia was not there.

"Where is she?" Margrethe asked.

The woman looked up, terrified, and awkwardly went to stand, cradling the child. "Your Highness," she said.

"No, please," Margrethe said, stretching out her hand, gesturing for her to sit down. "Do not get up. Tell me where your mistress is."

The woman sat down. She was flustered to have the baby in her arms and Margrethe standing over her. The room smelled of milk.

"I do not know, Your Highness. She was acting strange. She left the child with me. She seemed upset. She seemed to want me to take care of the child."

"Where is she?"

"She left. She seemed in a hurry to leave. I don't know when she is coming back."

Panic swept through Margrethe. "And you did not tell any-one?" Her voice was shrill and too loud.

"This baby has been crying, she will not stop crying. I did not . . ." The woman was struggling, the child squirming in her arms. She was nearly in tears.

"Do not worry," Margrethe said, making her voice soft. "Take care of the child. I will find her. Everything will be fine."

Margrethe left, wracking her brain. What if Lenia had hurt her-self?

She ran down the stone steps, past the great hall, searching fran-tically through the hush of the castle at night. The castle was so wide and empty, the cavernous corridors of marble and stone. It was like running through a graveyard. The busts of ancestors all around. The people who had lived once and were no more.

The queen's chapel was empty.

She turned and raced to the great doors that led to the sea. Two soldiers stood at the doors, immediately bowed to her.

"Have you seen Astrid?" she asked.

"She was here earlier. She is often out here at night—"

Margrethe took off running before the guard could finish, out the gate and down the pathway. The sea spread in front of her, shining like oil.

She arrived at the docks. The ocean was like a living thing, breathing in and out. Lenia was nowhere in sight.

Away from the docks, farther from the castle, there was the clutch of trees where she'd found the glimmering stone. Just past it, she saw a faint figure sitting, farther down the beach. Her blond hair was bright under the moon. The relief was so intense Mar-grethe almost passed out.

Silently, she made her way down to Lenia, careful to remain out of view, to let the trees shield her. As Margrethe approached, she saw that her friend was in a light shift, her hair blowing in the soft breeze. By the water like this, she looked almost as she had that morning, all those months ago, holding the prince. She was gazing out over the water, gesturing as if someone were there with her.

And then, as she moved closer, Margrethe gasped.

There, in the water, were mermaids. Five mermaids, all to-gether, near the shoreline. Their bald heads glittering, as if coated in diamonds. They had gathered around Lenia, looking up to her, speaking to her, and Lenia was kneeling before them.

Margrethe had never seen anything so beautiful.

Tears came to Margrethe's eyes and ran down her cheeks. She could feel herself trembling. For a moment, she forgot everything else. Only this: the mermaids glittering in the sea, under the starry sky.

Her feet were bare on the rocks. She crept closer. They were speaking. Even the faint sounds of their voices—she could not yet hear them—sounded like music. She remembered the poem she'd recently reread, telling of Odysseus lashed to the mast so that he would not die from listening to the Sirens' song.

As she moved closer, she could hear their voices, and they sounded like angels. She could see, then, that Lenia was crying.

"Lenia, you must do it. We are here to save you, Sister. Please let us save you."

Lenia shook her head, tears running down her face.

Margrethe watched, mesmerized. The mermaids' voices shivered through her whole body.

"We have been watching you. He is married now, Sister, and at dawn you are to turn to foam. That was the deal you made. Sybil told us everything. It is only a few hours now. We begged her to save you. She said there was one way to save you, and for payment she took our hair."

One of the mermaids pulled a knife from the water. A shining silver sliver, like the moon. "If you spill his blood, Sister, cut through his skin and let his blood spill on your legs, your legs will become a tail again, the spell will reverse, and you can return to us. That is the only way. You must spill his blood."

Lenia was frantically shaking her head, gesturing, struggling to speak.

"But, Lenia, you will die otherwise."

"Please, Sister!"

They were all talking at once now, crying, pleading, and Lenia was on the shore wracked with sobs. Margrethe could barely even think of Christopher now, though she knew somewhere inside her that he was in mortal danger. There was a part of her that would sacrifice him, herself, everything for this right now.

One of the sisters approached, the knife gleaming in her hands. She pushed up to the water's edge. As she moved, her tail slowly came into view, flashing in the moonlight.

Margrethe lost her breath then, remembering how she'd felt when she saw Lenia on the shore that first time. Nothing had been the same since that moment. The pure love and hope she had felt then. The unbearable beauty of it.

Lenia took the knife and turned. She reached back and tossed it in the air, past the trees. It landed in the sand, near Margrethe. Winking and glinting.

"No!" one of the sisters cried. "Lenia! He is only a man! He will die soon anyway. Think of all the years you have left to live."

"He did not love you, Sister. He is not our kind. Come back to us!"

As quietly as she could, Margrethe slipped across the sand and picked up the knife. It was heavy, so heavy she almost dropped it, and it burned to the touch.

Then she sank back down in the sand, to watch.

The sisters all floated in the water now, reaching for the shore, their arms long and shining. "Lenia, you cannot die for him," one of them said. "Please, it is nearly dawn."

Margrethe watched Lenia as she reached for her sisters' hands. She could tell by their faces—sad and beautiful in the starlight— that they all knew Lenia would never do what they were asking.

Suddenly, Margrethe snapped out of the trancelike state she was in, herself almost hypnotized by the sirens' voices. *Dawn,* the mermaid sister had said. The sun would come up soon, and the sisters were waiting now, all of them, for Lenia to turn to foam.

She had refused to kill Christopher to save her own life. Christina would stay behind, motherless, in the castle, bastard child of the prince.

It came to Margrethe, right then, what she had to do, and she turned back toward the castle and started to run.

CHAPTER TWENTY-FOUR

The Mermaid

THE SKY WAS A DEEP, BRILLIANT BLUE, MELTING INTO THE dark ocean, which was calm now, nearly still. The stars pulsed and shimmered, an orchestra of light. In the distance, the barest hint of color played on the horizon. The promise of a new day.

Now, sitting on the beach, Lenia remembered the first sunrise she saw, swimming toward land with the prince in her arms. The miracle of all of it—his warm skin, his beating heart, and the sky opening, splitting into colors she'd never before seen or imagined. How new and wonderful it had all been. By now, she had watched many sunrises in the upper world. All those mornings, just before dawn, when she'd wrapped herself in a robe and left the prince's bed as he was sleeping next to her, when she'd walked slowly through the sleeping castle to the gallery windows overlooking the sea. Standing there, still feeling his mouth and hands on her skin, smelling the perfume of the flowers, feeling the salt breeze that swept up from the sea.

She smiled, remembering.

Now there was nothing left to do but wait. Grief sparked in every bit of her body, every cell, but she savored it, that love and pain, the ache in her body to hold her daughter, because in moments it would vanish from the earth forever, and she with it. But right now, for this minute, she was alive.

In front of her, in the water, her sisters were quiet, too, waiting for the sun to rise. She knew they had sacrificed much in order to save her, but it had been her decision to come to this world, and she could not punish the prince for it.

Behind Lenia, the castle rose into the sky, and inside, she knew her baby was safe. She understood now that it was Christina she had felt when the prince kissed her and moved his body inside of hers. It was not the prince's soul that had entered her but this new one. This was her immortal life.

Thilla came toward her then, and the others followed. Lenia stood and walked slowly into the sea, and one by one her sisters said good-bye. Thilla, Bolette, Regitta, Nadine, and Vela. Her beautiful sisters, who would have done anything to save her but could not convince her to shed her beloved's blood.

A peacefulness came over her. Soon she would become nothing at all. This was the thing she had been most afraid of. She had given up everything she'd ever known for the possibility of love and eternal life, a soul. She stared up at the stars. The mystery of them, as mysterious as the ocean was, here in the upper world. None of these people could ever know what she knew, the world that lay deep within the sea. And she would never know, not now, the mystery that awaited them after death.

She would return to the sea, where she had always belonged, like all who had come before her.

∽

BUT SUDDENLY THERE were sounds behind her on the beach, footsteps and voices and crying. She turned to warn her sisters, but they had already cloaked themselves in mist.

It was Margrethe, with Edele just behind her. And in Margrethe's arms, Christina.

Lenia felt her whole body lurch with horror. *No!* Lenia gestured to them. *Go back!*

Even as she tried to stop their approach, Christina saw her, her blue eyes resting on her mother, and she reached out her tiny, shimmering arms.

No!

The sky was shifting, illuminating the mist that surrounded her.

"Lenia!" Margrethe cried. "I know what is happening. I know you are waiting to die here."

Lenia looked at Margrethe, confused, as Margrethe pulled something from her pocket.

"You do not have to die!"

The knife shone, like a sliver of the moon fallen to earth.

Lenia tried to scream, opening her mouth. *No!* All she could see was Margrethe, the knife, and her own daughter so helpless in Margrethe's arms. Panic rose in Lenia, sweeping through every vein.

"Lenia. I am a married woman now. His soul is my soul. His blood is my blood."

Just as Lenia launched her body forward, reaching for Christina, even as her own body began to shift and change with the first rays of the sun . . . Margrethe carefully handed Christina to Edele, then dropped to the ground, took the blade, and pressed it against her thigh.

His soul is my soul. His blood is my blood.

Edele screamed as blood flowed down Margrethe's legs.

"I will take care of Christina," Margrethe gasped. "I will raise her as my own child, and she will know her father, and she will grow up to be great and strong. I promise you this."

Lenia ran forward and dropped next to the princess, taking Margrethe's head in her hands.

"Why have you done this?" Lenia cried. And her voice, the words, rang out clear and bright in the air. Her voice. She clutched her own throat, nearly choking on the sound. She looked down.

Saw Margrethe's blood falling on her own legs. A wound glistened from Margrethe's thigh, and her blood, bright and shining, spilled over her, soaking her dress, dripping at Lenia's feet.

Christina was crying, Edele screaming for help.

The sun rose in the sky.

And then it came. The searing pain of her body dissolving. The sky was orange and pink and blue, a million colors melting together. She stared up at her crying daughter, and everything broke all at once: her heart, her skin, the sky, the whole world, shattering, and her daughter's cries above all of it.

She prayed then, for the first time, for nothingness. To turn to foam, become absorbed by the great ocean, and forget.

And then everything went black and, finally, her body was free from pain.

❧

SHE OPENED HER eyes onto the sky. Blinking at the sky. The sun on the horizon, glowing. She felt the earth beneath her. The sky an array of orange and yellow and blue. Long streaks across it, the stars hidden now.

She closed her eyes. She felt she was in a dream, wondered if these were the in-between moments as she left one realm and entered another, as her body melted to foam.

But nothing happened. The earth remained hard under her back.

She opened her eyes. Thilla was leaning over her.

"You've come back to us," she said. Her face was so beautiful, her huge eyes as close to human tears as they could ever be, brimming with relief and love. Her hair gone only made her face more striking, her shimmering skin . . .

"Come back?"

Bolette's face appeared next to Thilla's, and then Regitta's, and Nadine's.

In the distance, she could hear the castle coming to life.

Lenia sat up. She looked in wonder at her own skin, shimmering and hard, all the pain in it gone. Her powerful tail, curving onto the sand. Her tail.

For a moment, one moment, she felt everything there is to feel, all at once. The most intense euphoria coupled with the most searing grief. In a moment, she had lost everything, and gained everything back.

Or had she dreamed it all?

The world smelled different, tasted different.

And then she saw Margrethe lying on the ground just a few feet away from her, passed out. Edele fretting over her, ripping apart her own dress to stanch the wound.

She looked around for Christina, saw Vela sitting on the beach and holding the baby in her arms. Christina was staring up at her aunt, smiling.

In confusion, Lenia looked back to Thilla.

"She will be all right, Sister," she said. "Your friend. She hurt herself for you."

"I don't understand," she said. "What happened?"

His soul is my soul. His blood is my blood.

She looked more closely at Margrethe, her hurt leg, the blood on the sand under her.

"They will be coming now. The guards up there." Thilla pointed. "They are getting another human to take care of her. They heard her cries. We must go now."

"Go?"

"It is time for us to go, Sister," repeated Vela. "They will all be all right."

And then Lenia understood. Margrethe had saved her, but now she had to return to her own world.

The guards were running down to the water. The prince's new bride was missing. She was here by the water, wounded. The castle would be in an uproar.

There was no choice.

Lenia saw that things would be all right. That they would heal Margrethe, and Margrethe would care for Christina, and Christina would grow up beautiful and beloved in this castle by the sea. Would she look out at the water and sense something? Would she feel pulled to it? Maybe later in life, one day, when she was old enough to understand, Lenia could see her again. Maybe by then Thilla would be queen, and Lenia would be mated to one of her own kind, to Falke if he would still have her, and they would be surrounded by merchildren, and she could tell her own children stories about their half sister, who lived in the upper world with her human father, under the stars.

She looked back at Margrethe, whose eyes fluttered open and focused on hers.

There was so much Lenia wanted to say to her, but the sun was in the sky, the guards were approaching, and the court physician, the prince—they were all running to the water, and she had to think of her own people now, her sisters, who were slipping back in the water, waiting for her to return home.

She turned then to Vela, who held out her daughter to her. "Say good-bye to her," her sister whispered. "She will be safe here. She will live well."

Lenia cried out as she took her daughter, holding her close to her breast, inhaling her. It would be her last scent, one she would never forget. As Christina stared up at her, as her heart split open, Lenia realized she had been wrong before. She *could* feel more pain than she'd felt when Sybil cut out her tongue, when the potion ripped her body in two. There was this, now.

"Good-bye, my love," she whispered, willing the words into her daughter's heart, her soul, the web of light inside her tiny body that would keep this memory alive, even after death. Then Lenia spoke to Margrethe. "Please," she said. "Keep her safe."

Margrethe nodded.

Edele walked to Lenia then, nervously looking over her shoulder at the approaching men. "You need to go," she said gently. "I can take her."

Lenia nodded to her, this flame-haired girl, and carefully handed Christina over, making sure her blanket was tucked around her. She watched as her baby curled into Edele's arms and shut her glittering blue eyes. There was so much she wanted to tell her, to help her in the world, but there was no more time.

"Come, Sister," Thilla called.

And with one last look at her baby, and one last look at her first and only human friend, Lenia turned back to the sea, and pushed her powerful tail behind her.

The Princess

THE STORY OF WHAT HAPPENED THAT DAY WAS WHISPERED through the castle corridors and courtyards and along the benches of the great hall. The guests who were present for the meeting of the two kings, and for the marriage of Princess Margrethe to Prince Christopher, took the story with them, back to their grand estates, back to the snow-covered countryside, and up to what used to be known, in those days, as the Northern kingdom. The old woman who found the mermaid on the sand wearing nothing but a ruby necklace, the lady-in-waiting who took Christina from the mermaid's arms, the soldiers who saw a glimpse of the mermaid and her sisters as they disappeared into the sea, who claimed to see the mermaid glimmering from the ocean, her blue eyes glowing from the water as she turned back one last time before vanishing from their lives forever—they told what they saw, and the stories were repeated and changed over time.

Margrethe and Christopher raised Christina as their own daughter, and they went on to have children of their own besides, a boy and two girls, who grew up together in the castle by the sea, in the early days of the new kingdom. Eventually everyone forgot that Christina had ever belonged to anyone else. The mermaid had been in the castle for too short a time to have a child, people said—it could not have been more than a few months, after all—

and everyone remembered how Margrethe had disappeared into the birthing room for hours and hours, just before the wedding. No wonder the wedding was so rushed, some whispered. No wonder the baby was kept largely out of sight of the court until she was a little moon-haired girl so charming, and with such a pleasing voice, that no one thought anymore about the strange circumstances of her birth.

Margrethe often came upon Christina, in later years, staring out at the sea. Walking along the shore and dipping her feet in the water. Margrethe would wonder then if the girl had any sense of where she had come from, if she felt any pull toward the sea beyond what they all felt, always living in its shadow, always hearing the slapping of water against land and watching the moon and stars and sun reflected in it. But Christina seemed like a regular enough girl, though her skin continued to shimmer until she was an old lady and her voice bewitched everyone who heard it, throughout her life.

How can any of us tell when that thing comes that will make everything different? As she stood in the frozen convent garden at the end of the world, all those centuries before now, Margrethe had no idea that she was about to witness a miracle—the last mermaid to come to land, at the very end of the days when mermaids still longed to return to it. In her later life, Margrethe often thought about how had she not been looking out at the water at that precise minute, back when she was just a girl of eighteen standing at the end of the world, she would have missed the miracle altogether. Even as a very old woman, Margrethe would sometimes look up quickly from her books, the ancient tales she had loved to read since she was a child, afraid that she was missing something magical come to light for just one instant, before disappearing again.

They say that no one from the world of the sea ever came on land again after what happened to the sea queen's daughter, who suffered so much among humans, although no one knows for sure.

And as the story changed and grew and shifted into a legend of a little mermaid who fell in love with a prince and longed for a human soul, no one ever talked about what the mermaid left behind.

As most children do, Christina went on to have children of her own, and those children had children, and, as the world became larger and wider, those children spread throughout it, all of them burning with the same curiosity and love of adventure that had led King Christopher, as a young man, to look for the place where the world ends.

Now, many centuries after those days when the mermaid came to earth and then left it, after so many daughters and sons have been born, there are people all over the world who carry the mermaid inside them, that otherworldly beauty and longing and desire that made her reach for heaven when she lived in the darkness of the sea.

Acknowledgments

I WOULD LIKE to express my endless love and devotion to those who helped me create this book: Catherine Cobain, who bought a book about a mermaid from a list of ideas and thereby rudely forced me to write one; Elaine Markson and Gary Johnson, who helped so much in the conception of what this book would be and who pointed to the princess as a character worth exploring; Heather Lazare, who then bought that idea and (patiently and thoughtfully) helped me bring it to life; and Charlotte Mendelson, who (also patiently and thoughtfully) worked her magic from across the ocean; my friends Massie Jones and Rob Horning, who helped me brainstorm about long-ago wars and rival kingdoms, and Rob also for not only reading drafts of this book but also not minding *too* much when said drafts were still being created on train rides through Austria and the Czech Republic; my friends Mary McMyne, Joi Brozek, and Eric Schnall, without whose wondrous and constant input I might possibly die, or at least weep in a wistfully attractive fashion; and my friend Jeanine Cummins, who insisted that the mermaid be half the voice of this book and gave so much general input that really, if you don't totally love *Mermaid* it is probably her fault.

Thank you to my mother, Jean, father, Alfred, and sister, Catherine. They are not only tremendously supportive but fantastic editors and writers, which is very convenient.

Thank you to Two Alices and the Grail in Cornwall-on-Hudson, New York, and to Al-Hamra in Berlin, Germany, since I wrote most of this book at and in them.

Thank you to everyone at Broadway Paperbacks and at Headline.

And thank you to Mr. Hans Christian Andersen, for being so inimitable, so wonderful, and so totally, gorgeously weird.

Reader's Guide

1. *Mermaid* is based on Hans Christian Andersen's *The Little Mermaid*. Have you read the story? Have you seen the Disney film? What are some of the differences and silmilarities between the other versions and this one?

2. What do you think of retellings of fairy tales? How do you account for their popularity? Do you think there's any special power in taking a known story and envisioning it in a new way?

3. How would you describe the mermaid world in this book? Is this an attractive world to you? Why or why not? How does it compare to the human world in the book?

4. What does Lenia find so compelling about the human world? Does she have an accurate view of it?

5. Think about Lenia's choice to return to the sea witch and trade her voice for legs. Would you ever make such a sacrifice—for love, for salvation, or for any other reason? Why or why not? Talk about the theme of sacrifice in the book. Who is making sacrifices and for what purposes?

6. Compare Lenia and Margrethe. What do they have in common, and how are they different? What do you think about the relationship that develops between them?

7. How would you characterize Margrethe and the choices she makes? Does she change throughout the book?

8. If you could switch places with Lenia or Margrethe, whose life and world would you rather inhabit for a day, and why?

9. Describe Prince Christopher's relationships with Lenia and Margrethe. Does he behave honorably toward them both? What do you think of him?

10. Mermaids are an incredibly popular subject in many cultures. What do you think accounts for their appeal? What makes mermaids such a rich subject for the imagination? Can you think of other books in which mermaids play an important role?

Also by Carolyn Turgeon

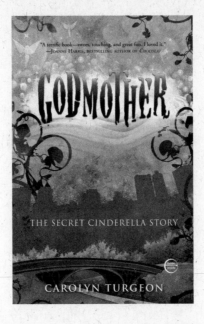

The true story of Cinderella's fairy godmother.

"Turgeon writes beautifully. She tells this deliberately ambiguous story with delicacy and wit. This is a magical novel, in many ways." —*Boston Globe*

GODMOTHER
The Secret Cinderella Story
$13.95 (Canada: $15.95)
978-0-307-40799-3

Available wherever books are sold